# A SLOW SORT OF COUNTRY

VIKING
Penguin India

# A SLOW SORT OF
# COUNTRY

Cherian George

VIKING

VIKING

Penguin Books India (P) Ltd., 210, Chiranjiv Tower, 43, Nehru Place,
New Delhi 110 029, India
Penguin Books Ltd., 27, Wrights Lane, London W8 5TZ UK
Penguin Books USA Inc., 375 Hudson Street, New York, N.Y.10014 USA
Penguin Books Australia Ltd., Ringwood, Victoria, Australia
Penguin Books Canada Ltd., 10 Alcorn Avenue, Suite 300, Toronto,
Ontario M4V 3B2, Canada
Penguin Books (NZ) Ltd., 182-190 Wairau Road, Auckland 10, New Zealand

First published in VIKING by Penguin Books India (P) Ltd. 1993

Copyright © Cherian George 1993


All rights reserved

10 9 8 7 6 5 4 3 2 1

Typeset in Sabon by dTech Services Pvt Ltd, New Delhi

*For
my sister
fifteen years too late*

# Chapter One

'THEY DON'T WEAR trousers. They wear skirts. No, not skirts, but a white cloth, mostly white at any rate.' Lalu Koshy's letters to his friend, Pragasam, in Malaysia, were confused. Lalu was confused by India. In his confusion Lalu exaggerated what he saw to fantasy. 'But they wear their white cloth athletically . . . it slips into and over all the right places in all the right ways and at all the right times. It is a magical piece of cloth.' He merely meant versatile. He wrote magical.

'Don't brood,' said Mamma Koshy.

'And sit up straight,' said Pappa Koshy.

The Koshys' irritability with their new environment expressed itself in absent-minded scolding. With two children, a newly acquired cow and a sloppy servant, there was always something to say.

'The price of kerosene has gone up again,' said Mrs Koshy, blowing out her cheeks. 'It was half this price in Malaysia. And your father is a pensioner now.'

'It is beginning to rain,' said Chechamma, the sloppy servant.

'Bring the clothes in,' said Mrs Koshy. 'It didn't rain without warning in Malaysia.'

'What a din,' said Mr Koshy, who was in his study. 'I can hardly concentrate.'

'It is the rain,' said Mrs Koshy.

'It is not the rain,' said Mr Koshy.

'Get the sheet before the calf soils it. And that shirt! It has been blown on the wall.'

'I think I need help.'

1

'Tie up the calf,' said Mrs Koshy.

'God has given me only two hands. He has given the calf four legs,' said Chechamma.

'Pappa bring the umbrella.'

'Life is so different here,' Lalu was writing. 'In so many ways. We don't have friends here. Only relatives. In Malaysia, we had no relatives. Only friends. That's one difference . . . .'

'Save my washing! Where's the umbrella?'

'It is still unpacked,' said Mr Koshy.

'But it was in the black trunk and I unpacked the black trunk yesterday.'

'I clearly remember putting the umbrella into the green suitcase,' said Mr Koshy.

'And where is the green suitcase?' asked Mrs Koshy impatiently.

Mr Koshy didn't know.

'I hate getting wet . . . but if I have to, I will,' said Mrs Koshy. It was a sort of answer.

'It is not the rain I mind, but the rain and the sun,' said Mrs Koshy. 'It is not honest this or that. You can fall very ill in this sort of weather.'

The muddy calf had danced all over the white sheet. The shirt which had rested briefly on the lower boundary wall, had been blown into the next compound. Chechamma who had thrown the washing over her shoulders, was distracted by falling coconuts. Trailing the washing, she went to pick up the coconuts. Mrs Koshy shouted new commands. 'God has given me only two hands. He has given the calf four legs,' repeated Chechamma morosely.

'I told you the umbrella was in the green suitcase,' said Mr Koshy, holding up a list in which he had carefully noted what had been packed where. He was a methodical man and proud of his method, often insanely proud.

'That cow will catch a cold,' said Mr Koshy. Chechamma was standing bare headed in the thunderstorm and it was of Chechamma that Mr Koshy seemed to be speaking. She

2

looked like a bedsheeted wraith. There were coconuts in her arms. She was muttering to herself.

'Chechamma is mad,' Lalu wrote. 'She is the maddest servant of our little mob of servants. But she is beautifully mad, so funnily mad. She is a fairy thing, but with the flattest of flat feet at times . . . .' The suggestion that they were waited upon by a retinue of servants, was fantasy. Chechamma was their maid-of-all-work.

Chechamma let the coconuts fall to the ground. She loosened her hair. A drenching in a thunderstorm could also be made to serve as a proper bath.

'Go on with your letter-writing,' said Mrs Koshy sharply. There was no saying what Chechamma would do. She could shed some part of her clothing without warning.

'Our servant, Chechamma, bathes in the open when it rains,' Lalu continued. 'Mamma is afraid she will do something scandalous one of these days. But they are all like this. Not just the servants. Everyone we know. They are quite unlike us.'

But Lalu wondered whether such honesty would give Pragasam a chance to gloat? Pragasam had always said that Lalu wouldn't like India. Lalu chewed the top of his pen. He would need to keep his end up with a little fantasy. He was good at fantasy. He thought fantasy the smoothest kind of ink there is.

'But India is so large,' he wrote.

> Everything is bigger than anything I have known in Malaysia. There is a Maharaja here. I believe he rides an elephant. I haven't seen any tigers but this only because we haven't gone on any safaris. And there are people, people everywhere. You can't get away from them. Not in parks, not in walks. There are armies on the roads. Their many, many feet make huge drumbeats on the roads.

3

Mr Koshy announced in a half-choked voice that he had found another leak in the drawing-room. A pool had begun to form between the armchairs and the Grundig radio. Mr Koshy complained that the landlord, Madhavan Thampy, had not warned him of the leaks, nor was the landlord of a mind to set the roof right. 'The Municipality,' the landlord kept saying. 'They drink my blood.' He was referring to municipal taxes.

Mr Koshy brought a bucket. Now there were three buckets in the drawing-room.

'I wonder when we will have our own house,' said Mr Koshy, closing the door that opened out on the back veranda. There was something indecent about a woman bathing in the open. Pictures of belles at village wells were one thing but such scenes in the flesh were quite another thing. It was a noisy bath. Bathing in the rain apparently brought on *frissons* of some kind and Chechamma kept up a steady gurgle.

'When will the woman finish?' asked Mr Koshy.

'I wish we could find another servant, another house,' said Mrs Koshy.

'And another land,' said Mr Koshy shortly.

So his father regretted coming, Lalu thought. But then he had a gift for unhappiness. He wallowed in regrets, the soupier the better.

'I knew there would be no peaceful retirement for me,' said Mr Koshy, who had recently begun to confide in Lalu. Lalu found these confidences both exciting and depressing. It was good to be treated as a half-grown-up. But it was depressing to know that so much unhappiness seemed to go with the grown-up state.

'That woman washing!' said Mr Koshy to Lalu. 'What a sight!' He moved a bucket with his leg. One drop of water splintered on the bucket's edge. 'And we don't have any friends. We are too new to have friends.' Mr Koshy looked thoughtful. 'The landlord claims to be a friend.'

'He drops in often,' said Lalu.

'That's what I meant.'

Mr Koshy looked out of the window. 'And do you know I think I have lost a shirt. I saw it blown over the boundary wall. Don't tell Mamma now. She will only get frantic. There will be time to get the shirt back when the rain stops.'

'Unless somebody finds it first,' said Lalu.

'There is nobody out in the rain,' said Mr Koshy.

'There are people everywhere at any time,' said Lalu.

Mr Koshy smiled. That was the sort of thing he himself might have said. They were beginning to see India the same way.

The calf was frisking about in the compound. In an excess of high spirits, it had danced into the outer veranda.

'I didn't know that calves were so frisky,' said Lalu. 'This one is so much like a young puppy.'

'I believe it is well looked after,' said Mr Koshy. 'The milkman was telling me that no one ever allows a calf to drink so much of its mother's milk, as we do. Usually it takes just a minute to get the flow started, and no more. When the calf dies, it is stuffed. The dummy fools the mother. How, I can't imagine.'

'How happy the calf looks!' said Lalu. 'We must buy it a bell. A tinkly bell.'

'It is not a cat,' said Mrs Koshy. Then after a pause she added, 'Those hard blobs will take some cleaning. I hope the rain doesn't melt them. They are so much easier to sweep up if they are hard.'

The rain came down harder. There was another leak. Another bucket was fetched. Mr Koshy observed that that was the last bucket they had. 'We may have to use a flower bowl next,' he said.

'Or grandmother's brass *kolambi* (spittoon),' said Lalu.

'Yes, or that,' said Mr Koshy.

The compound was already ankle-deep in water. This was another of Mr Koshy's complaints against the landlord. He

5

had neglected to put in any drainage. The neighbours on either side had been similarly neglectful, but their houses were on a raised terrace. They looked smug during the rains, for they were looking out of a Noah's Ark. The landlord had said that the Tiruvananthapuram City Corporation had approved the plans for the houses in the neighbourhood without insisting on drains. The Corporation knew its business. And he knew his. Mr Koshy had said that that was no answer. He would complain to the Corporation. 'The Mayor,' the landlord had said, 'knows that I control a vote bank of six hundred.' Mr Koshy hadn't taken the argument any further.

The rain pounded on the roof like jungle drums. The leaks became spouts. The water in the compound lapped three inches below the threshold. In the house, they had the sensation of being afloat. The neighbours looked on pityingly from their terraced homes. Neither Mr Koshy nor Mrs Koshy was popular with the neighbours. Mrs Koshy had too much to say to them. Mr Koshy had too little.

Chechamma had abandoned her bath. She had no idea that rain could sting so painfully. She tumbled into the kitchen, the bedsheet a squishy train. She had forgotten the coconuts which now bobbed in the water outside. Water seemed to roar in from the skies and from the neighbouring compounds. Two more inches . . . .

Mrs Koshy was at her calmest during crises. It was the minute upsets of everyday living that got her down. 'Put the fridge up on the Nestlé boxes,' she said with calm authority. Chechamma was twittering with nerves. Mrs Koshy's tone steadied her somewhat. Mr Koshy lent a helping hand and the fridge, queen of the kitchen, was hoisted to the top of the Nestlé boxes. 'Careful with her,' said Mrs Koshy, as if intoning a prayer. 'We won't be able to afford another in a hundred years.' She girded herself to face the waters.

The cow had been untethered and led into the kitchen. Chechamma said she had never permitted even so much as a cat to enter the kitchen. 'Dry yourself,' said Mrs Koshy severely. Chechamma looked at her questioningly. The *double entendre* in Malayalam could also be taken as a command to shut up.

'The landlord is going to pay for this,' said Mr Koshy. 'I swear.'

'The washing has disappeared,' said Chechamma, looking out into the compound.

'Nothing ever disappears,' said Mrs Koshy. 'The water goes no further than our compound. The washing must be somewhere in the mud.'

'Haven't I troubles enough, Oh Lord?' said Mr Koshy in his most tragic voice.

'The calf has disappeared,' said Chechamma.

'It hasn't,' said Mrs Koshy. 'I tied it up behind the kitchen . . . while you were bathing.'

'You think of everything,' said Mr Koshy, in ungrudging praise.

Lalu had knocked over one of the buckets in the kitchen. Mrs Koshy noticed that. It would be a subject for reprimand later.

'Devi is not home yet,' said Mrs Koshy. Devi was their daughter.

'She will be safer wherever she is,' said Mr Koshy.

'Safer of course. But I need help,' said Mrs Koshy. 'Empty the buckets, Lalu.'

It was astonishing how many rats, rat snakes and bloodsuckers there were on the outer veranda. Flushed out of holes and burrows, they sought refuge in the house. The rats sat motionless in corners; the rat snakes hauled their bulks about in quick plunging movements; the bloodsuckers feigned death. Lalu lost his self-possession. He dropped the buckets and fled indoors.

'Where are the buckets?' asked Mr Koshy.

Lalu pointed to the outer veranda.

'Hmm,' said Mrs Koshy grimly, looking out into the veranda. 'We have visitors.'

One of the rats climbed into a bucket. The rat was escaping from a snake that wasn't in fact pursuing it. The bucket overturned when the rat leapt into it. The bucket, with the whimpering rat inside it, rolled away into the flood waters. Kicking out of the bucket, the rat swam expertly for the veranda. In the water, for a few moments, the rat was a thing transformed. Its smooth velvet coat, its clockwork movements, gave it a sort of handsomeness.

'I'll make the landlord pay,' said Mr Koshy. 'I didn't know I shared the house with so many. A zoo, it is a zoo we have here.'

'Water will get into our crates,' said Mrs Koshy, 'if the waters keep rising at this rate.' She looked up at the sky. The sluice gates were still open.

'When animals come into the house, the rains will be uncommonly heavy,' said Chechamma. Her hair was tied into a peaked knot above her forehead.

'Will it rain any harder?' asked Lalu who could not believe that the rains could come in any greater intensity.

'Just try to keep your head dry,' said Mrs Koshy. 'Chills begin in the head.'

A tile fell with a sharp report into the living-room. 'The roof is coming down,' said Mr Koshy. 'The landlord is not going to get away with this.' The rain flooded in through the open invitation in the roof. Winds whipped out of nowhere. A bloodsucker shifted by an inch. The three rat snakes coiled and uncoiled themselves with ugly deliberation. The rats huddled together. The cow in the kitchen began to low. Chechamma tried to relieve the strain on the bulging udders by squeezing the cow's teats. Irritated by her fumbling, the cow kicked her. Chechamma cursed. She massaged her shins, morosely watching the rising waters.

Chechamma looked warily at the trees around the house. There were two coconut trees, a tamarind and a giant jak tree. If any of these trees were uprooted in the storm, Bhagwan help them all!

The coconut trees were bending in the wind, supple and yielding, a good sign. The tamarind was young and firmly rooted. The jak, huge and spreading, seemed unworried by the wind and water.

'Let's shift the crates,' said Mr Koshy. 'I've got my books in the crates in the pantry.'

Mrs Koshy, who had long since considered the battle for Mr Koshy's attention, if not his affection, lost to his books, made no reply. She would have rejoiced to see her rivals float away in the storm waters.

'I was thinking of my kitchen things,' said Mrs Koshy.

'Pots and pans,' scoffed Mr Koshy, 'I can't face life without my books.'

'It will take more than you and me to shift the crates of books,' said Mrs Koshy.

Lalu now came with news that a car had stopped at the head of the drive.

'Maybe it is the landlord,' said Mrs Koshy. 'Come to save his property probably.'

'Maybe it is the Municipality,' said Mr Koshy. 'They approved the plans for the house without putting in the drainage, didn't they? Now they fear a scandal.'

It was Devi. She had come with three porters and had brought them in a taxi.

'You shouldn't have,' said Mrs Koshy weeping without restraint. 'Three men and you in one taxi!' But now their crates could be shifted to the attic.

'But, but,' stammered Mr Koshy, who lived in wonder at the shrewdness of his womenfolk. 'This is incredible. You are incredible.'

Devi said trees were falling all over the city. The giant Flame of the Forest, an ageless landmark opposite the Chandrasekharan Nair stadium, had collapsed on three persons in a roadside *kudil*. The roof of the Chief Minister's house had been blown away, according to a rumour in the bazaar. Humbly, the Chief Minister had joined the ranks of destitutes.

Mr Koshy snorted. Chief Ministers' roofs did not behave like that at all in real life, nor for that matter did afflicted Chief Ministers.

The porters swiftly moved the crates to the attic. Mr Koshy smiled. The floods were less threatening now. At least his books were safe.

The storm waters lapped somewhere near the lower lip of the threshold. Occasionally, some strong wave would heave some water over the threshold. More water came into the house from the roof than from the flooded water moat that girdled the house.

'I still blame the landlord,' said Mr Koshy. 'He should have told us all about the house, about the flood drill most of all.'

Their work over, the porters entertained themselves by worrying the rat snakes. They prodded the rats, driving them towards the snakes. The rats huddled together. One of the porters hit the largest of the rats on the back with a stick. It was a stinging crack but the rat did not move. Another crack. Then another. The rat seemed insensible to the pain. Yet it was bleeding profusely. The porters laughed coarsely.

'Let's pay them off,' said Devi, upset by their cruelty.

The house seemed to breathe uneasily.

The tormenting of the giant rat was cruelty from the jungle. And the ugliness of the bloodsuckers and the rat snakes and the fear that the ugliness brought, were also of the jungle. The blobs of sewage in the water, the landlord's indifference to drainage, the washed-up backyard sludge, were of the urban jungle. Neglect was a form of cruelty too. The story of the Chief Minister joining the ranks of the destitutes, was a farce, an insult to the intelligence. He should have in this hour, taken command. If only a story, to Mr Koshy it was a story that summed everything up.

'Forty rupees!' said one porter. 'Did we save only forty rupees of your belongings?'

Mr Koshy who hated arguments with the proletariat, now offered eighty rupees.

10

'Eighty rupees!' said the porters together. 'You are teasing us.'

Mr Koshy said they would have to name their price. The porters whispered together and announced a figure of three hundred.

'A month's pension,' Mr Koshy thought despairingly.

'Too much,' said Mrs Koshy. 'You know it is too much.'

'All right,' said the darkest of the porters. 'Pay us nothing. Only allow us to put the crates back where we found them.'

'That will be double work for no pay,' said Mrs Koshy.

'It won't be,' said the Dark One, hopping with anger. 'I will throw the crates down. I will spill their insides into the water.'

Mr Koshy shrank away from the argument.

'Not a rupee more than eighty,' said Mrs Koshy.

'Bhagwan help us all,' said Chechamma, rushing into the room. 'The jak tree is falling.'

'Which way?' Mrs Koshy asked, rushing to see for herself.

The jak tree was swaying drunkenly in the wind.

'Bhagwan, Bhagwan,' came the cries from neighbouring houses.

'Let it not fall,' prayed Mrs Koshy. 'But if it must fall, let it fall away from us.'

'Bhagwan, Bhagwan,' the cries from neighbouring houses became louder.

'We must leave the house,' said Mrs Koshy.

'I told the landlord these trees were dangerous,' grumbled Mr Koshy.

Barefoot, Mrs Koshy led her family into the flood waters. The rain had stopped, but strong winds flung up webs of spray.

'We need gum boots,' said Lalu, looking at his bare toes in the water.

'Where will we go?' asked Devi.

'We will stay out of the house till the tree has fallen,' said Mrs Koshy. 'And then return . . . .'

11

'If there is a house to return to,' said Mr Koshy.

Lalu pointed to the frightened faces in the balconies of the neighbouring houses.

'Come down,' shouted Mr Koshy.

'How can we!' whimpered a woman. 'This is our house.' Death, she was saying, rather than the disgrace of homelessness.

'For the sake of the children,' said Mr Koshy.

'This house is all we have,' said the woman.

They had saved all their lives to build their house on high terraced land.

'You can rebuild a damaged house,' said Mrs Koshy. 'You can't rebuild a broken neck.'

'Bhagwan, Bhagwan,' wailed the woman and her six children. 'What have we done to merit this?'

'No more than we have done,' said Mrs Koshy.

'And we had built our puja room first,' said the woman.

'In a civilized country,' said Mr Koshy, in a tone which implied that he was not in a civilized country, 'that woman and her brood would have been brought out by force.'

'Surely that woman doesn't want to die!' said Devi.

'That will teach them to gloat,' said Lalu.

'This is no time for spite,' said Mrs Koshy.

Knee-deep in mud, the Koshy family looked anxiously at the skies. Would there be more rain. The wind came in wicked gusts. All manner of flotsam swirled about their legs, blades of grass, bits of coconut husk, and, more dreadfully, dung, both animal and human. They wove patterns in the water, following some erratic current, but always the epicentre of their movements, was the Koshy family. Invariably, after a few criss-crossings and bold surgings away from them, the flotsam returned to the Koshy family, tickling their flesh, and seeking to cling to them like affectionate barnacles.

'Where are the porters?' asked Mrs Koshy. The porters hadn't followed them out of the house.

'They could be entertaining themselves with the rats,' said Devi.

'Not all our crates are nailed down properly,' said Mrs Koshy, not willing to bet on the honesty of the porters.

'Ooo, the water is cold,' said Chechamma.

A wind sang out of the eastern sky—and the tops of the coconut trees were stung into frenzy. The tottering jak bent low, its lowermost branches sweeping the ground. Its spasms were almost human.


'How much longer?' asked Chechamma.

'Maybe a few minutes. Maybe few hours,' said Mr Koshy.

The neighbours quit their balconies. They had decided against going down with their homes. Only ships deserved that kind of sacrifice.

And then the Koshys saw a strange sight. The porters, armed with rope and tackle, were wading towards the jak tree. Taking careful aim, the Dark One swung the tackle towards the tree, trapping the tackle in one of the forked lower branches, directly above the trunk. He tugged at it, first gently and then forcefully. The hold was secure. They paid out the rope, length by length, backing away to the furthermost end of the compound, plip-plopping through the water. The Dark One passed the rope round his waist and knotted it firmly. The other porters wound the rope across their chests, and then at a signal they began to heave together.

The neighbours reappeared in the balconies. They looked pleased.

'What in heavens' name!' exclaimed Mr Koshy.

'Pull,' said the Dark One. 'All together.'

'Pull,' said the others. 'Pull, pull, pull.'

'Stop,' said Mr Koshy.

'Stop, stop,' said Mrs Koshy.

'Pull, pull, pull,' said the Dark One. 'Pull, pull.' The straining men panted in rhythm with the expiring tree.

'My kitchen,' said Mrs Koshy, wading squishily towards the porters.

'Our house,' said Mr Koshy bouncing after her. 'My books.'

'It is too late to talk about the three hundred rupees,' said the Dark One. 'Pull, pull, pull.'

The root system of the jak had been weakened by years of flooding. The roots had lost their grip in spongy mud. In ten minutes the jak was brought low. There were moments when the jak, to its credit, seemed to resist the men, but this only spurred them to greater effort. Finally, the jak slid oozily out of the earth; its roots lay exposed like a tangle of spider legs. The tree fell clear of the Koshy home, but one large protuberant arm slapped into the kitchen. A part of the veranda roof and two sides of the kitchen fell after the tree.

'Murderers,' shouted Mrs Koshy.

'The calf,' said Chechamma. 'You have killed the calf.' A falling piece of zinc roofing had hit it on the head. The cow was safe and lowed lugubriously.

'You can make a stuffed dummy of the calf,' said one of the porters.

'We'll make a stuffed dummy of you,' said Mr Koshy. These were his last words to the porters before he went to call the police. His shoulders hunched, his arms clasped behind his back, his hair rumpled by the wind . . . this is how a man looks when he is surprised by pain.

'The porter drove a hard bargain,' said the woman in the neighbouring balcony. 'Four hundred rupees.' But the tree had fallen away from her house. She had the roof over her head intact, which was more than they could say about some people. Mother and children tittered in self-congratulation.

# Chapter Two

'THREE FEET EIGHT,' said the *Manorama* newspaper.

'Four feet,' said the *Kaumudi*.

They were estimating how high the flood water had risen. It was part of the tradition of rivalry between the two newspapers that the *Kaumudi* always insisted on the taller story.

'Six feet,' said Mr Koshy.

'Six feet?' asked Lalu.

'Yes, six feet. It is always six feet for corpses.' Mr Koshy liked his stories tall and black—rather like the black slave that he somewhat fancifully insisted his great-grandfather had kept.

The flood waters took three days to recede. The Chief Minister went round the city on the third day. The rumours weren't true: the roof of his house hadn't been blown away in the storm. His house had kept its head, the Chief Minister joked. He liked the joke-metaphor. But, said the people of Tiruvananthapuram, it was the Chief Minister's head that had blown away in the storm and he had taken three days to find out.

The Chief Minister visited the Koshy home on the fourth day. He was accompanied by three policemen and six officials, all with notebooks. One police car flashed a red light. The car whined in a way that set Mr Koshy's teeth on edge. Thampy, the landlord, scurried along behind the Chief Minister and this set Mr Koshy's teeth on edge as well. These days Mr Koshy's teeth were very easily set on edge.

'Very bad drainage, sar,' Thampy said.

'Hmmm,' said the Chief Minister, noncommittally.

'I'll send a petition, sar.'

15

The Chief Minister nodded to an official who began to scribble in a notebook.

'I've sent many petitions, sar,' said Thampy.

'Six feet of them at least,' said Mr Koshy, his anger making him excitable.

A senior official glared at Mr Koshy. You spoke to the Chief Minister only with his leave.

'Six feet?' asked the Chief Minister.

'Only a joke, I think,' said Thampy unsmilingly.

'This is not the time for jokes,' said the senior official.

The Chief Minister nodded solemnly.

Joker, bloody joker, thought Mr Koshy.

'Good big tree,' said the Chief Minister, planting one leg on the jak tree.

'There were birds in the tree every evening,' someone said. 'They will not come again.'

'The kitchen is gone,' said Thampy.

'Save the jak wood before water soaks into it,' said the senior official. 'Jak wood makes good tables and chairs.'

Good coffins most of all, thought Mr Koshy.

Scores of people came to meet the Chief Minister. He made a small speech, standing on the small parapet outside the Koshy home. There was some whispering which stopped only when the senior official nodded to the police who began to finger their lathis. The Chief Minister used the English word 'tragedy' six times in four sentences.

'He didn't say anything about compensation,' said Mr Koshy when the Chief Minister had gone.

Thampy smiled. He knew what Mr Koshy didn't know. Compensation was settled in the back room. Six tragedies in four sentences meant a good compensation. The flood was a tragedy. It was official. The Chief Minister had spoken.

'We will talk about all that later,' said Thampy. 'We have a lot to talk about.'

'Yes, a lot,' snapped Mr Koshy. 'Our lives are ruined. That's what I want to talk about mostly.'

'You heard what they said,' Thampy said in a supercilious tone. 'This is not the time for jokes.'

Mr Koshy stared after Thampy, afraid that he had heard right. Thampy wasn't sorry for anything. He had no sympathy to spare.

Oh God! thought Mr Koshy. He had a family to provide for. He had always thought that a tiresome business. Now it seemed more tiresome than ever.

Thampy sent a team of his men later that day.

'They may have come to repair the kitchen,' said Mrs Koshy hopefully.

Mr Koshy said he didn't think so at all.

'There are two bullock carts waiting outside,' announced Lalu.

'And the men have axes,' said Devi.

The men had come to cut up the jak tree. Jak wood sold well.

'Perhaps they will work on the kitchen later,' said Mrs Koshy, unwilling to abandon all hope.

'Perhaps,' said Mr Koshy, making a very long word of it.

The men worked like a gang of ants on the jak tree. They sawed, they hacked, they tore, they broke, The majestic tree was butchered into lots of ten kilos. The ten kilo lots were loaded on bullock carts.

'The birds have lost their choir stalls,' said Chechamma.

The Koshys knew exactly what she meant.

That night Lalu had a dream about bullock carts. They were rather like the tumbril-like carts that took goats to the slaughter house. He heard the creak of ungreased axles, the shouts of bullock cart drivers, the snorts and champing hoofs of the bullocks, all accomplices in crime, and then the chop-chop of the butcher and the whimper of goats as they fell severed head first into puddles of blood. It was a confusing dream. Lalu talked in his dream. 'Pappa, why are you doing nothing?' he kept saying.

Mrs Koshy lay awake most of that night. She heard Lalu

17

talk. Devi too heard Lalu talk. Mrs Koshy hoped that Pappa was asleep and Devi hoped that Mamma was asleep. 'Pappa, why are you doing nothing?' It wasn't a question that well brought up children ever asked.

Mrs Koshy drifted into sleep, thinking of the Chief Minister's visit. The word 'tragedy' hummed in her brain.

Devi did not sleep till two in the morning. It was the first bout of sleeplessness she had ever known. She felt oddly and sadly grown up.

Thampy had much to answer for. He had built his house without drains. Worse, he had built his house without a thought for the shastras, the scriptures. Thampy had been in a hurry. The land on which the house stood had been grabbed from a widow. The house had been built before the widow could gather her wits about her.

The house had its back to the morning sun. Chechamma said there would always be trouble in a house that turns its back on the sun. Nothing but nothing should stick its bottom out at the sun. The evening sun should fall like a shadow in the backyard. As the saying has it, the morning sun should nibble a house in the nipples, and the evening sun pinch it in the backside.

Chechamma's babble irritated Mrs Koshy. 'Ill luck has nothing at all to do with the sun, the moon and the stars,' she said.

'It has, Ammachy,' said Chechamma in a resolute voice.

'It hasn't, you poor, poor girl,' retorted Mrs Koshy.

Chechamma called in a witness, the village *mesthri* (mason). The *mesthri* narrated the story of Chackochayan's house. Chackochayan's house had been a mistake. The evening sun fell in heavy washes on its front veranda. The house was built in a rat-trap of land between two hills. It was closed in by a hill spur on one side and a grass mound on the other. There hadn't been a way to locate the house except to face it

18

to the west. Chackochayan had been warned against it. But he was a stubborn man. He had said that superstition should give way to a shorter and nicer word—science. He had been left to his science, left to make a fool of himself. But he had made more than a fool of himself.

'I suppose the hills landslipped into his house,' said Mrs Koshy, sarcastically.

'Worse,' said the *mesthri*. 'Within a year of moving into the house to the very day, Chackochayan fell from a hill. It was a long tumble.'

'A long tumble,' echoed Chechamma. And this was taken to be heaven's verdict on the poor free-thinking Chacko-chayan.

'And I made his gravestone,' said the *mesthri*. 'He is buried at the foot of the hills, not far from where he fell. But this time the morning sun falls from the front.' It was a *Panchatantraish* story, short, pointed and with a scorpion-sting moral.

'Chackochayan was a drunkard,' said Mrs Koshy, 'and drunkards mustn't go hill climbing.'

Chechamma and the *mesthri* looked at each other. This was going to make a very long argument.

The *mesthri* smelt the wind with one nostril. He plugged the other nostril with a forefinger.

'What time is it, Ammachy?' he asked.

'Five o'clock.'

'See the long shadow the sun throws already. It is a crippled shadow, like the crooked fingers of a thief.'

'A pall rather,' said Chechamma.

'And it smells bad, this wind. There is trouble in this wind. It picks up a lot of bad air from the crust of the earth. This house smells of ill health. Even the earth here breathes strangely. You can almost hear it pant. Funny things have happened to the earth here. It is bleached and unhealthy.'

'See, see,' said Chechamma.

'I see and smell nothing,' said Mrs Koshy, determined not to understand the mumbo-jumbo.

'The shadows are lengthening,' said Chechamma.

An owl hooted in a nearby tree. The *mesthri* pretended to start. 'Even the owl is fooled by the thickening shadows.'

The owl hooted again.

'Listen,' said the *mesthri*. 'It is like a voice from the spirit world.'

The *mesthri* was trying to work up an atmosphere. An owl could not hoot, a crow could not caw, without being made part of a white magic pageant.

The *mesthri* sat down heavily on the ground. 'Look up,' he said, pointing at the reddening sky and at a bird that hung in the sky. Its black feathers shone in the evening glow.

'Now look down,' said the *mesthri*, pointing to the ground. The bird seemed to cast a shadow as small as a fist on the ground below. 'See how the bird throws its ghost-shadow. It is the sky speaking to the earth.'

Mrs Koshy shrugged her shoulders.

She won't buy my magic, thought the *mesthri*.

'That is a raven,' said the *mesthri*. 'A bird of uncommon dignity.'

A small, black cloud of crows had gathered round the raven. The crows wheeled and turned, dipped and banked, half respectful court, half sky ballet.

'They are only looking for lice,' said Mrs Koshy in deliberate caricature of what she saw.

'If that's the way these birds look for lice, Ammachy,' said the *mesthri*, 'then they deserve to be eaten up alive by lice.'

The *mesthri* walked to the front door of the house. The *mesthri* placed his palm on the door and made it skip across the length and then the breadth of the door. 'It is just as I thought,' he said. 'The measurements of this house are all wrong. All wrong.' He meant ill-omened.

'Do you want to tear the house down and build it all over again?' asked Mrs Koshy. 'And rebuild our lives too?'

'Sometimes we have to live with the world as we find it. Sometimes not. It is hardest to know what to leave alone and what to tear down.'

'But you are willing to tell us?' asked Mrs Koshy.

'Forgive me, Ammachy,' said the *mesthri*. 'I speak as the words come to me.' Mrs Koshy cracked her knuckles loudly, as if saying she thought that a poor excuse.

'Will I annoy you more than I have already if I ask whether you plan to stay in this house?' asked the *mesthri*. 'It isn't yours.'

Mrs Koshy snorted. 'I have had hardly any time to think. The storm has gone maybe, but not the storm in my head.' She was saying that the *mesthri* should keep his tactless questions for later. The *mesthri*, a man of rough manners, adding tactlessness to tactlessness said, 'A roof above one's head is not a small thing.'

'That is hardly what I meant,' said Mrs Koshy.

But the *mesthri* would chase his hare. 'A tenant has his rights. To what God has given the sarkar has added. And sometimes I think that not even God can take away what the sarkar has given. It is easy to be generous with other people's property and sarkars are very good at this kind of generosity.'

'I do not want so much as a needle-point of another's property,' said Mrs Koshy. 'And let every cuckoo in the neighbourhood know that.'

'If you are going to stay for a while, Ammachy,' said the *mesthri* coming suddenly to the point, 'I can make an east-facing door for this house. Only to fool the spirits, you understand. You will leave and enter by the door but only first thing and last thing each day. The door won't come very cheap . . . .'

'Such a door shouldn't come cheap,' mocked Mrs Koshy. 'It would look to heaven and a good way beyond.'

'I will make a pretty door of it.'

'We do not have the money to put in doors merely to please the sun and the moon,' said Mrs Koshy.

The *mesthri* hunched his shoulders sadly. 'Then you must do things your way and I must do things my way, Ammachy,' he said. It sounded almost like a judgement.

Tactfully, Mrs Koshy said that she heard the kettle coming to the boil in the kitchen and she went indoors.

The *mesthri* got up, his legs creaking under him. He looked up at the sky. 'The raven is still there,' he told Chechamma.

The raven banked slowly in the wind. A very fluffy cloud rolled towards it and the raven seemed to want to hang like a pendant from the belly of the cloud. Black against white cloud against an orange-gold sky.

'The raven is performing for nothing and nobody,' said the *mesthri* sadly.

Chechamma began to sweep up dry leaves in the yard. She put a lot of spurious energy into the work. She was angry that Mrs Koshy had snubbed the *mesthri*—she had also snubbed Magic itself. Mrs Koshy gave commonsense a bad name. 'Nothing but dry leaves,' muttered Chechamma. 'Nothing but dry leaves. And dry minds. Dry leaves and dry minds.' Chechamma swept with a heave-ho, heave-ho flurry. 'Always the dry leaves fall and always I sweep them up. The leaves fall again and again I sweep up. That is the lot of a servant. But one day I shall break out.'

'You are disappointed with the Koshys?' asked the *mesthri*.

'Foreign! What a sorry business this foreign is! This family thinks different. Why, they look different!'

'They have no right to!'

'Indeed they do not!'

Chechamma swept the dry leaves into a heap. 'You stay there,' said Chechamma to the leaves, 'till I throw a match at you. Don't you go dancing in the wind! You are mine now.' And she added under her breath, 'Mine to burn.'

'The Koshys have the money but will not use it right,' said the *mesthri*.

'It is indecent,' said Chechamma, returning with the matches. 'It is indecent how little they know, how little they want to know.' She threw a lighted match at the leaves. 'Every week for years and years we have always had a bonfire. Bonfires frighten mosquitoes and haunting ghosts.' The *mesthri* nodded. The theology was sound. 'But last week the master said that the smoke stung his eyes and he wanted to make a small bonfire. As if there is such a thing as a small bonfire. Bonfires must roar and crackle . . . .'

'Like a cremation pyre!' said the *mesthri*. 'If the ghosts are to be singed out.'

'I made the usual bonfire and called it a smaller bonfire. The master couldn't tell the difference. He was grateful. He said the smoke no longer stung his eyes.'

The *mesthri* poked the leaves with a toe. There was a healthy crackle.

'An odd family,' said Chechamma.

'Why do you stay on with them?'

'They pay me well. They feed me well.'

'I will say this for "foreign". They know how to treat servants.'

'They also leave me alone.'

'That is also something.' He was thinking of the bossy Malayali housewife who brings a steamroller strength to her rolling pin.

'But I don't like to be left alone all the time,' said Chechamma.

'Oh?'

'And I don't leave them alone either,' Chechamma said, arms akimbo.


Two days after the Chief Minister's visit, Thampy was summoned to the District Collector's office. The day of the appointment was given but no time was given. The Collectorate was usually under siege by bewildered appointment seekers.

But Thampy knew his way about the Collectorate. He

knew that peons are the kings of the corridors. When a peon challenged him and asked him to produce his entry pass or 'get out', Thampy smilingly produced his 'entry pass'. 'Signed by no one less than the Governor of the Reserve Bank of India,' he joked. It was a five rupee note. The peon let him pass.

He got to see the tahsildar within the hour.

The tahsildar pushed a sheaf of papers across the table to him.

'The compensation is ready,' said the tahsildar.

Thampy was too polite to ask how much. He would soon know how much.

'Sign here. And here. And here.' Everything was in triplicate.

The tahsildar licked his forefinger as he turned the pages.

Thampy licked his lips.

A messenger boy brought two cups of tea. Thampy knew that this meant a discussion. A deal had to be struck.

'Drink,' said the tahsildar, putting away the signed papers in a file marked *Compensation, Chief Minister's Relief Fund* in maroon ink.

'The Chief Minister is generous,' said Thampy.

'It was a tragedy,' said the tahsildar. 'The Chief Minister said so himself.'

'Yes, yes. Many times over.'

'But we had to hear it from him,' said the tahsildar, playing self-importantly with a pen.

'Of course,' said Thampy.

'The Chief Minister has ordered a compensation of ten thousand,' said the tahsildar. 'That is a lot of fruit for one bird.'

'It sounds like a lot of fruit but compared with how much this bird has lost . . . .'

'Almost everyone says that,' said the tahsildar unsympathetically.

'I don't want to sound ungrateful,' said Thampy.

'Would you like cash or cheque or National Bonds?'

'Cash,' said Thampy quickly.

'National Bonds aren't a bad investment at all. Almost ten per cent interest. And if you buy them from my nephew, my nephew will get a cut.'

'Oh I see!' said Thampy, his face falling.

'You don't like National Bonds!'

'No.'

'National bondage, someone called it.' The tahsildar laughed knowingly.

'There must be an escape from national bondage,' joked Thampy.

'There must be,' said the tahsildar, digging in his ear with the government issued pen. Such pens do not write, but the butt end digs well. Bureaucrats in abstracted moods explore every orifice above the neck with them.

Disgusting, thought Thampy. It occurred to Thampy that the fellow was also digging for baksheesh.

'Do you know that funnily the rules do not allow you to keep all the money?' asked the tahsildar.

'It is my house,' said Thampy stoutly.

'But you do not live in it,' said the tahsildar.

'I would have if . . . .'

'There are very few ifs and buts in tenancy laws. Either you live in a house or you do not.'

Thampy opened his mouth and then closed it. He was face to face with a master baksheesh-scrounger.

The tahsildar smiled. 'Usually those who come into good money are generous. You know, party-tarty, drink-shrink . . . . Of course party-tarty is good but what you save on not giving a party-tarty is better.'

'How much?' asked Thampy in a defeated voice.

'A party-tarty costs three thousand at least.'

The tarty no doubt costing more than the party, thought Thampy sourly.

Thampy whistled. He pretended to be astonished at

the figure. In truth it was no higher than the usual going rate for such cuts. 'Three thousand!' he exclaimed.

'If you had to give ten thousand to the tenant, how much would you have left? Take away ten thousand from ten thousand.'

'You are right,' said Thampy meekly.

'You wanted cash you said?' asked the tahsildar. He started counting out the money. 'In hundreds?'

'In hundreds.'

The tahsildar counted out seven thousand.

'Ten thousand,' he announced.

'Only if you count some notes as two,' said Thampy.

'You have signed for ten thousand.'

'So I have,' said Thampy sarcastically.

The tahsildar handed over the money with his left hand. He was irritated and wanted to show it. 'I have three daughters to marry off. I could have asked for four, five thousand . . . and you would have paid. And you must know that not all the money comes to me.'

'How much net for you?'

'Five hundred,' said the tahsildar. 'It is the Chief Minister's Relief Fund, you know. He comes first.'

'I almost forgot,' said Thampy. He chased away a fly that was trying to settle on his lips. He put a lot of hot contempt into the gesture. Flies have such sticky legs. They go where there is muck and misery. They seemed to Thampy, only one evolutionary turn away from the babu with his sticky baksheeshes, rules, digging pens, and triplicates. And babus are just as impossible to swat.

Thampy scowled at the peons in the corridor.

On his way home, Thampy broke seven coconuts at a small street-corner shrine in Kumarapuram. He insisted on strict ratios and bargains with the gods. There would have been ten coconuts if there had been ten thousand rupees.

The priest at the shrine collected the broken coconuts and blessed him by splashing a *pottu* in sandalwood paste on his forehead.

Thampy rang the bell at the shrine. He kicked at a dog that tried to nibble at a piece of broken coconut. The dog exploded in a yelp that Thampy found satisfying.

'Do you have change for ten rupees?' asked the priest.

The priest did not produce a ten rupee note. He wasn't asking for change at all but for baksheesh. The gods too demand their baksheesh.

Thampy fumbled in his shirt pocket. The priest pointed to Thampy's waist. His large leather purse was strapped to his waist. He kept only small change in his shirt pocket. Thampy ignored the impertinence of the priest. He gave the priest five rupees.

'The gods must be fed and clothed,' said the priest. Some Indian gods are Indian poor. The gods are made in the image of the people who worship them.

'And protected from cringing dogs,' said Thampy. He gave the priest two more rupees but with very poor grace.

Thampy sat down on the cement rim of the shrine and cupped his head in his hands. He felt a strange presentiment of trouble. One thousand from the jak wood, seven thousand from the compensation. He hadn't done too badly from the storm. But the Koshys worried him. How much did they know of tenancy law, the robust tradition of tenant lawlessness in Kerala? If the Koshys rebuilt the kitchen they could stake a claim to the house. They had only to put a brick in and they would soon be singing about 'the house the Koshys built' — with some help from double-tongued lawyers.

Thampy rang the shrine bell. If the gods have ears, let them hear his nerves speak.


It was his lowness of spirit that took Thampy to the Thekkinmoodu junction. Men looking for a certain kind of entertainment went to Thekkinmoodu junction.

Thampy knew the moves. He waited under a lamppost, his

legs more than somewhat apart. Soon he heard a pretty voice tell him, 'You look sad. I know a way of making you happy.' It was a tinkly voice. Goat-bell tinkly.

Thampy looked sideways at 'Tinkly'. Tinkly was young. He inspected her rapidly. She looked washed and clean. There was jasmine in her hair.

'How much?' he asked.

'Just the company.'

Tinkly was lying.

'Tell me?' Thampy didn't want any bad-tempered black-mailing scenes later.

'I never bargain over my body.'

Tinkly was clever.'Come home,' she said.

Tinkly led the way, about six feet on. She was discreet. 'Home' was a well-known house of ill-fame. Thampy knew the set-up. Thin walls. Thick chuckers-out. Overflowing wash basins. Scaly shower rooms. But the girls were good value.

Thampy insisted on new bedsheets.

'You are staying the night?' Tinkly asked.

'Do I have to stay the night for new bedsheets?'

'You are right. You don't.'

Tinkly disappeared downstairs.

The walls were cardboard thin. Perhaps they were cardboard. He could hear squeaky voices from the next room. And then a slap, slap, slap, perhaps of thighs. Thampy could almost smell the cheap perfume and the sandalwood soap.

Tinkly came back with the sheets and pillow cases.

'Sit down,' said Tinkly. 'You are a big man. I am a small woman. We mustn't tear anything.'

Tinkly climbed out of her evening dress which was a sarong with a long, lacey blouse.

'Let me say hello to your small man.'

Tinkly had a sparrow body. She hopped all over him. She made much of him.

'Ah, what is this?' she asked, poking playfully at Thampy's

purse which was securely strapped round his waist. 'This is more than most men have.'

Thampy no less playfully steered her hands away from the purse.

'Lights on or off?' asked Tinkly.

'On.'

'Toddy?' asked Tinkly.

'Yes,' said Thampy. He was breaking a rule of his. He never had toddy with a tart. Tarts never seemed to know when or how to stop. But he felt he couldn't say 'no' to Tinkly.

They made a long night of it. Tinkly made intelligent, at least non tart-like, conversation in the intervals between their bouts.

'I wasn't always in this trade, you know,' she said. 'I lost my house in the rains. And a husband. I have two children. What else could I do?'

'I lost part of a house in the rains!' murmured Thampy, drinking from his bottle of toddy.

'Maybe if I can find a husband . . . .'

'This is a strange place to look for a husband,' said Thampy.

'God found me my first husband. Maybe the devil will find me my second husband.'

'What do you mean?' asked Thampy.

'I met my husband in a church. He had a good voice. A strong voice. And he was strong all the way down. He died saving our two children when our house collapsed in the rains.' She sniffed.

'You are a Christian?'

Tinkly showed Thampy a small metal cross that hung from a chain round her neck.

'But I am disappointed in the Christian God. A god who allows his own son to die so painfully is a strange god. If he can do that to his son, he can do that to any of us. I will go back to my Hindu gods.'

'Try Ayyappa,' said Thampy now flushed with drink. 'But

29

first try some more toddy. Try everything once. Christian, Hindu. Back and front.' He laughed noisily.

A Christian whore, thought Thampy. He fumbled for the cross. With the thin metal cross between his teeth, he seemed to surge most healthily.

'Are you married?' asked Tinkly.

'Yes,' said Thampy. He was lying.

'Oh,' said Tinkly, retrieving the cross from Thampy's mouth. 'Thoo, thoo, what a lot of sticky spittle.'

Thampy fell asleep in Tinkly's arms.

Tinkly roused him at four in the morning. They did it again. Thampy said that he felt so young in her arms.

'How much?' he asked as he prepared to go.

'Nothing,' said Tinkly.

'Nothing!' Thampy shouted. 'Impossible.'

Tinkly wouldn't allow Thampy to open his purse.

'But you need the money,' said Thampy.

'Sometimes a woman needs more than money.'

Thampy bear-hugged Tinkly and kissed her on the eyes.


When he got home Thampy discovered that he had been robbed. Most of his 'compensation' was gone. Five thousand of it. His anger was baboon-like. He tore back to the whore-house.

But the chuckers-out were firm. 'You are drunk,' they told him. Thampy was drunk.

Thampy tried to force his way in. The chuckers-out pushed him back into the street not too ungently, but they threatened to use more force if he came back.

Thampy said that he would go to the police.

'Go on,' one chucker-out taunted. 'Go to the police.'

It was five in the morning. Thampy reeked of toddy and cheap perfume. The chuckers-out were trying to say that the police were not likely to believe a disreputable story from a disreputable man at so disreputable an hour.

'Let me see Tinkly. There might be a mistake and she might be able to explain.'

'And who is Tinkly?' mocked the chuckers-out.

Thampy described her with many sad gulps—sparrow body, tinkly voice.

'That's Rosamma.'

'Let me see her.'

'You are not the first one who wants to see her. She is sort of busy now. And will be busy for some time more.'

'I must see her.' Thampy was pleading.

'But you have been seeing her all night. Are you in love with her? Or do you want to throttle her? With Rosamma it is usually either one or the other.'

'What do you mean?' asked Thampy.

'What do I mean?' The chucker-out laughed. 'I mean how did her husband die this time? From fire or water or the tricks-of-nasty-pricks?'

The chuckers-out had a lot of trouble calming Thampy. 'I want to throttle her,' he kept shouting. 'I want to throttle her.'

But it was just as the chuckers-out had said. Thampy didn't go to the police. Such victims usually have their respectability to think about.

# Chapter Three

LALU REMADE HIS life in his letters to Pragasam. 'Our fridge was smashed in a storm,' he wrote.

> But we are not going to buy another. Food kept in a fridge smells of yesterday. We buy today what we eat today. And there is plenty of water in the compound. A fridge seems so unnecessary when you have a relay of servants who keep bringing you the freshest things from the bazaar. Plantains with the sap still running, mangoes still smelling of the warm earth, fish that still have kick in them . . . .

But the unreconstructed truth was sadder: Mrs Koshy was in deep mourning for the smashed fridge. She blamed herself for enthroning 'the queen of the kitchen' on rickety Nestlé boxes. The boxes had splintered like matchwood when the jak branch had slapped down on the fridge. The fridge had fallen over and landed on its back. How right her friends in Malaysia had been to advise her against the top-heavy Westinghouse! The cobweb of wiring and tubes at the back which, as Mr Koshy explained to her, was what made the fridge tick, was squashed. The door was twisted and the top of the fridge looked 'chewed up'. It was unlikely that either the beauty or the engineering of the fridge could be put right. Well, thought Mrs Koshy, her mother had managed well enough in her time without a fridge, and she had raised nine children. She would have to learn to face life without a fridge. It wasn't impossible. It had been done. But this was only the unsentimental part of her speaking. Her tears when they came, came in a stinging flood.

'Let us go back to Adoor,' Mr Koshy said. Adoor was Mr Koshy's 'native' village. To Mrs Koshy it was a place of few charms: she said that she could not bring herself to like a place so sleepy and dusty, and so infested with flies and relatives.

'Adoor is green and open and we will breathe easily once more,' said Mr Koshy. 'We will have no bossy landlords there.'

'Adoor has its ways and we have ours,' said Mrs Koshy. She was saying that they could not go back to the uneasy rhythms of village life after twenty-five years. Mr Koshy knew that too. His talk of going back to Adoor was no more than just brave-sounding talk. It comforted him to think that there was something to fall back upon.

'We have been over this argument before, Pappa. Nothing has really changed.'

'Nothing?' asked Mr Koshy, looking at the fridge.

'Nothing,' said Mrs Koshy, ignoring the evidence before her.

'I still say Adoor,' said Mr Koshy. He liked to pursue an argument almost for its own sake.

'No,' said Mrs Koshy, hotly.

'I suppose,' said Mr Koshy, looking at the still muddy floor, 'you know what to do next time there is a flood.'

Mrs Koshy blew her nose noisily. After a while she said, 'I don't think the fridge is beyond repair.'

'Even if it were not, where will you find the men to do the job?' Mr Koshy asked, rapping out the words like an oath. 'Westinghouse, latest model. There's not a man in town who has seen a Westinghouse, any model.'

'But in Madras . . . ' began Mrs Koshy.

'Madras is two nights by train,' said Mr Koshy. 'And no doubt there will be place for the fridge in your travelling-bag.'

'Then I'll have the fridge for a cupboard,' said Mrs Koshy. 'There must be a way of repairing the door.'

'There must be. Tiruvananthapuram has many tinkers,' said Mr Koshy. 'Tinkers, that's all they ever will be.'

'Tinkers have their uses,' said Mrs Koshy. 'We can't all be philosophers.' It was a sly dig at Mr Koshy.

'In all decency,' said Mr Koshy, 'I think the fridge should be buried. With the calf.'

'But the fridge isn't dead yet.'

'We can argue about that. But I tell you, I nearly am, and on this I won't have an argument.'


'These people are so different,' muttered Chechamma. Other families she had worked with had had regular brawls with her. That made for equality. But this family hardly noticed her, except as a work-machine. She was not all hands and feet. No servant was. She had a mouth and ears and they needed to be kept happy, with a little gossip. Gossip was companionship. But the Koshys never gossiped with her. There was no gossip in this house. In her ill temper, Chechamma clanged the saucepans in the kitchen. The noise always annoyed Mr Koshy. It was Chechamma's way of calling attention to herself.

'How can I think in this din?' asked Mr Koshy. He put his pen down and waited for the din to stop. He was writing his diary. It was to him a sacred hour.

'I have told Chechamma a hundred times that Pappa can't stand noise,' said Mrs Koshy. 'Lalu, shut the door.'

Lalu slammed the kitchen door shut. Mr Koshy groaned.

'You know, don't you, that if I do not write my diary for the day, I have a headache! It is my conscience protesting!'

'Of course,' said Mrs Koshy, her lip curling.

Mr Koshy's was more diary-as-literature than diary-as-record. He never wrote about any domestic happening, except when it lent itself to 'literary' writing. The flood and the fallen jak tree had not been worthy of record.

Mr Koshy had just settled down again to his diary, when the cow began to low. Mr Koshy put his pen down and supported his head in his hands. The cow was mourning its calf. She had been lowing all night. There had been some respite since dawn, but now she had started again.

'Bhagwan!' said Chechamma. She threw three extra pinches of salt into the sambar. Mr Koshy had been prescribed a salt-free diet for his blood pressure.

'You should be calling in the skinners,' said Chechamma, banging a saucepan for attention. 'The cow won't fall silent till you get a dummy calf for her. There are *parayans* (outcastes) who will make the dummy calf for us.'

'No,' said Mr Koshy.

'Disgusting,' said Mrs Koshy, who had nursed the calf through a severe attack of colic.

'Then you must live with the noise,' said Chechamma, scoldingly. Another pinch of salt went into the sambar.

The cow's lowing filled the house. No door could shut it out.

'Perhaps there is something in what Chechamma says,' said Mrs Koshy after ten minutes of this bombardment.

'Perhaps there is,' said Devi.

'Perhaps there isn't,' said Mr Koshy. Mr Koshy liked to be the last to give in to what he called 'local barbarities'.

Devi and Lalu applied to Mrs Koshy for some cotton wool. The lowing cow was beginning to grate on their nerves. It was more than noise. It was the blackness of death. Devi was troubled.

As usual, Lalu found relief in his letters. His father used to say that a writer wrote best when the mind was full. But not, thought Lalu, when the mind was full to bursting as his was now. Lalu took after his father. For Lalu, writing was therapy; even the little chores of getting down to writing, the laying out of the desk, the setting of pen to paper, the pulling in of the straying mind, were acts of healing. And then there was the escape into another world where the writer was king, a world where people could be made to behave, where the rude could be snubbed and the wicked brought to order, where landscapes could be remade and where floods need not happen. Lalu was learning to like the drug.

'That damned noise,' said Mr Koshy. 'I say sell the cow.'

'A cow without a calf won't fetch anything,' said Chechamma, from the kitchen.

'I don't like the servant joining in conversations that she has no business to overhear in the first place,' said Mr Koshy.

'It is a small house and this is the way with servants here,' said Mrs Koshy.

'That cow will drive us mad,' said Mr Koshy, meaning Chechamma this time.

'That is just what I have been saying,' said Chechamma. 'Let me call the skinner.'

Mrs Koshy turned in appeal to her husband.

'On condition that I see nothing,' said Mr Koshy.

'They charge more for rotting animals,' said Chechamma.

'They would,' said Mr Koshy.

When the skinners came Mr Koshy left the house hurriedly.

'Don't go near them,' said Chechamma to Lalu. 'They stink.' Of their trade, she meant.

There were two workers and as was usual in Tiruvananthapuram, two to supervise. One of the supervisors was drunk and did not for one moment leave off cursing the workers for their clumsiness.

It was astonishing how quickly putrefaction had set in. 'As if our job isn't dirty enough,' said the workers. 'Now we have to compete with maggots.'

The stench brought you close to giddiness. Chechamma led the cow away, wishing to save it the sight of the exhumation. The neighbours hung out of the balconies, whispering and pointing, except when the wind went their way.

Devi wondered at the oddity of their ways in this new land. It was home. Yet, they were strangers at home.

The workers knifed open the belly of the calf, making one long cut from throat to groin. Their hands disappeared inside the slit belly and drew out chunks of the entrails, slowly but expertly. They spat heavily as they went about their work.

The entrails were then buried. Then the head of the calf was cracked open with a stone. The inside of the head was scooped out with an iron *thavi* (a cup-shaped spoon). The calf was then tied by its legs to a pole and the pole was lifted to the shoulders of the two workers.

'Bastard,' said the drunken supervisor, for no particular reason. 'Maggots. The bastard is crawling with maggots.'

Mr Koshy, with a greatly mistaken sense of timing, was returning home at this moment. He ran into the procession inside the compound.

'Stand by, sir, stand by, sir,' said the drunken supervisor to Mr Koshy. 'This calf has more smells than a bed of roses.'

Mr Koshy had a weak stomach and was very sick. 'This house reeks of decay,' he said as he bent over the sink.

Her father's headlong tumble into invalidism worried Devi. He had been a fairly robust, tennis-playing sort of person in Malaysia. In India, in two months he had taught himself to be an invalid.

Early the next week, Madhavan Thampy paid Mrs Koshy an angry visit.

'You look as if you have bitten into a kanthari chilly,' said Mrs Koshy in a tone that she used only to scold very difficult children. She was telling Thampy that she wasn't going to allow him to frighten her.

'You save me the trouble of having to explain my mood to you,' he said.

'Maybe our mood matches yours,' said Mrs Koshy.

As Madhavan Thampy saw it, a man is either a winner or a loser. Let a man start winning and he will go on winning. Let him start losing and he will go on losing. The gods of failure and of success, were cannibalistic. They fed on their own, and the fatter a god got the more he gobbled. Thampy was afraid he had started losing, and losing badly. A tart had made a public fool of him. A tahsildar had got the better of him. And now, the Koshys, a bleating family of sheep, threat-ened to knock him down and run him over. When sheep became unruly in this way, it was time to worry.

Thampy's brow furrowed. 'Let me be as direct with you as you have been with me. You know there are stories . . . .' He paused.

'Stories?'

'You hired the porters.'

'Yes.'

'They pulled the tree down. On my house. The neighbours say that it was no accident.'

'You are not saying we paid them to?'

'Perhaps I am.'

'That's a low thing to say,' said Mrs Koshy.

'The tenant makes the most of a convenient act of God. He repairs the house. He claims the house for himself. The law takes the side of the tenant. Our lawless law.'

'Extraordinary!' was all that Mrs Koshy could say.

'A house is a great prize. It can excite terrible dishonesty. Brother can swindle brother . . . I may have to hire porters of my own to persuade you to leave. I am a blunt man. You must excuse my bluntness.'

Mrs Koshy was taken aback at the nakedness of the threat. Her chin jutted out angrily. The shape of Mrs Koshy's chin was usually a reliable guide to her feelings.

'And one final thing . . . . Your servant took the cow to graze in the maidan this afternoon.'

'But we buy all the grass the cow needs,' said Mrs Koshy.

'Oh, I can't say . . . but I know the cow broke loose. Your servant had a nasty fright. Very nasty. She has gone home.'

'Home? But she lives ten miles away.'

'She can walk. So can the cow.'

'So she has stolen the cow then,' said Mrs Koshy. 'With some help from you.'

'I wouldn't put it like that,' said Thampy.

'And I thought I had bought her,' said Mrs Koshy, ruefully thinking of the two blouses and new sandals that she had given Chechamma only last week.

'The cow or the servant?' asked Thampy.

Thampy's over-fine wit made Mrs Koshy very angry.

'I'll fight you,' she said.

'In court?' taunted Thampy.

'Everywhere,' said Mrs Koshy.

'It is not the law but the claw that settles disputes in our land. If you don't understand that, you don't understand anything.'

'There is a law above that is bigger than all your claws clawing together,' said Mrs Koshy. 'If you don't understand that, you understand nothing.'

Devi thought that her mother was magnificent. As soon as Thampy had gone, Mrs Koshy unpacked her kitchen stuff. She took it out of the crates that the porters had thrown it into. She laid out the saucepans and spoons, pots and bottles neatly in the small storeroom which now did service for the kitchen. She counted the spoons: thirty-two, they were all there. She hung the four saucepans from nails that she drove into the wooden door.

'We are staying,' she said.

'But the house is ill-omened,' said Devi.

'It is fear that is ill-omened,' said Mrs Koshy.

Together Mrs Koshy and Devi prayed before the Gethsemane Christ in the living-room. Mrs Koshy prayed fervently. She prayed for strength, rather like the Gethsemane Christ.

'Do we know what we're doing?' asked Devi.

'Do we ever?' replied Mrs Koshy. 'Chechamma . . . what a let down!'

'I told you two blouses were too good for her,' said Devi half jokingly.

Mrs Koshy smiled a very thin smile. 'It is a very animal world, isn't it?' she said. She meant it as a statement of

39

appalling fact.


The tanners brought the dummy calf in two days.

'This should fool any cow,' said one tanner, proud of his handiwork. 'But where is the cow?'

'The servant stole it,' said Mrs Koshy.

'You can't steal a cow and not be punished,' said the tanner. 'The cow is holy . . . . Have you been to the police?'

'We have,' said Mrs Koshy. 'The police are never in a rush.'

'Unless you make it worth their while,' said the tanner. 'Bhagwan is the only real policeman in this lawless land.'

'But Bhagwan has done nothing yet,' said Mrs Koshy.

'He will,' said the man. 'You can't steal a cow, you can't.' He shook his head.

The tanner was counted among the most despised among the so-called untouchables, cruel word. His community ate cattle flesh and worked on cattle skin. They inspired horror among caste Hindus. But even for the untouchable the cow was holy.

The tanner patted the dummy calf on the head. 'It was hard work,' he said, 'there was a lot of scraping away to be done. The work has almost blunted my best knife.'

Mrs Koshy looked at the calf's eyes. Only the sockets remained and the skin around them looked stretched and frayed.

'The eyes don't seem right,' said Mrs Koshy.

'The calf doesn't need them,' said the tanner.

'Eyes rot,' said the second tanner.

'But the smell . . .' said Mrs Koshy. 'The cow may not take to the calf.'

'Dry the calf in the sun. The sun soaks up all smells,' said the first tanner. 'The cow doesn't have as keen a smell as you think, Ammachy.'

'About that we shall say nothing till we have the cow back,' said Mrs Koshy. 'It will be the cow that will judge your work.'

She was subtly running down the work of the tanners. The tanners had not named their price. Mrs Koshy was hinting that they shouldn't ask for too much.

'They kill the calf, and steal the cow,' said the first tanner. 'And you allow it to happen, Ammachy?'

'It is easy to steal but hard to keep what you steal,' said the second tanner. 'A man can eat a dozen eggs but can he keep them inside him?'

'Of one mouth,' said the first tanner coarsely, 'of one mouth, man has control. Of his other mouth, he has none.'

Mrs Koshy blushed. 'Tell me how much you want for your work.'

'We would do it for nothing,' said the first tanner. 'But we must live, Ammachy.'

'So must we,' said Mrs Koshy.

'Fifty rupees, Ammachy.'

'Twenty-five,' said Mrs Koshy.

'Pay us twenty-five, Ammachy. And give us the rest as a gift,' said the first tanner.

'We never bargain,' said the second tanner. 'But these are hard times.'

'You allow these worthless dogs to talk like this?' said a neighbour, looking over the boundary wall. 'Work you call it. I call it sin.' He was a pious Namboodiri Brahmin.

'Master, you keep out of this,' said the first tanner.

'There was a time,' continued the Namboodiri, 'when people like you did not come within a hundred yards of people like me. Now you bark at us.'

'There will be a time when people like you are locked up,' said the first tanner.

'May I never live to see that time,' said the Namboodiri. Turning to Mrs Koshy, he said, 'You have lived abroad too long. You have forgotten what proper behaviour is. This neighbourhood has been spoilt for ever.' He disappeared into his home.

'They are all like that, Ammachy,' said the first tanner sadly.

41

'Here's forty rupees,' said Mrs Koshy. She felt sorry for the tanners. Insult was no part of the bargaining.

'Ammachy, say that you are giving twenty-five rupees as our wages. And fifteen as gift.'

'But why?' asked Mrs Koshy.

'Bhagwan will punish us for bargaining with our betters,' said the second tanner.

How much better? wondered Mrs Koshy, as she counted out the money.

# Chapter Four

'WE MUST CLEAN the *thattinpuram* (attic),' said Mrs Koshy. She made it sound like an order. Mrs Koshy said that she didn't like any part of the house to stick out a dirty tongue at her.

Mrs Koshy led her family up to the attic. 'Nasty business,' she said, looking around her. The rat droppings lay in florid little mounds. Mrs Koshy said that they looked like black cauliflowers. 'And this evil little garden was growing right above our heads!' She spoke reproachfully, as if about a low trick that had been played on her.

The Koshys noticed that the cockroaches did not scuttle away at their approach. 'They are as brave as roosters,' said Mrs Koshy. 'And almost domesticated.'

Mr Koshy had a handkerchief wrapped bandit-style around his nose. Only Lalu dared to breathe normally.

The Koshys worked sweatily all morning. Mrs Koshy was a slave driver. Sometimes the family trooped to the small attic window to fill their lungs. One, two, three . . . Mrs Koshy led the exercises.

In the afternoon, the attic swooned with heat. With a nice sense of timing and of diversion, Lalu discovered a photograph of a holy man in a cell-like room not two steps away from the wooden stairway. The photograph was framed in almost comically ornate gilt. It was garlanded with tulsi leaves, as lithographs of a god or a *netavu* (hero-leader) usually are. The photograph was covered with a thick layer of lamp black.

Lalu rubbed away the soot from the photograph. His innocent eyes saw no more than a tangle of flesh. If Lalu had known what to look for, he would have seen a couple locked in a complicated embrace. The woman was explosively exaggerated owing to her nearness to the eye of the camera. The man lay in a red hot pile under her. A skull and a serpent head hung like black fruit from the top half of the photograph: they were, most transparently, camera trick objects that had been cropped in later. An ash smeared man sat cross-legged beside the couple. Austerely, he noticed nothing of the funny business around him.

The holy man was of uncertain age, youngish rather than young. He wore two strings of beads round his neck. He supported the strings in his hands.

'A guru of some kind,' said Mr Koshy, looking exclusively at the guru. 'Those are rudraksha beads that he has around his neck. But I see no caste marks. No sign of what sect he belongs to. It can't be a very orthodox sect.' Mr Koshy spoke with a detached archaeological sort of interest. That was how he usually discussed people nowadays.

'This house has a history,' said Mrs Koshy. 'Houses shouldn't have histories. You can't move in with ghosts. We must leave the attic to its own life.' She leaned on the word 'life' sarcastically. She turned the photograph to face the wall.

'Perhaps a god-man,' murmured Mr Koshy.

'God-man indeed!' said Mrs Koshy. 'Men who fail as men try to set themselves up as gods. Neither one nor the other. That's the way to the madhouse.'

Then, most disapprovingly, Mrs Koshy led her family down the narrow, roughly carpentered stairs from the attic. She had expected the attic to be dirty, not decadent.

What happened next, happened all at once. First, Devi, who had fallen behind, screamed that a brown swarm of cockroaches was attacking her. Devi stampeded into Mr Koshy. Mr Koshy fell down the steep stairs. He landed all on one side and lay quite still.

'I've killed Pappa,' wailed Devi.

'Ice. Bring some ice,' said Mrs Koshy.

No one reminded her that the fridge was smashed.

'I said, bring some ice . . . . All right, some fresh well-water then,' amended Mrs Koshy.

Mrs Koshy was at her best in a crisis. She sent Lalu for the doctor. 'Tell Dr Vareed to hurry.' She cradled Pappa's head with one hand, and with the other the back of Devi's head as if it were a flower-stalk that needed holding up.

'No,' whispered Mrs Koshy into Devi's ear. 'It is just that Pappa has been so . . . so very so. He will be all right.' 'So very so' was one of Mrs Koshy's very own phrases. It meant something between difficult and under-the-weather.

When Dr Vareed came, he said there really was nothing to worry about.

'But what happened?' asked Dr Vareed.

'I saw hundreds of flying cockroaches,' said Devi. 'They were like grinning aeroplanes.' Terror has its own inventions.

'It was very hot in the attic,' said Mrs Koshy.

'Maybe,' said Dr Vareed, 'it was just that those things in the attic had never seen a pretty face, and didn't know what to do when they did. I like my explanations simple.'

And perhaps just a little flirtatious, thought Mrs Koshy.

Devi blushed. 'How is Pappa?' she asked, changing the subject.

'He just fell at an odd angle,' said Dr Vareed. 'Lots of bed rest and quiet and he should be all right, I think.' But he didn't sound as though he entirely believed his own words.

'Did I die?' asked Mr Koshy, opening one eye slowly.

'I am all to blame,' said Devi.

Mrs Koshy hugged her daughter. 'We should have known that you were afraid of those ugly things,' she said.

'Nerves, have you got something for his nerves?' said Dr Vareed.

'We have about six inches of whisky,' said Mrs Koshy.

'Quite enough,' said Dr Vareed.

'Two glasses,' said Mrs Koshy.

Mr Koshy refused the whisky when Lalu brought the bottle

from Mrs Koshy's broom cupboard.

'I can't drink alone,' protested Dr Vareed. But he did.

'Pappa is trying to sit up,' said Mrs Koshy.

'I've had the most refreshing sleep,' said Mr Koshy.

'It was a little more than that,' said Mrs Koshy.

'Did I fall from the stairs?' asked Mr Koshy. 'Or was I pushed?'

'Pappa's memory hasn't altogether come back,' said Mrs Koshy, tactfully.

'And why are you drinking my whisky?' asked Mr Koshy, staring at Dr Vareed.

This is awkward, thought Dr Vareed.

'You've attacked the bottle heavily,' said Mr Koshy.

'But you have never cared for the stuff,' said Mrs Koshy.

'Whisky is a wonderful gargle,' said Mr Koshy, sinking heavily into the pillows.

Mr Koshy closed his eyes. He seemed to drift into sleep.

'Pappa wasn't himself at all,' said Devi. 'He never embarrasses people. His manners are good.'

'He has become delicate,' said Dr Vareed. 'He will take some time to recover from his fall, I fear.'

'I'll always blame myself,' said Devi.

'Your father was close to the edge already,' said Dr Vareed. It was a doctorly ambiguity.

Dr Vareed gulped down what remained of the whisky. He slid the glass under the bed, as if he were hiding uncomfortable evidence. 'Can you send Mr Koshy away for a while?' asked Dr Vareed. 'To a quieter sort of place. His nerves . . . .'

Mrs Koshy interrupted him. 'Yes, his nerves . . .' she said. She didn't think herself strong enough for another discussion of Mr Koshy's nerves. 'He can go away to my brother-in-law Avrachen's perhaps. Avrachen has a large house. He can give Pappa a quiet room. Pappa so very much wants to be left alone. He gets tired of people very quickly nowadays.'

'You must protect him as much as you can,' said Dr Vareed.

Mother him rather, thought Mrs Koshy.

More easily said than done, thought Devi.

Mr Koshy's life in Malaysia, had been calm and orderly. It ran on the rails of a timetable. Mr Koshy kept a neat desk at the office. He played two sets of tennis, no more, no less, every day. He read the *Straits Times* for an hour, timing himself by his watch. Mr Koshy's friends joked that his heart did not so much beat as go tick-tock. His life had been ruled by the clock. In India he had to unlearn the habits of a lifetime. He had lost his watch within a week of his coming to Tiruvananthapuram. He had soon lost his niggling sense of time. Thereby, he told Devi once, he fell in his own esteem. And a man can suffer no worse fate, he had said, than to come down in his own esteem.

When Mr Koshy was asleep, and Devi and Lalu had gone to bed, Dr Vareed told Mrs Koshy the story of the house. To Mrs Koshy a house with a history, like a woman with a past, is trouble.

'These gurus are setting themselves up in business everywhere,' said Dr Vareed. 'Self-made god-men for the most part. It is almost a cottage industry.'

Dr Vareed said that it was only last week that he had examined the cadaver of a god-man in 'exposition'. The god-man's right hand was raised, half benediction, half Nazi salute: the god-man's followers claimed that this was how the god-man had gone into samadhi. But the hand had in fact been worked into the raised position while the body was still warm. The worshippers had come in droves. It said a lot for the audacity of the god-man's followers that they had permitted Dr Vareed his medical examination. Perhaps they had grown careless. There were some MBBS's among the god-man's followers and none of them had objected to the faked post-mortem spectacle. A god-man makes his own rules even in death.

'Just as I was saying,' said Mrs Koshy. 'Those who think

47

they have tricked men soon believe they can trick God as well.'

The story of the guru of the attic photograph was extraordinary and Dr Vareed told it all. Mrs Koshy blushed at the lack of expurgation.

The guru had started as a painfully shy man. He had found a job as a government clerk and like a good clerk he had buried himself in paper. Just the job for the painfully shy you might say: but six months of 'paper work' and he found himself becoming a piece of paper himself, flimsy, thin and bloodless. Soon he had had enough of hiding behind paper.

To the great horror of his family he resigned his government job, the safest kind of job there is in the land. He gave away almost everything he had, his furniture, his money and, rather pointedly, his office shoes and clothes. Madhavan Thampy, the landlord, was on the point of throwing him out when a group of firangi 'Hindus' adopted him. The firangs were a mixed lot—two Americans, a Scandinavian, and an English couple. There was also an enigmatic young woman from the French Alps, who traced her paternity to Tenzing and Hillary. 'Both at once?' people would ask her. 'They knew a way,' was her reply. 'They reached the top of Everest at once, didn't they?' A pretty theory, but the girl had no Gurkha features.

A noisy cult grew up around the guru. The bhaktas wanted to make an instant guru of the man. He should have broken free but some childish element in him liked the fussing. But the guru didn't seem attached to any of his devotees. He hardly noticed when one came or another left. He had nothing to say to any of them. When they told him their troubles, he listened patiently, but he never said anything even to a pointed question. Once an American devotee, enraged by his silence had struck him. She had slapped him again and again, drawing blood. The guru had howled like a child but had done nothing to defend himself. The American devotee stayed on to become the most doting of the guru's devotees. Soon his devotees learned to enjoy him as they would a baby. They dressed him, fed him and even bathed him. They fought for the honour of massaging him. The bhaktas played with his body without embarrassment. Some of the more fanatical even fed on the remnants of the guru's meals, *icchil* in Malayalam.

Dr Vareed said that in the months before the guru took his own life, the house had become a gathering place for bhaktas of every kind, almost an interesting sort of zoo. Hefty six footers in saris; busty Scandinavians in military uniforms; earnest Vedantins in south Indian *mundu* and *jibba*, you never knew who you would find in the house and in what proportion of maleness and femaleness. Dr Vareed said he had treated a hairy Italian with fierce tattoos on the arms, assuming the patient's maleness until . . . Dr Vareed cleared his throat.

In its last days the cult went somewhat literally to 'pot'. It became a drug den. There were the strangest stories. Of black arts and worse. Of drug-crazed violence. Dr Vareed was told that he could stop calling. The cult had found a quack who dealt in drugs, not medicines.

The guru became a prisoner of the cult. He was the cult mascot and they wouldn't let him go. He was fed drugs and forced into the strangest black rites. Suicide was the guru's way of escape. He hanged himself from the jak tree. This was his route out of hell. The cult tried to hang on to the guru's body. So long as there was a chance of Resurrection there was hope. But the neighbours called in the police on the fourth day when the stench was unbearable. When the police came, the chelas fled. After a hasty post-mortem, the police cremated the guru under the jak tree.

To Mrs Koshy, Dr Vareed's story seemed to bring together all that she disliked, feared even, about the world. Godlessness, drugs, foreign corruption, cheap money and cheaper women, moral failure . . . . She had always seen her home as a tidy little refuge from the various madnesses of the world. It was a shock to know that her home had been a wicked sort of playground for every kind of lunacy. She even thought that Devi's whirring cockroaches made sense.

Mr Koshy was taken growling and groggy, in a taxi, to the Avrachen home. Devi went with him. Mr Koshy slept like a child in Devi's lap. He had dwindled into a sick man. Devi looked at her father's face. It was strangely smooth—as if it had never known a blade. Even his features had softened. He looked so sadly unmanned.

'Is the doctor still at my whisky?' he asked when they reached the Avrachen home.

'No, we have taken it away from him,' said Devi.

'Good girl, you are a brave one. Was there a struggle?'

'No, Pappa.'

'You don't look hurt.'

Mr Koshy fell asleep again in the spare bedroom of the Avrachen home. He slept with his mouth open, a thread of saliva hung from his chin. Devi wiped it away with her handkerchief.

'Are they going to operate on me?' he asked, the next time he woke up.

'What for?' asked Devi.

'Then why did the nurse dab my face with cotton wool?'

'There was no nurse, Pappa. It was only me.'

'You? In a white uniform and cap?'

Devi's saree was green.

'Pappa, you are seeing things.'

'More clearly now than before,' he replied.

Thankam, Mrs Koshy's sister, was a brisk and rather matronly figure. She liked to take charge of people. She told Devi in a whisper that Mr Koshy needed constant care. She suggested a nurse.

'We must ask Mamma,' said Devi.

'She will want to do it herself,' said Thankam. 'To save money. But we need a nurse.'

'So there was a nurse,' said Mr Koshy. 'Devi, you can't fool your father.'

'There will be a nurse,' said Thankam.

'There was a nurse,' said Mr Koshy. 'I saw her. Tell her not to play games with me. It tires me.'

Devi patted her father's hand and said that he wasn't to talk. The doctor had wanted him to rest.

'But how can I rest with a nurse playing hide and seek with me? Ask the doctor that?'

Devi slipped away as soon as Mr Koshy fell asleep. Her father would need a lot of looking after. Devi felt sorry for Lalu. The boy needed a father, not two mothers. She needed a father too—even at eighteen. But it looked as if Mamma would have to manage without husbandly support. Thank goodness, she was not given to brooding. Thought gave misery new dimensions.

'How's Pappa?' asked Mrs Koshy when Devi came home.

'He's still hearing and seeing things.'

'His grandmother had the same problem.'

'Perhaps it is the medicine that Dr Vareed gave him,' said Devi.

'We would be lucky if it is just the medicine,' said Mrs Koshy. 'You haven't seen everybody on Pappa's side of the family.' Mrs Koshy had never cared very much for what she called 'Pappa's side of the family'. Her side of the family was open, generous and fun-loving. His side of the family was narrow and censorious. They made a religion of their gloom. Some of them, inevitably perhaps, had become extremists in their religion, marrying man-made gloom with god-made gloom.

'Thankam Ammachy thinks that Pappa needs a nurse,' said Devi.

'A nurse costs money.'

'Thankam Ammachy was afraid that you would say that. But Dr Vareed says that a week of bed-rest might be enough.'

'We wouldn't be talking of a nurse if it's going to be only a week of bed-rest.'

'What are you saying, Mamma?'

'I'm saying that it will take more than a week of rest. Devi, we're on our own now. Pappa won't be a help for some time now.'

'Yes,' said Devi, suddenly tearful.

'You don't know perhaps how difficult finding a husband for you is going to be, if it is generally known that Pappa is not all right in the head. A nurse talks. And there will be gossip. I won't have a nurse whatever Thankam might say. In Malaysia, Pappa was a government employee. We were well looked after. Here we have these to look after us.' She spread out her hands. 'And these,' she added, clenching them. 'But for all that a woman's hands.'

'Twenty-five years as a government employee and perhaps Pappa is fit for no other life,' said Devi.

'He cannot use his hands except to hold a pen.'

'Poor Pappa,' said Devi.

'Poor all of us.'


Thankam ran her household on a litany of dos and don'ts, some of them stranger than others.

No one was allowed to sit in the 'lion chair' that stood in a corner of the drawing-room. The chair had belonged to her father, Appachen of revered memory. It was a very special chair. Thankam varnished it regularly and inspected it often for woodlice.

The chair had lion legs. And the legs ended in paws. It had a leather back. Its seat had a deep dip that put some in mind of a thunder box. But it wasn't anything of the kind of course.

Nor was anyone allowed to use the malacca cane that rested like a sceptre across the great leonine arms of the chair. The malacca cane had also belonged to Thankam's father. The chair and the cane were 'relics'.

Avrachen grudged the relics their special place in the household. That he was not permitted to use the relics did not make him better disposed towards them. He thought the chair's lion legs pretentious. And the deep heart-shaped dip in the seat a silly affectation. No one had a bottom shaped like a heart.

When Mr Koshy came to stay, he irritated Thankam immediately by lolling about in the lion chair. Just as irreverently, he played with the malacca cane.

'He is doing it on purpose,' said Thankam.

'He may have forgotten your rules,' said Avrachen. His tongue was usually half in cheek when he spoke to his wife.

Once Mr Koshy fell asleep in the chair. He drooled spittle as he slept. Thankam was most distressed.

Avrachen said that it at least proved that the chair was comfortable. 'I can't tell of course.' He meant that he had never sat in the chair. His tone was ironic.

'It isn't as if I haven't dropped hints,' said Thankam. 'I have said that Appachen's lion chair is not very sturdy. Hasn't supported the weight of a human body for years and years, not since Appachen last sat in it. But Koshy didn't seem to understand. He might have been deaf.'

'He is so mixed up nowadays,' said Avrachen.

'Though sometimes I think he is posing. Koshy has always wanted to do nothing except read his tedious books and now he has discovered a way of doing it. And poor Sosamma has to struggle alone with the children and the house.'

Thankam had little forgiveness for anyone who upset the sacred order of her household.

'Do you know that Appachen used to sit in this chair when he wanted to take an important decision? He said the chair had been blessed by a holy man from the Tamil country. Our marriage was decided in this chair.'

Avrachen thought that this perhaps explained many things about their marriage. He had married a woman with lion legs.

'We have to be as gentle as we can with Koshy,' said Avrachen, 'he is recuperating after all.'

Thankam looked with beady eyes at the sleeping figure in

the lion chair. 'I will not advise him to recuperate in Appachen's chair.'

'But if it has a special magnetism . . .' said Avrachen.

'Your lack of comprehension makes me very sad,' said Thankam hotly. She was more angry than sad.

The new domestic arrangement did not please Mr Koshy either. He made no effort to make himself in the least agreeable to Thankam and Avrachen. 'If this is a rest cure, where is the rest?' he asked Dr Vareed in the hearing of Thankam.

Thankam said she endured the darts only for the sake of Sosamma. Sosamma couldn't really be expected to cope with a disturbed household and a disturbed husband at the same time.

Mr Koshy was conspicuously fidgety. He washed his hands whenever and wherever he could. He opened books and closed them with many loud snaps as if determined to announce his restlessness to the household.

Mr Koshy had been a man of some *gravitas*, but not it seemed any more. Can a tumble down a flight of stairs change the wiring inside a man's head so strangely? Thankam wondered.

'You must rest,' said Thankam to Mr Koshy in the stern tones of a nurse.

'I can't rest. The roof is so different. The floor is so different. The smells are so different . . . .'

'Different, but I dare say better,' said Thankam, who hated to hear it said that her house did not smell as nice as any other house. She was very house proud.

'I miss the children,' said Mr Koshy, using another unbeatable argument.

'But you didn't always,' said Thankam. 'Children are noise and we want to give you a holiday from children and noise.'

'Or do you want to give Sosamma a holiday from me?' asked Mr Koshy.

'There might be something in that,' said Thankam.

'But marriage allows no holidays. You don't know what you are suggesting.'

Ishwara, groaned Thankam, O Ishwara.

The very next day Thankam found Mr Koshy reclining in the lion chair again. Preposterously, the malacca cane was under his feet. Thankam thought she could roar like a lion. It was so ungrateful of Koshy to insist on the lion chair, especially as he had at least four kinds of chairs to choose from—a comfortable bamboo rocking-chair, a dutch colonial *chaise-longue*, an easy chair with extendable leg rests and a 'deep well' arm chair into which you could sink and sink and sink.

Thankam decided that she had to be firm.

'That chair is not for sitting on.'

Mr Koshy leaned back and raised his head in interrogation. 'Why?'

'It isn't the sort of chair you take it for.'

'Oh! I saw the cat curled up on it.' He pointed to the cat that lay like a sulky, couchant lion on the floor beside him. He had merely displaced the cat.

Thankam conceded that the cat did sometimes curl up on it. But a cat is a cat.

'Do I have less rights than a cat?'

'You know that is no way to talk.'

They proceeded to quarrel.

Thankam said that she wasn't asking much. Just a little consideration.

Mr Koshy said that no part of the house could be out of bounds for him. Just good manners, pleaded Thankam. Mr Koshy said that he could not be remade. Would not be remade. And he wouldn't allow a chair, even if it were a lion chair, to call him to order. 'I sit on a chair. I do not allow a chair to sit on me.'

Thankam snatched the malacca cane away. Very pointedly, she began to polish it with a duster cloth. 'For Sosamma's sake,' she said. Mr Koshy did not budge. He wiggled his toes teasingly. It was disgraceful.

Thankam lost control of herself. It was the wiggling toes

 Cherian George

that did it. It was such a mocking gesture. Like so many jeering heads. Thankam caught hold of the back of the chair and tried to ease Mr Koshy out of it. Mr Koshy sat in the chair like a very determined limpet. The cat to whom the chair really belonged was astonished by what it saw. It arched its back and then began to spit. It clawed at the chair.

'Good pussy!' said Thankam encouragingly. The cat spat at Mr Koshy. Mr Koshy retreated half in anger, half in confusion. Mr Koshy really couldn't handle two cats at once. Three cats if you counted the lion of the lion chair.

Thankam picked up the cat. She stroked its back.

Mr Koshy took his defeat poorly. He kept to his room. He ate little. He slept little. He spoke little. His silences were unnerving.

In her triumph Thankam was contrite. She apologized at least twice over. Mr Koshy hardly heard her. 'He is much worse now,' said Thankam to Avrachen. 'I didn't mean to be so abrupt. But those horrible wiggling toes!'

'Koshy must go back home,' said Avrachen.

'What shall I tell Sosamma!'

'Tell her the truth!'

'I can't!' moaned Thankam. 'It is so shameful.'

'It is,' said Avrachen, without compassion.

# Chapter Five

'Has it taken to the stuffed calf?' Mrs Koshy asked anxiously.

'I think so,' said Lalu. 'Cows are stupid.'

'There will be no problem, Ammachy,' said Chechamma. Mrs Koshy and Thankam ignored her stonily. Thankam was visiting her sister.

The cow, looking little the worse for her adventure with Chechamma, munched steadily into the pile of hay before her. Chechamma kept stroking the cow's back. Her clothes were torn: her hair messy: she looked more slatternly than usual. 'Ammachy, forgive me,' she kept repeating. 'Madhavan Thampy master said I could keep the cow and I was fooled.'

'He said you could steal the cow,' said Mrs Koshy.

'He said that you were strangers in the land . . . that you were easily cheated.' Chechamma began to pound her chest with both hands, quite in the style of mourning at a funeral.

'God is not so easily cheated,' said Thankam, in the tones of a minor prophetess.

'I have learnt my lesson,' said Chechamma. 'Look at my clothes. Look at myself. To keep the cow alive, I had to starve myself. I ate nothing so that the cow might eat something. When it rained, I covered the cow with sacking, with newspapers, to keep her dry. Now the cow looks well, but look at me.'

Chechamma had found out that it was easier to steal a cow than to care for it. There was nothing to stealing a cow, Thampy had told her. You had merely to walk it out of the gate. But would they not send the police after her? Chechamma had asked. No, Thampy had said, he would look after all that. These people were strangers to Tiruvananthapuram. They could as well complain to the wind for all the notice the police would take of them.

Chechamma had walked all night with the cow, reaching her home at Nedumangnad at dawn. Cow and maid had stopped several times on the way to rest. Chechamma had been content to drink from wayside rivulets—there were many of these on the Tiruvananthapuram–Nedumangnad road. Chechamma drank, scooping up the flowing water in her palms. But the cow was a much more daintily brought up creature. Used to drinking from a bucket, it would not drink any other way.

There were more manifestations of its sensibility when they got home. It would not graze on the stubbly village maidan. It would not compete with goats and bullocks for fresh, sprouting grass. It preferred to starve in dignified isolation. It did allow itself to be milked but this was only because Chechamma had got help from the village milkman. The milkman reported every morning and evening, and had to be paid for his services. The milk the cow gave became scantier and scantier. The milkman said that it really wasn't worth his while coming any more. Chechamma was in despair. Her sisters blamed her for adding to the burden of the family by bringing home so worthless an animal. Her mother, whose mind had begun to wander in old age, said the cow carried a curse because it was stolen. 'Sell her,' one of Chechamma's sisters had urged her. 'Sell her to the butcher if you must, but I won't have useless stolen property around the house.'

Chechamma was aghast. The cow had calved only once before; these were the years when its milk would be most plentiful. Chechamma in her despair had turned to Thampy who said, 'If you cannot feed a cow, you must sell it.' He had then shut the door in her face. In Chalai bazaar, Chechamma had stopped to buy a five kilo pack of cattle feed, the kind that the cow was used to. And that was how the last of her money had gone. Chechamma had walked home in the rain, toiling under the weight of the feed.

'Cattle feed,' her sister had mocked. 'But no human feed!' Their anger was real, for they thought it wicked of Chechamma to buy cattle feed, when the children went hungry. Her sisters had refused to serve her any food that night.

'Theft, no good ever came of theft,' her mother had kept repeating witlessly.

Chechamma had slept outside their hut that night, unable to bear the nagging of her sisters. She took the cow its feed the next morning. What was her astonishment when the cow after sniffing the feed briefly, turned up its nose at it. Was it sick? She had consulted the milkman when he came on his rounds.

'Nothing wrong with the cow,' he had said. 'But what is this?'

He had examined the feed which was unusually moist. He had then smelt it.

'Someone has pissed into this,' he had said. Chechamma had left the feed inside the hut. One of her sister's babies had rolled over incontinently in the night and had sprayed the cattle feed pack with piss. The cow had known at once.

Three days later after a particularly spiteful quarrel with her sister, Chechamma had decided to return the cow.

'There will be police jail for you,' one of her sisters had warned.

'I'm in jail already, my sisters' jail,' she had retorted.

She had not looked back once at her gesticulating sisters.


'Chechamma wants to be taken back,' Thankam told Mrs Koshy. 'She really ought to be handed over to the police.'

'Servants are all alike,' said Mrs Koshy. 'They will steal when they can.

'I count my *chattis* (cooking-pots) every week,' said Thankam. 'It wasn't honesty that made Chechamma bring the cow back. It was poverty.'

'That she didn't sell the cow for its meat, shows that she is not all bad,' said Mrs Koshy.

'We seem ready to forgive her,' said Thankam.

'Servants are impossible,' said Mrs Koshy. 'We can't do without them, but when they are with you, they drive you mad. Besides, bad usually gives way to worse.'

And that was how Chechamma came to be taken back. Chechamma had to endure a severe talking to by Thankam. She was told that she wasn't to speak above a whisper. Indeed, she was never to speak unless spoken to. Chechamma nodded dumbly.

'And throw away those clothes of yours! They stink!' said Thankam.

'You can have an old blouse of mine,' said Mrs Koshy.

Chechamma's tears came copiously.

'And I don't want you talking to the vendors in the neighbourhood,' said Mrs Koshy. 'They are always ready for a chat.'

'I never talk to men I do not know,' said Chechamma.

'It is also wise not to take things that do not belong to you,' said Thankam.

There was a fresh rush of tears. Mrs Koshy had to lead Chechamma away to the kitchen.

As if in expiation of her recent wickedness, Chechamma threw herself into a frenzy of work about the house. She swept the courtyard, washed the clothes, bathed the cow, all without the usual pother and noise. She then set to sweeping and mopping the rooms, washing the window-panes, dusting even remote ledges hitherto untouched by broom or mop.

'I don't think she can keep the pace up,' said Devi.

'I wouldn't want her to,' said Mrs Koshy.

'Pappa is already complaining of the dust storm,' said Devi.

'He has had two baths today already,' said Mrs Koshy.

But nothing could stop Chechamma's steam engine energy. After a quick inspection of the attic, Chechamma declared that the attic needed a thorough cleaning. She said that they had abandoned the place to scorpions, centipedes and spiders for too long. The attic, Chechamma argued, could be used as a storeroom. Mrs Koshy agreed but not with any enthusiasm. Ever since Mr Koshy's fall from the attic stairs, she couldn't think of the attic without discomfort.

The house soon echoed to a thousand sounds from the attic. Mr Koshy mumbled a prayer, convinced that a band of frantic noise-makers had invaded the house. He waited tremblingly for some irruption from the ceiling. Mrs Koshy said that it was only Chechamma cleaning the attic.

'I knew you would say something like that,' he said.

'But it is,' said Mrs Koshy.

'Of course it is,' said Mr Koshy, sarcastically.

Chechamma attacked cob-webs, white-ant hills and the all pervading dust, with truly splendid energy. She pursued tarantulas and black widows from wall to wall, hitting out at them with her coconut husk broom. After she had done for one particularly large tarantula, she inspected its ripped abdomen and spinnerets with relish. She attacked cockroaches with the same ruthlessness, cutting off their escape routes with skill and precision. Some cockroaches tried, as cockroaches will, to escape by flying into the rafters but always Chechamma seemed to anticipate these movements. She felled them before their frantically whirring wings carried them out of reach of her coconut husk broom. Chechamma's broom swept, sliced, chopped, squashed and crushed, depending on whether she chose to use the stick or the coconut husk end of the broom. That Chechamma had grown up with a coconut husk broom and was acquainted with its multiple uses was plain enough.

However, Chechamma was unexpectedly tender with the soft-skinned geckos. The gecko was harmless and it was a local superstition that killing a gecko brought bad luck. The silly things shed their wriggly tails at the first hint of trouble. Chechamma could not help smiling at this pathetic feint. She helped lizards lost or frozen in mid-passage, to safety.

There were two large dormer windows in the attic, hidden behind rolls of discarded jute carpeting and linoleum. Chechamma waded to the windows through knee-deep tailoring odds and ends. She pulled down stacked rolls of jute carpeting, careless of the dust around her. Finally, when she had the windows clear, she flung them open, letting in sunlight and fresh air. She filled her lungs with air, then breathed out in little puffs. Her hands had begun to blister. But she would press on till the attic was livable once more, and not for lizards alone. Her guilt about the cow she had stolen was less oppressive now. She had won forgiveness of a kind through work.

'This place is cleaner now,' Chechamma called out from the attic.

'Are there lizards in the attic?' Devi asked. Devi had a horror of lizards.

'Lizards don't hurt nobody and nobody should hurt lizards,' replied Chechamma. But to Devi this was hardly the point.

'Are there centipedes?' called out Lalu. He had heard it said that centipedes made good, if unusual, pets.

'I've killed them all,' said Chechamma.

'Not even Chechamma can kill them all,' said Mrs Koshy.

'Dead centipedes have such a rotten stink,' said Lalu.

'Ugh,' said Devi.

The attic was to the Koshys, mother, daughter and son, a place of ill-omen. It was dusty. It crawled with strange insect life. Its invisible hand had pushed Pappa down the stairs. Mrs Koshy had tried to forget the attic.

'Malaysian houses did not have attics, thank goodness. They were sensibly put together,' said Devi.

'Perhaps Malaysia was sensibly put together,' said Mrs Koshy.

Mrs Koshy thought that attics are most unlikable when they threaten to compete with the house itself. They really have no right to steal character from the rest of the house, certainly not to spread gloom in the way this attic did. The attic, in Kerala houses, the gloomy *thattinpuram*, is the last place to be civilized. It is never a straightforward business of good housekeeping alone, as poor Chechamma seemed to think. Winning back this attic is more than a matter of sweeping away the cobwebs and routing the cockroaches and the lizards.

And then they heard Chechamma shriek.

'She must have seen a centipede,' said Lalu.

'It will take more than one centipede to frighten Chechamma,' said Mrs Koshy.

'Or it must be ghosts,' said Lalu.

'Yes,' said Mrs Koshy, 'Chechamma has that sort of mind.'

Chechamma came rushing down the stairs. She looked angry. 'I saw the shameless picture. A woman hotter than a hot she-buffalo. And a man where he has no business to be. And a tantrik waiting for his turn with the woman. I tell you, Ammachy, Shatan himself has been visiting the *thattinpuram*.' She spoke between gulps. 'I can smell his evil. The *thattinpuram* is *ashuddham*. The skull and the serpent head tell me all that I need to know. I will never again step into it.'

Tantra is full of vigorous but rather dotty orgies of which ordinary folk do not approve. Nothing frightens them so much as its devil-raising rituals. Houses have been known to burn like coconut oil torches, and bridegrooms reduced to wedding night impotence by its magic.

'And now you will scare the children,' said Mrs Koshy. 'Chechamma, go into the kitchen if you can't contain yourself.'

'I want to serve you,' said Chechamma. 'To work the skin off my hands for you . . . but do the gods give me half of half a chance?'

Chechamma went into the kitchen, looking defiant. She knew she was right to warn them. She 'knew' what they didn't know: idols and other things holy have a deep life of their own, but so too did *ashuddham* objects. Tantriks have a way of making the forces of the deep listen. These are the facts of life, which every Malayali absorbs with his mother's milk.

In the kitchen, Chechamma broadcast her nerves, by banging pots and pans, as if protesting against what she had seen.

'The new Chechamma didn't last long,' said Devi. She was saying that Chechamma belonged to an older Kerala, a Kerala that could not change. The pots and pans sounded again. Chechamma was heard saying that she should never have cleaned the attic. 'Already I feel the curse of the *thattinpuram* in my bones.' The pots and pans supplied noisy punctuation marks.

'We've a duty to fight such silliness,' said Mrs Koshy.

Mamma is sturdy common sense, thought Devi. But Devi was also half afraid that her mother's talk of duty, of fight, came of poorly handled stress. It was nice to know that her mother wasn't going under, but it would be just as nice to know that she wasn't becoming a warrior.

Mrs Koshy thought of her husband, sleeping through all their troubles. She was alone. There was Devi, of course, but it would be selfish of her to burden Devi. Worries wore down a girl. Devi had to look her best to find the right husband. It was a subject on which some eloquence was possible.

It was night already. The swiftness of nightfall in Kerala continued to astonish the Koshys. It was as if a switch in the heavens were put off.

Forming a train, Devi's arms round her mother's waist, Lalu's arms round Devi's waist, mother, daughter and son went down the stairs. Now they had only one another to steer by.

Devi felt something soft fall on her shoulder. She let it be, fearing what she may discover.

It was only when they were downstairs that Devi dared to look at her shoulder. There was a horrible tell-tale lizard stump. The lizard had slithered into Devi's blouse, and did not give itself away until a little later. The family would always remember the hugely undignified scene.

Chechamma laughed to herself. The 'sastras' were quite emphatic. Discover a lizard on your person and trouble you will have in plenty. Lizard lore was a department of learning by itself.

'The cow has fallen ill,' Chechamma announced in stricken tones, a week after she had brought it home. To Chechamma the cow was more pet than livestock. Mr Koshy said that the cow and Chechamma had much in common.

'This is the working of the curse of the *thattinpuram*,' Chechamma added in an undertone, as if continuing her unfinished argument with the Koshy family.

Mrs Koshy decided she wouldn't hear her.

Chechamma said that the cow's stomach was an explosive bag of gas. 'Everything it eats comes out in a waterfall,' said Chechamma. 'The poor thing is covered with its own green, watery dung. It can hardly stand up.' It is a sign of trouble when a cow is 'grounded'.

The vet from the government veterinary department was sent for. The vet said that he was busy for a whole week and that their cow would have to wait its turn.

Chechamma cursed the vet. 'No doubt he thinks that animals are less trouble dead. May every well run dry when he is dying and needs a drink!'

'Maybe we should ask Avrachen,' said Mrs Koshy. Avrachen knew his way about the jungle of government departments.

Avrachen said that a government department needed grease to work. He arranged for a little 'grease'. He sent the vet a bottle of toddy and some cardamom from his estates.

The vet came in a jeep. He carried a nylon bag and a torch. His assistant carried a pink official register. The vet shook his head after seeing the cow. He looked at his assistant who also shook his head.

The vet had to skip out of the way of a sudden waterfall.

This only confirmed his judgement. 'Bhagwan!' he said. 'Does this bloody cow have a stomach at all?' With many precautions, the vet peered into the cow's mouth and rear. His assistant held the torch and watched for any warning contractions.

'It is sad,' said the vet. 'The cow will never calve again.'

'But what disease is it?' asked Mrs Koshy.

'A kind of cancer,' said the vet.

'What is cansher?' asked Chechamma.

The vet explained. 'It rots the stomach and the womb. It spreads from cell to cell like a fire.'

Chechamma said that it was most unfair.

The vet agreed that cancer was most unfair.

'Is there nothing we can do?' asked Mrs Koshy.

'You can take the womb out,' said the vet. To Mrs Koshy and Chechamma this seemed a remedy worse than the disease.

'Well,' said the vet's assistant, 'you could sell the cow for its meat.'

'We will never do that,' said Chechamma piously. 'We are not cow killers.'

'If you change your mind,' said the vet's assistant, scribbling a name on a piece of paper torn from his pink register, 'I know a butcher who does it painlessly.'

'Is your butcher's chopper made of rubber?' asked Chechamma angrily. She thought it wrong that an animal doctor should even know a butcher. This was just as wrong as it was for doctors and undertakers to work together. They had or ought to have entirely different vocations.

Later, Chechamma said there was no such thing as 'cansher-mansher'. It was a disease that existed only in government registers. The cow was only suffering from a heavy stomach flu and bad digestion. Sometimes the grass that the grass women brought for the cow contained valari weed that irritated the stomach. The upset was frightening while it lasted but it would soon pass. 'That vet knows less than any common village lad about these things. These government animal doctors are just butchers with another signboard.'

Chechamma said she would pit her knowledge against that of the vet's. 'My no-learning against his book-learning!' As her anger grew, so did her suspicion that the doctor was in league with the butcher.

'Give me a chance, Ammachy,' she pleaded. Chechamma was also asking for another chance to redeem herself. Mrs Koshy nodded. Mrs Koshy had been brought up to trust doctors, but cancer seemed an extravagant diagnosis. And the man had only a torch and a pink register to help him to the diagnosis.

Chechamma brought the village medicine man to look at the cow. He did not shake his head. He did not diagnose cancer. He told Mrs Koshy that the cow had caught a cold in the stomach and this had churned up the stomach and many neighbouring parts.

'Three times a day for three days,' he said, measuring out a white powder. 'Cows like it.' He explained that the powder contained neem seed and leaf and a gooseberry tincture.

To Chechamma he whispered that a *bhootam* (evil spirit), probably from the *thattinpuram*, had entered the cow. He said that he would send her *prasadam* from the Devi temple in the village. The cow had to be fed the *prasadam* three times a day for three days. This was the real cure.

Chechamma sensed victory over the government vet already. The Koshys would have to take back their contempt for the 'spirit' world.

Chechamma quickly made the *erethil*, the cow shed and barn, into an infirmary. Oils and *arishatams* (health tonic), the use of which only Chechamma seemed to know, crowded the single shelf there was in the *erethil*. She drew water for the cow from the well, arguing that unseen poisons lurked in tap water. She checked the grass that the grass women brought for valari. One *thotta-vaadi* (forget-me-not) was enough to destroy a digestion for two generations. Piously she fetched the *prasadam* from the Devi temple three times a day.

She kept some back for herself—on the principle that a nurse needs spiritual bolstering as much as the patient.

On his second visit the medicine man recommended rock salt for the blood circulation. A poor circulation makes for sluggishness. Chechamma went to Shankamukham beach to buy fresh rock salt from the salt stills along the coast. On the way back she stopped at a wayside Devi shrine to pray.

'May she get better soon,' she prayed with trembling-lip fervour.

'Is it your child that you are praying for?' asked a temple attendant.

Chechamma hesitated briefly. 'Yes,' she said. Well, it was the truth, after a fashion. Besides, any other answer would have involved a complicated explanation.

'May the Devi hear your prayer!' said the attendant.

Chechamma dropped a rupee into the open palms of the attendant. The attendant brought a piece of coconut *prasadam* from the inner sanctum.

'Is it for me or the cow?' Chechamma asked absent-mindedly.

'The cow?' echoed the attendant.

Chechamma giggled all the way home.

Chechamma stitched a cloth jersey for the cow. It ended in a long-eared cap for the head. The jersey was for the stomach and was intended as a second skin, to keep out colds and whistling winds. The cap was to ward off spirits.

The cow began to recover on the second day. Its stomach was better disciplined. Its appetite returned. It stood up. Its ears flapped playfully. Chechamma blessed the Shankamukham Devi.

When the vet called on the third day, Chechamma tried to hustle him out of the *erethil* as quickly as she could. She feared his evil eye.

'I think,' ventured Mrs Koshy cautiously, 'the cow is much better.'

'I think not,' said the vet. 'There is clotted blood and pus in its urine.'

Mrs Koshy didn't know what to make of that.

'You know what that means!' said the vet.

Mrs Koshy didn't.

'It may have started haemorrhaging,' said the vet. He used the English word. 'Or will start soon.'

'My God!' said Mrs Koshy.

'Don't let his long words frighten you, Ammachy,' said Chechamma stoutly. 'Give me two more days.'

The cow continued to improve on the third day. Chechamma felt the cure was complete when the cow playfully butted her. Chechamma took the cap off. 'I don't want you to look ridiculous,' said Chechamma, stroking the cow. But the jersey stayed. Chechamma said that it would stay for another week.

Chechamma was happy in a very self-congratulatory way. She trumpeted the story of her victory over veterinary science to all who would listen. And most of the neighbourhood was willing to listen.

'Did he really recommend the name of a butcher?' was the question that rang round the neighbourhood.

'Yes, indeed!' said Chechamma.

'Shame, shame, shame . . . .' Chechamma was thumped on the back for her courage. She had earned a lot of *punyam* (credit) for herself by saving a cow from a butcher's knife.

But on the morning of the fifth day Chechamma found the cow on the floor of the *erethil*. Its head was on the floor too. There was a pool of blood and mucus around it. The cow had died during the night.

The cow was a painful sight. Chechamma was a painful sight.

Mrs Koshy tried to comfort her. 'The curse of the *thattinpuram*, I know that it is the curse of the *thattinpuram*,' muttered Chechamma. It was the curse of the *thattinpuram* that had defeated her, not 'cansher'.

Thankam sent two of her estate labourers to remove the cow. The labourers threw the cow into the back of a lorry. The cow corpse was rock hard. The lorry rattled.

'Do you want to remove the jersey?' asked the labourers.

'No,' said Chechamma.

'All right,' said the labourers, 'but I tell you it won't be cold where the cow is going.' They were saying that they would burn the cow.

The last that Chechamma saw of the cow was its hooves facing up. Sad, protesting hooves.

In the *erethil*, Chechamma told the stuffed, eyeless calf, 'Sometimes I wish I didn't have eyes either. Better darkness than to see such sadness.'

Chechamma felt as orphaned as the calf.

# Chapter Six

'INDIA,' WROTE LALU to Pragasam,

is a place where nothing is allowed to remain
ordinary and flat. We live in a fairy tale. Pappa was
an ordinary sort of person in Malaysia. His God
was a Sunday God. He said his prayers of course
but always as if he couldn't wait to rush away
elsewhere. He prayed only because Mamma expected him to pray. But look at Pappa now. He
walks with God. He speaks to God. Sometimes I
think he is God. I used to think the God of our
Sunday School strange. And the Allah of Friday
prayers stranger. How we used to giggle at the
bellowing from the mosques! But Pappa has found
the strangest God of all. Pappa's is an odd God all
right. And Pappa is not dull and flat anymore. He
sees more. There are depths in his eyes. Depths in his
conversations. He looks at you differently . . . .

Lalu had rewritten his father into a fairy-tale.

'Koshy is getting stranger by the hour,' said Thankam to Avrachen. Thankam insisted on visiting her sister almost daily.

For no more reason than that the last book he had been
reading had been an exposition of Zen, Koshy now insisted
on speaking only of Zen.

'The "Ah" of all things,' he said. 'The beauty of the rose is
only "Ah".'

'Help me,' said Thankam.

Dr Vareed prescribed sedatives. Avrachen called it defeatist medicine.

'Pappa you must take your medicine,' said Devi.

'Sedatives!' exclaimed Mr Koshy. 'What a silly idea!' But he swallowed the pills Devi gave him.

'We must take his books away from him,' said Thankam to Mrs Koshy. 'They are so bad for him.'

'When Pappa had a nine-to-five job, he had to keep a grip on himself,' said Mrs Koshy.

'But look at him now,' said Thankam.

'Look at me now,' said Mr Koshy. 'The two eyes are the third eye.'

'It is so maddening,' said Thankam.

'It is meant to be,' said Mr Koshy. 'Cats are meant to spit. And mad men are meant to be maddening.'

'Pappa is so difficult over trifles,' whispered Thankam to Mrs Koshy. 'I try to be patient.'

'You are tired of us already, Thankam,' said Mrs Koshy.

'Oh, no, Sosamma,' said Thankam quickly. But Thankam knew her sister had come close to the truth.

'Thankam has worried eyes,' said Mr Koshy. 'But worse, she has worry lines in her face. She must take care the worry lines do not deepen. Worry lines reach all the way to the grave . . . .'

'I wonder if Avrachen can take Pappa to his estates in Munnar for a while,' said Mrs Koshy. Munnar has a bracing climate.

'I don't think that would be wise at all,' said Thankam. 'You know it is a long story.'

'Indeed,' said Mrs Koshy, afraid that Thankam would begin one of her many stories of Avrachen's faithlessness. The tea pickers at Avrachen's estates in Munnar were always ready to please the boss. Even with so vigilant a chaperon as Thankam, there were times Avrachen disappeared for many hours into the trackless tea gardens. A Eurasian overseer punningly described these as disappearances into the bush.

'No one can reason with Pappa in his present mood,' said Devi.

Mrs Koshy said she was beginning to live on her nerves. Madhavan Thampy was impossible and her husband seemed to want to behave like an exasperating sort of child.

Thankam suggested that their brothers, Mathaichen and Kunjunj, stalwart landlords both, be called for a family council. 'Our brothers are used to being obeyed,' said Thankam. 'And to settling some arguments with *mammoties* (shovels). And a *mammoty* is just the thing for Madhavan Thampy.'

'What can your brothers do that I can't?' Avrachen asked Thankam. Avrachen always felt diminished in the presence of his brothers-in-law.

'You are a glutton for sleep,' said Thankam. They were on the edge of an argument over the tea-pickers of Munnar. Thankam was speaking in code. Avrachen sought more than sleep in the arms of the tea-pickers. Thankam had once confided in her sister that it made her feel unclean even to think of the tea-pickers. There was so much disease about in the hills. Yet, almost in the spirit of a martyr, Thankam had borne Avrachen two children, both boys. What more could a husband ask of an ill-used wife?

'Is a husband less than a brother?' asked Avrachen.

Thankam and Avrachen appealed to Mrs Koshy. Their quarrels were sometimes conducted with an umpire. The preferred umpires were a visiting relative.

'A brother is a brother and a husband a husband,' said Mrs Koshy. It was a very careful neutrality.

'All right, all right. Call your brothers if you want to,' grumbled Avrachen.

'Sosamma,' said Thankam to Mrs Koshy. 'You and I must pray for patience. We have to be patient with our husbands.'

'God loves wives more than He loves husbands,' said Avrachen dourly.

'Pappa has become very fragile,' said Mrs Koshy, trying to take the conversation away from husband-and-wife bickering.

'Soft,' said Avrachen. 'There is no place for softness is this land.'

'Sometimes I think that someone has cast a spell on him,' said Thankam. 'A black magic spell.'

'The church doesn't approve of such talk,' said Mrs Koshy.

'Church ceremonies are also magic,' said Avrachen.

'White,' said Mrs Koshy.

'I know a priest who for twenty rupees a time will chase away a haunting spirit,' said Avrachen.

'Sosamma,' said Thankam. 'I think you should consult a *mantravadin* (shaman) about your house. There may be many unappeased spirits there. After all a man died there. A godman.'

'I have never heard such nonsense,' said Mrs Koshy.

'You have stayed away from our land for too long,' said Thankam, almost pityingly.

'Pappa won't approve,' said Mrs Koshy.

'His Zen is magic too,' said Thankam. 'But bad magic.'

'We'll be the laughing stock of the neighbourhood,' said Mrs Koshy. 'Church on Sundays and now this.'

'You'll be surprised how few will laugh,' said Thankam. 'A ceremony like this brings the whole neighbourhood together. It won't be plain exorcism. That would be too crude. It must be a sacrifice for peace, peace in the family, peace in the neighbourhood.'

'You make it sound almost respectable.'

'It is,' said Thankam. 'It is the only real religion we Malayalis have and ever will.'

'But, Thankam, have you ever tried to use magic to solve your problems?' asked Mrs Koshy. She disliked yielding the initative wholly to Thankam. It was a habit from childhood rivalry.

'I have used *mantravadins*,' said Thankam quietly.

'You have?' asked Avrachen in surprise. 'What for?'

'That my sons might never know what their father does with his spare time,' said Thankam with sudden bitterness.

'Is that a riddle or an answer?' asked Avrachen.

Mrs Koshy took Thankam by the arm and led her away to the kitchen.

'I'll have an answer,' Avrachen shouted after her. But he made no effort to pursue Thankam. They were an odd couple. They had worked out the rules of their kind of marriage. To refrain from angry pursuit was one of the rules.

Kunjunj was a tall man with a sallow complexion. He was the eldest in the family. He had not married. Many had speculated why, but none of the theories, some wildly imaginative, stood up to fair scrutiny. He liked female company. So 'that' was ruled out. Kunjunj became abruptly cold and hostile when the subject of marriage was broached with him. At sixty-four he was a bachelor, a contented bachelor.

Mathaichen, the younger of Mrs Koshy's two brothers, was the prolific one. He had married early, at eighteen, rushing to the altar to avoid scandal. He had known his wife carnally before marriage and, he boasted, with unflagging energy thereafter. In twenty-two years of marriage, he had fathered nine children, seven boys and two girls. He insisted that the seven boys testified to his virility, though his friends laughed at the whimsicality of the theory.

'Hmmm,' said Kunjunj, when he met Mrs Koshy.

Mrs Koshy began to cry.

'Is it so bad?' asked Kunjunj. 'Oh Lord!'

'And Koshy?' asked Mathaichen.

Mrs Koshy cried all the more.

'Oh Lord!' said Kunjunj. He had never known his sister to cry.

'Koshy is not himself,' said Thankam.

'He isn't . . . is he?'

'He is half way there, I am afraid,' whispered Thankam.

'Breaking things?' asked Mathaichen.

'Nothing like that,' said Devi. 'He has become quieter, more reflective.'

'Religion?' asked Kunjunj.

'Zen,' said Devi.

'So long as it is another way of worshipping Christ,' said Mathaichen.

'It isn't,' said Devi.

'What!' said Mathaichen, aghast. 'You must call in a priest.'

'Let us talk to him first,' said Kunjunj. 'Priests are not what they once were. They talk. Talk creates scandal and scandal I won't have.'

Mr Koshy was sitting up in bed, reading Christmas Humphreys on Zen. He gazed at his visitors in a gentle way: he was a Zen master now. Beside Kunjunj, Mr Koshy looked small, soulful and demure.

'It is the books that he reads that are to blame,' said Thankam. 'They make up his mind in many silly ways.'

'Christmas Humphreys!' said Mathaichen pronouncing the name in broken syllables. Mathaichen did not read English easily. 'Sounds Christian enough to me.' He flipped through the book, pausing at the illustrations. 'But I'm not sure of these pictures,' he said after a while, staring at a photograph of the mother temple of Soto, seat of Zen, the Zendo of Soji-ji. 'Strange spellings. Too many z's and j's. It doesn't sound right. It isn't right.' He spoke as if he suspected a confidence trick of some kind.

'I've never understood what he reads,' said Mrs Koshy.

'I've never understood Koshy,' said Kunjunj, making it sound like a damning judgement.

'He isn't strong enough for our land,' said Thankam.

'A cut worm is two worms. A cut man is dead,' said Mr Koshy, wistfully.

'This is what I have to live with,' said Mrs Koshy.

'This is serious,' said Kunjunj.

'Serious,' echoed Mathaichen.

'Zen masters express themselves oddly,' said Devi.

'Of that I have no doubt,' said Kunjunj.

'What shall I do?' asked Mrs Koshy. 'What shall we do?'

'I know what we must do to Madhavan Thampy,' said Kunjunj. 'But about him . . . .' He pointed with a shrug of his shoulders at Mr Koshy.

'Sometimes he talks like a child,' said Mrs Koshy.

'He forgets that he is the father of two children,' said Mathaichen.

'He is the head of the family . . . but if the head is soft!' said Kunjunj. He led the way to what was called the family boardroom, the *pathayam*. Kunjunj seated himself at the head of the table. Avrachen and Mathaichen flanked him.

'I should have been called sooner,' said Kunjunj.

Avrachen thought he was being accused, unfairly so. 'It was harvest time. We didn't want to call you away . . . .'

'A full granary isn't everything,' said Kunjunj, running his eyes round the table. Snubbed, Avrachen fell silent.

Ungraciously, Thankam nodded. Like Mrs Koshy she thought her side of the family superior to her husband's. Avrachen's family was 'old money' Her family was landed 'aristocracy'. Kunjunj was well bred, though she had to admit that Mathaichen's manners could be very common.

'I hear that Madhavan Thampy called twice,' said Kunjunj.

'He has become so threatening,' said Mrs Koshy.

Kunjunj looked fierce and leathery. 'Let Thampy huff and puff till he bursts,' he said, 'but we will continue to live in this house as long as it suits us.'

Thankam purred her approval. This was family solidarity at its best. The pack standing together and baying together. Selfishly, she was glad that Kunjunj hadn't married. His passion for his family certainly was sublimated energy. Thankam thought of poor, fuddled Mr Koshy. There were two of him now—the simpering invalid and the Zen abbot. Poor Sosamma, she was married to both of them.

'But won't Madhavan Thampy harass us?' asked Mrs Koshy.

'There will be no harassment,' said Kunjunj.

'It is just that Madhavan Thampy has no idea what he is up against,' said Mathaichen. 'When we explain matters, he will understand.'

'And the smashed outer kitchen?' asked Mrs Koshy.

'We'll repair it,' said Kunjunj.

'And the drainage?' asked Mrs Koshy.

'We'll put in the drainage,' said Kunjunj. 'Two deep soak pits.'

'And the money for them?' asked Mrs Koshy. She knew she was being tiresome, but she had to know. Sometimes Kunjunj could be very impatient of detail and leave things in the air.

Thankam thought her sister's questions graceless. In a superior tone of voice, she said, 'We never talk money at a family council.' Thankam looked at Avrachen. A 'loan' from Avrachen was usually the answer. Both Kunjunj and Mathaichen sponged on Avrachen mercilessly. They never applied for money to him directly. Thankam was the conduit. Many years of bullying and brainwashing by Thankam and her family, had reconciled Avrachen to his role as the nitwit provider.

'I doubt whether Madhavan Thampy would want us to put in drains,' said Kunjunj in a sly voice.

Mathaichen smiled knowingly at the remark. It was a tease. It was evidence of their worldly wisdom.

'Why shouldn't he?' asked Mrs Koshy naïvely.

'Because,' said Avrachen quickly, eager to prove that he knew just as much about these things, 'because it might be the first step towards owning the house.'

'I would never want to do that,' said Mrs Koshy.

'It is not a house after your own heart, is it?' asked Mathaichen.

'No,' said Mrs Koshy. 'Besides, it doesn't belong to us.'

'Of course, I almost forgot,' said Mathaichen. 'But we

mustn't be overwhelmed by that. We will have Madhavan Thampy whining at your feet like a pariah dog if you stand on your rights as a tenant.'

It was a simple plan. The Koshys would repair the kitchen and put in the drains and soak pits. Avrachen would find the labourers for the work. The Koshys would leave the house when it suited them and it would not suit them for a very long time. In Communist Kerala tenancy laws took the side of the tenant. The landlord was the interloper.

'We were planning to buy a house,' said Mrs Koshy, not entirely comfortable with her brothers' strategy.

'Just so,' said Kunjunj.

Mathaichen smirked. Avrachen smirked too. Kunjunj was a sly customer. Madhavan Thampy had caught the proverbial *puli vaal* (tiger's tail). He had, in another idiom, caught a tartar.

'I don't understand,' said Mrs Koshy.

'She wouldn't,' said Mathaichen.

'You may be able to buy Madhavan Thampy's house,' said Kunjunj.

'At a knock-down price,' said Avrachen, enjoying his pun.

'I wouldn't like that,' said Mrs Koshy

'A roof is a roof,' said Kunjunj. 'And try to remember that we have to find a husband for Devi. No one will marry into a family without a house to call its own.'

'And some sons-in-law even expect to be supported,' said Mathaichen.

'That is impossible,' said Mrs Koshy, in some alarm.

'There is a wealthy family of landlords in Kuttanad,' said Mathaichen. 'They have two sons. The elder son doesn't care for marriage. The younger son is looking for a bride. He is twenty-one. The right age.'

'What does he do?' asked Mrs Koshy.

'He is just a rich man's son,' said Mathaichen. 'But he has plans to join politics.'

'Then he may need to be a rich man's son-in-law as well,' said Thankam.

'They are, I think, rich enough not to have to think of that,' said Mathaichen.

'Politics is money, isn't it?' asked Mrs Koshy.

'Some win, some lose,' said Mathaichen. 'This family plays to win.'

'Shrewd are they?' asked Thankam.

'Shrewd enough not to want to marry a girl with a small dowry?' asked Mrs Koshy.

'But how small is small?' asked Thankam.

'Five thousand,' said Mrs Koshy.

'Cold cash?' asked Mathaichen.

'Cold cash,' said Mrs Koshy, thinking this was how she had bargained for her cow.

'By the way, what is this Zen?' asked Kunjunj.

'A Chinese philosophy Devi tells me,' said Mrs Koshy.

'Nothing to do with Chinese Communism, I hope,' said Mathaichen. 'This landlord's family has always fought the Communists.'

'In the end, only Koshy will know what his ideas mean,' said Mathaichen.

'If so, thank the Lord,' said Kunjunj. 'So long as the muddle doesn't have a name.'

On this note of thin humour, the family council ended.


Madhavan Thampy prided himself on knowing something about the law: he had attended six months of classes at the Law College in Tiruvananthapuram before he had left college to join Mahatma Gandhi's Non-cooperation movement.

Thampy had been beaten up by the Diwan's police thrice. The Diwan, Sir C. P. Ramaswami Aiyar, true knight of the Empire that he was, thought a lot better of the Indian Civil Service of which he considered himself an honorary member, than he did of the Indian National Congress. Sir C. P.'s reply to Gandhiji's non-violence was the boots of his Malabar Police.

The Malabar Police had beaten up Thampy thrice. It was in the third and most vicious of these beatings that Thampy had had one of his testicles punctured by a policeman's lathi. Thampy had thought less well of non-violence after the beating. He didn't think it a philosophy for men, real men. The policeman's swagger stick had quite deliberately sought out a soft target and broken it like an egg.

With independence, Thampy could have applied for a freedom fighter's pension, but male vanity forbade. He was afraid that an embarrassing physical examination would be necessary. Long weeks in hospital in an effort to repair the testicular damage had made him morbidly afraid of having those parts handled. Doctors could be rough and nurses giggly. Thampy felt the world was always laughing at him for his missing testicle. In some measure this was true, for his curious history was common knowledge in so small a town as Tiruvananthapuram. He was always anxious to prove that he was as much, if not more, a man as any of those who laughed at him. It was this anxiety that in some part explained his fractious manners.

When Mathaichen called on him, Madhavan Thampy forbade him to repair the house.

'Then I will have to ask for permission in writing,' said Mathaichen. 'You cannot stop me from writing letters to you and sending them to you by registered post.'

'But I can refuse to receive such letters,' said Thampy.

'Then I'll have a record of your refusal.' Mathaichen was even with Thampy, trick for trick.

'You realize that repairing the kitchen and putting in the drains will cost you more than five thousand rupees. I will not allow it to be set off against the rent.'

'My sister's comfort matters more than the money,' said Mathaichen.

'They don't have a house of their own, of course,' observed Thampy.

'No.'

'Their daughter isn't married yet?'

'No.'

'It is usual to want a house of one's own before looking for a son-in-law.'

'I suppose so.'

'But I would warn you against any designs on my house.'

'I'd warn you against rudeness.'

'I'm a very blunt man,' said Thampy.

'But never quite a bully,' said Mathaichen, sarcastically. 'Do you know Kunnukuzhi Mohan?' asked Mathaichen. Kunnukuzhi was a rowdy part of Tiruvananthapuram, and Kunnukuzhi Mohan was the gangster 'lord' of Kunnukuzhi.

'Bhagwan curse the time when I came to know him,' said Thampy.

Thampy feared Kunnukuzhi Mohan. Many years ago their paths had crossed. Kunnukuzhi Mohan had threatened to smash Thampy's surviving testicle, putting the threat as ribaldly as he could. Thampy had kept out of Kunnukuzhi Mohan's way ever since. Kunnukuzhi Mohan liked to say that he prayed for his enemies every day, prayed that they might not come to any mortal harm at his hands.

'Kunnukuzhi Mohan told me that he will be glad to get you,' said Mathaichen, rather enjoying Thampy's discomfiture. 'He said something about an unfinished job. He said that he wanted to knock off the other one too.'

'The scavenger dog!' said Thampy.

'I had to go to him,' said Mathaichen in mock-apology. 'For my sister's sake. Sometimes to fight a small fire we need a big fire.'

'Small fire!' howled Thampy. Thampy had been called many names, but never 'small fire'. He was certain that Mathaichen was joking about the missing testicle.

Kunnukuzhi Mohan, said Thampy, was the son of a sweeper-woman. His father was cut down in a street brawl when Mohan was only two. His mother had survived by offering herself in the market-place. 'For four annas,' said

Thampy as if speaking from personal recollection, 'you could have the woman—and her diseases. The son of such a woman now hops in and out of the houses of ministers. Like of course keeps company with like.' His was a terrible anger.

Kunnukuzhi Mohan invited Avrachen and Mathaichen to visit him at his bungalow. Avrachen said this was impudence. Could Mohan so quickly forget that he had once worked as a chaprasi in one of his estate offices?

'It is strange,' said Mathaichen, 'that some people should fret about visiting Mohan but think it all right to sleep with tea-picking women. What fleas does Mohan have that the tea-picking women don't?'

Thankam had been complaining to her brothers again. Avrachen wished he could in very plain speech tell them that any man who had known the ministrations of tea-pickers, would hardly want to be boxed in by a stale marriage. Two leaves and a bud was almost an erotic simile. The tea-pickers knew all about picking two-leaves-and-a-bud in bed as well as anywhere else. For fear that he would betray himself by foolish speech Avrachen made an excuse to leave the room.

'It is not proper for me as an elder of the family to visit Mohan,' said Kunjunj to Mathaichen. 'But you can go. You are not yet an elder.' He spoke without irony.

'Mohan said that he would send the car round to fetch us,' said Mathaichen.

'I wouldn't think that necessary at all,' said Kunjunj. 'And should he ask you to stay for a meal?'

'I eat only with my equals,' said Mathaichen, irritated by Kunjunj's big brother tone.

'You must try to make your case without seeming to beg,' said Kunjunj.

'What topsy-turvy times we live in!' said Mathaichen, determined to keep his end up in the conversation. 'Consider, would our father have waited on a low-born like Mohan?

Father had dignity, the dignity of his five hundred acres and hundred servants.'

'We are among the oldest of Syrian Christian families,' said Kunjunj, 'but in the end even ancient families must come to terms with the times they live in.' He sighed.

Later that afternoon the driver of a shiny red Mercedes Benz asked for Mathaichen. The driver said that he had been sent by Kunnukuzhi Mohan.

'But we had agreed that you wouldn't travel in Mohan's car,' said Kunjunj.

'Would it be polite to send it back?' asked Mathaichen.

'All right,' said Kunjunj. 'You can go in the car. But come back in a taxi.'

The driver of the Benz held the door of the car open and waited till Mathaichen had settled in before he closed the door. The door shut with a murmurous click. A refined and smooth driver. A refined and smooth car.

'Our Master is waiting for you, sir,' said the driver, conversationally, but his tone was not familiar. That the Master should wait for him, was a sign of special favour.

'Hmmm,' said Mathaichen. So, Mohan was 'our Master' now.

'Our Master told me that you are one of his oldest friends,' said the driver.

Give me strength, prayed Mathaichen.

'I have known him a long time, yes,' said Mathaichen aloud.

'Our Master never forgets a friend.'

'He doesn't?'

The driver missed the note of interrogation.

'Nor an enemy,' he continued.

'You know him well?' asked Mathaichen, determined that this time the question, sarcastic in intent, should sound like a question.

'I'm only his driver, sir.' It was the only possible answer.

Conversation languished.

Then the driver said, 'Sir, this is a new Benz.'

'It is a very bright red,' said Mathaichen.

'Our Master's choice.'

'Of course,' said Mathaichen.

Kunnukuzhi Mohan was waiting for Mathaichen at the door of his terraced-roof mansion. Mohan was a short, dark man. His head was built like a bludgeon, a particularly rounded bludgeon. His neck was an impressively sturdy pillar. However, it rose from a weak chest and a disgracefully pendulous paunch. Good living was taking its obvious toll.

Mohan grasped Mathaichen affectionately by the shoulders. Mathaichen thought the greeting right. A hug would have been familiarity. A namaste too formal. Mohan addressed Mathaichen as 'sar' which is Malayalam for 'sir'. That was properly respectful. Mathaichen was disarmed.

'A fine house,' said Mathaichen. 'I was admiring your car. A lovely colour.'

'Bhagwan's gifts,' said Mohan.

'Bhagwan has been kind to you.'

'For the first part of my life He gave me nothing,' said Mohan. 'Now He gives me everything.'

Everything, thought Mathaichen, so he imagines he has everything. 'When He gives,' said Mathaichen, 'He gives without measure. When He stops giving, He stops altogether.'

'He has a sense of humour,' said Mohan.

'But not of proportion,' said Mathaichen.

Mohan laughed heartily.

'Or of justice,' said Mathaichen.

Mohan laughed less heartily.

Mohan's reception room was all teak and satinwood. The heavy ebony furniture was arranged on gaudy linoleum. In the centre of the room under an ornate rosewood canopy, there was a scarlet lipped Ganesh.

'I don't use this room much,' said Mohan modestly.

'It is a fine room,' said Mathaichen.

'People are impressed,' said Mohan. 'It is good for business.'

'I won't ask what that is,' said Mathaichen slyly. 'You have done well in life.'

'The riches came easily,' said Mohan. 'But will they go as easily as they came?'

'Beware of income tax raids,' said Mathaichen, maliciously feeding Mohan's insecurity.

'I've nothing to hide,' said Mohan. He looked at Mathaichen a little crossly.

Mohan led Mathaichen through the reception room to what he described as his 'private' room. The private room contained no furniture. There were coir mats spread on the floor.

'This is also my shrine room,' said Mohan. There were lithographs of gods and goddesses on the wall. Multicoloured bulbs flickered at the base of each lithograph. Each lithograph was garlanded with white jasmines.

'You are thankful to the gods,' said Mathaichen.

'I try to be,' said Mohan.

'If you grow any richer, the gods will start worshipping you,' said Mathaichen.

Mohan did not care for Mathaichen's levity. 'Not in the shrine room,' he said, rather stiffly. 'It will bring bad luck.'

Mathaichen felt snubbed. Bad management of the conversation had allowed Mohan to gain a sort of advantage over him.

'I came to talk to you about my sister,' said Mathaichen. 'Madhavan Thampy is her landlord.'

'There is more trouble in his one testicle than other men have in hundred,' said Mohan. 'A very poor choice of landlord.'

'Very,' agreed Mathaichen. He told Mohan the whole story. 'My sister is afraid. We cannot come to her help from Kuttanad, every time she needs us.'

'She can count on me,' said Mohan, solemnly.

'I'm most thankful to you,' said Mathaichen. Too late he remembered Kunjunj's warning about seeming too obviously the supplicant.

'I have a score to settle with Thampy myself,' said Mohan.

'That makes things a little simpler for both of us,' said Mathaichen.

'I helped Thampy once, more than any man would. And in return he insulted me. It is a sad story.'

Mohan said that he was not married because no respectable family considered him respectable enough. He had given up trying. However, these very families which had turned him down, were ready enough to use him for his influence. They were even ready to receive him as a guest in their homes. But ask for their daughters or sisters and he could read discomfort in their suddenly twitchy hands.

'A sad story, truly,' Mohan repeated, surveying the gods on the walls, as if calling them to witness his sadness.

Madhavan Thampy, said Mohan, continuing his story, was a son of one of the more obscure cadet branches of the Travancore royal family. He was insanely proud of his 'royal' connections. But Thampy had come to Mohan for many favours. His family had many scattered farms and paddy fields, many of which had been encroached upon by land-hungry peasants. Mohan had, by a mixture of cunning, threat and violence, secured close to a score of evictions, thus saving Thampy and his family the expenses of dilatory judicial idiocies.

Thampy and his cousins had been loud in their thanks. Thampy had more than once hinted that Mohan should marry into his family. Thampy had said that he had two cousins who had fallen upon hard times. Come to think of it, he had two half-sisters who seemed just right. He praised their looks. In another age, he said, they would have made their mark at court. They had beauty, birth and breeding. Money they had none, but this of course Mohan could supply.

'It is a story of treachery,' said Mohan, looking at the gods, as if appealing for justice.

Mohan, no fool, had discovered soon enough that Thampy had no half-sisters. Thampy had been praising phantoms to Mohan. There had to be some mistake, Mohan had thought. Bhagwan grant that there is some mistake, Mohan had prayed. Thampy's phantom sisters had come to haunt his dreams. Sometimes, lustfully, he had taken them to bed: as he held them by their waists, for shamelessly he had taken both of them to bed at once, he could not but remark that there was something about well-born flesh that tickled both lust and vanity.

Mohan had confronted Thampy. Thampy had tried to put him off, but on being pressed he had confessed to the truth. Thampy had told Mohan that he thought him an excellent match for any of his 'royal' cousins and half-sisters, but that he had come up against the caste pride of an ancient line.

'Thampy did offer me in the end a cousin in marriage. Thampy has royal cousins for all occasions. This cousin was the cast-off concubine of an elderly uncle.'

'The scavenger!' said Mathaichen.

'And this scavenger,' said Mohan, pointing to himself, 'and this scavenger agreed to have her.'

'Impossible!'

'She was of fair Nair stock. Full of breast. Round of face. I liked her.'

'As a concubine . . . ?' said Mathaichen.

'No, I would have married her.'

'She turned you down?' asked Mathaichen, incredulously.

'She wouldn't marry a scavenger,' said Mohan.

Mathaichen at once regretted his expletive use of the word.

'For all my wealth, I'm still a scavenger in the sight of a concubine.'

'Unfair,' said Mathaichen.

'That's how they put people like me in their place,' said Mohan.

'They?'

'The upper castes and their gods.' He pointed to the pantheon.

'They are yours too.'

'They are theirs first.'

'Caste is rubbish,' said Mathaichen.

'It is and it is not,' said Mohan, somewhat more honestly. 'I want to forget it but it gets in my way all the time. Sometimes I think it is as much with us as the air we breathe.'

Mohan said that he had threatened to kill Thampy. 'With my bare hands,' said Mohan. 'But murder is messy.' The police were always pushed into acting when there was a murder, though they seemed happy enough to see the world destroy itself in other ways. Mohan devised a simple plan of revenge: he encouraged the very families whom he had evicted from Thampy's lands to return. The families in question though greatly bewildered by Mohan's change of heart, grabbed back what they could. Thampy went to the police. That was one measure of his defeat. The police always took care to come a day or two too late.

Thampy had begged Mohan to help. He had offered Mohan another cousin. 'I shall break every bone in her body if she refuses you,' he had said.

'But I said no to Thampy,' said Mohan. 'No fox is caught in the same hole twice, not even an out-caste fox.'

'So Thampy was ruined,' said Mathaichen, supplying the morally satisfying ending.

'No, the courts helped him to get back some of his lands. They took ten years to do what I did twice over in a month.'

Thampy had got his own back by gossiping about Mohan. 'A bride from my family for the scavenger!' Thampy was heard to say. 'When he wanted to marry one of my uncle's cast-off concubines, I told him that the concubine had said that she employed scavengers not married them.' These ferocious quips reached Mohan who felt both anger and shame,

89

the shame of the inferiority branded on his kind over the centuries.

Mohan said he had sought consolation in money. He had become a Public Works Department contractor. He had been quick to learn the art of winning tenders. Sneak 'previews' of quotations could be arranged at a price. Doctoring of quotations was not impossible. Mohan was content to keep the margin of his profit small. Greed for quick profits in the short run always made larger gains impossible, and Mohan was set for the very long run. He also became a master in a neglected branch of psychology—the psychology of the government servant. Nothing so alarms a government servant as an obvious bribe. The left hand drawer ought not to know what the right hand drawer receives. Mohan left his fat envelopes in the back of a car or inside a birthday gift of a new *mundu*. He never talked over the phone to his contacts. He never wrote them letters. He never recognized them in public places. He did his business without fuss. The bureaucrats were grateful and the tenders came his way easily.

'You are shocked at what I tell you,' said Mohan.

'I've heard worse,' said Mathaichen. He had not.

'But an untouchable's money is not untouchable,' said Mohan.

'That is so,' said Mathaichen.

'An untouchable without money is doubly untouchable,' said Mohan. 'Doubly.'

'It is a cruel world,' said Mathaichen.

'Only if you allow it to be cruel to you,' said Mohan. 'I'm not a cruel man, because I know what it is to suffer.'

Mathaichen laughed uncomfortably. These were unsuspected depths.

'Will you have a drink?' asked Mohan.

Mathaichen remembered Kunjunj's warning. Notoriously, Syrian Christians are known to mimic high-caste Hindu prejudice.

'I've known others hesitate too,' said Mohan.

'Of course, I'll have a drink,' said Mathaichen with forced heartiness.

Mathaichen chose whisky, Mohan local arrack. Mohan said that he hadn't developed a taste for the firangi stuff. Two hours later Mathaichen was still drinking. Five neat whiskies in two hours was rapid going, thought Mohan, abstemiously nursing his second arrack. Mathaichen's eyes had begun to goggle somewhat. He rubbed his belly often, as if coaxing away a protest from that quarter.

'Our family history goes back fourteen generations,' said Mathaichen. In his cups, Mathaichen always talked of family history.

'Every family goes back fourteen generations at least,' said Mohan. 'It has to.'

'But I said family history,' said Mathaichen.

'A history of what?'

'The usual things, I suppose: Hard drinking. Very hard lovemaking.' Mathaichen laughed.

'We have similar histories then,' said Mohan.

Mathaichen was taken aback by this remark. Mohan had got it all wrong. 'And public service,' added Mathaichen. 'We've had a lot of that in our family. Postmasters. Headmasters. Two bishops at least.'

'Our family too has always been in public service,' said Mohan. 'You can do without bishops, but can you do without scavengers?'

Mathaichen spluttered.

'Does the whisky taste different now?'

'Why, no!'

'Your kind are not prejudiced against my kind?'

'Why should we be? Why should I be?'

'An important difference—of course you don't speak for your family.'

'I haven't asked them.'

'You don't have to ask them. You know already. But it is good enough for me that you are not prejudiced.'

91

'I'm not,' said Mathaichen, stoutly.

'You wouldn't mind a test?'

Mathaichen gulped down his whisky, as if preparing his nerves.

'Will you,' continued Mohan, 'will you consider my marrying your niece?'

'How dare you?' shouted Mathaichen, rising shakily to his feet. 'How dare you?'

'Yes, how dare I?' said Mohan calmly.

Mathaichen shambled to the door. 'I have never been so insulted,' he muttered. 'I did not expect this from a friend.'

Mohan followed Mathaichen, helping him with door knobs and latches. In the outer veranda he was even saved from a fall. 'It is all that whisky in me,' said Mathaichen. 'And the suddenness . . . .'

'Yes, the suddenness,' said Mohan.

The red Benz was in the porch. The driver leapt to help Mathaichen.

'I won't be using the car,' said Mathaichen, pushing the driver away. The driver's arm came away from its truss-like support of Mathaichen. Mathaichen fell all of a heap.

'You need the car after all,' said Mohan.

'Kunjunj told me not to use it,' said Mathaichen, speaking with the honesty tipsy men are prone to.

'But Kunjunj also told you not to drink anything that I might give, didn't he?'

'But the whisky is bottled in Scotland,' said Mathaichen.

'Yes, tell Kunjunj that. And because neat, pure.'

The driver settled Mathaichen in the back seat. Mathaichen leaned out of the window and said, 'I have been a beast.'

'I hardly noticed.'

'About Madhavan Thampy?' asked Mathaichen, after an awkward pause.

'I have given you my word.'

'Oh, what a beast I've been,' said Mathaichen as the car purred down the drive.

'Our Master is a wonderful person,' said the driver.

'He is,' said Mathaichen earnestly.

'He has a long memory for friends . . . and enemies.'

'I hope I'm still a friend,' muttered Mathaichen. He had to stop the car twice to be sick.

They despise me, thought Mohan, they despise us. Yet when was the last time he had received one of his own kind at home? He couldn't remember. He had been anxious to bury his origins, shed his shadow. Mathaichen had spoken of fourteen generations of family history, of the trite, small-time glory of head clerk, headmaster and village headman. His family had known perhaps four into fourteen generations of degradation. There was some glory, inverted glory, in suffering. He had many pictures of gods and goddesses in his house. But did he have a photograph of his mother, the woman who had sold her body in the bazaar that he might live? He thought of the unknown men who had lived with his mother, any one of whom could have been his father. He could hear his mother's screams still as she yielded to them. Perhaps a more sensible son would have put her picture up on the wall with the goddesses. Would the goddesses fly out of the frames in protest? He poured himself another attack. 'Up yours,' he said, raising the glass to his plump pantheon. *Pidichoh* was the precise Malayalam phrase Mohan employed.

# Chapter Seven

'YOUR FATHER,' SAID Dr Vareed, 'your father doesn't want to be cured.'

'But he must be . . .' said Devi in alarm.

'Well, he is happy . . . .'

'But it's a very selfish happiness,' said Devi.

'We have to coax him out of his Zen world before he comes to like it too much,' said Dr Vareed.

'Oh God!'

Mr Koshy had been brought home from Avrachen's. Mr Koshy had insisted. He had tantrums, sometimes a tantrum a day of the sort, Avrachen joked, that keeps all doctors away. Thankam thought them more staged than real. Her smile had become thinner and thinner. Mr Koshy used to lock his arms around his shoulders the instant Thankam came into the room and unlock them only when she left. 'A bad sign,' Dr Vareed had said.

'We so very much wanted to help,' Thankam told Mrs Koshy.

'Of course,' said Mrs Koshy.

'He was very much like a brick wall with us,' said Thankam.

'Pappa has never had very much conversation,' said Mrs Koshy.

'Avrachen has taken it very ill,' said Thankam. 'Avrachen is paying for the kitchen and the drains, after all. Is a little politeness too much to ask in return?'

'Pappa has been most tactless with Avrachen.'

'I have never known Avrachen to complain about helping less fortunate relatives but . . .' Thankam hesitated.

'He doesn't like to throw money at a brick wall,' Mrs Koshy finished. 'Neither do you.'

'I wonder,' said Thankam, 'if you and the children can make up for Koshy?'

This was most unexpected, thought Mrs Koshy.

'I mean, could you show yourselves more grateful to Avrachen?'

'Aren't we doing enough?' asked Mrs Koshy, an edge to her voice.

'Avrachen doesn't seem to think so.'

Mr Koshy knew that it wasn't really Avrachen. Thankam wanted her do-gooding to be noticed.

'Thankam,' said Mrs Koshy on cue. 'We are not a demonstrative family. You have behaved beautifully towards us.' Mrs Koshy held Thankam's hands and squeezed them.

Thankam glowed. In her sad life, the smallest thank you meant a lot.

Later Mrs Koshy discussed the conversation with Devi.

'We have come to depend on Avrachen and Thankam for so much,' said Mrs Koshy. 'It is almost charity. I've never known charity before. I do wish Pappa would hurry up and get better.'

'Dr Vareed says that Pappa is in no hurry at all.'

'We can all see that,' said Mrs Koshy. 'And so many things wait on him. Your marriage . . . .'

'It can wait.'

'It cannot. Then there is our quarrel with Thampy. In less than three months in Kerala, we have got into more muddles than we had in twenty-five years in Malaysia.'

Mrs Koshy stared out of the window. Everything in the garden seemed sculpted in black, the bougainvillaeas, the mango trees, the drooping cashew. Fireflies chased each other in and out of the house, till they collapsed in exhaustion in tree branches, their lights guttering. After the rains, there was peace now. But how could she forget how the rains and the wind had driven her family out of their home? It was as if she were in the presence of a wild animal that had gouged her, hurt her, but was now all false meekness. A cruel and dissembling thing.

'If we had been weaker, Thampy would have crushed us utterly,' said Mrs Koshy. 'Kunjunj and Mathaichen understand him. Thank God for that. I would never have known what to do.'

'It is painful to fight all the time,' said Devi.

'It makes you feel so animal,' said Mrs Koshy.

'We have become fighters now,' said Mrs Koshy. 'Well, call Lalu. It is time for prayers.'

'Pappa has already gone to sleep,' reported Lalu when he came.

Mrs Koshy, Devi and Lalu knelt before the small family altar. They moved their lips fervently in prayer. Prayer seemed a form of sanity.

'Save us from more quarrels,' prayed Mrs Koshy.

'Give us strength,' prayed Devi.

'Make my Pappa well,' prayed Lalu.

The Christ of their altar seemed to stare past them. As if he had heard it all before.


Mr Koshy continued to be a very delicate valetudinarian. He drank weak tea in slow sips all day long, and grumbled ferociously when the supply ran out. It was impossible to engage him in sensible conversation: he would nod off midway or he would stare at the ceiling. When he talked it was in the opaque language of a Zen master. He was still on Christmas Humphreys and Dr Suzuki. They were his 'friends' and he said that he didn't care for any other kind of company.

'Devi,' he said one day, 'don't listen to Avrachen.'

'But why?' asked Devi.

'He keeps bad company,' Mr Koshy said, drawing Devi to his side. He was suggesting by his manner that he was telling her a dark secret.

'I didn't know,' said Devi.

'The family is usually the last to know,' said Mr Koshy in a whisper.

Was her father merely chasing another phantom, Devi wondered.

'Avrachen has a sniffer dog,' continued Mr Koshy. 'The dog sniffs every visitor.'

It was nonsense, thank goodness, thought Devi. Thank goodness? Pappa was still very sick, wasn't he?'

'And Dr Vareed spies on me,' said Mr Koshy.

'Pappa why do you talk like this?' Devi buried her head in his hands.

'I have to warn you,' said Mr Koshy, trying to disengage himself.

'Pappa be yourself again,' said Devi, weeping, 'Be my Pappa again.'

'I am your Pappa.' There was a puzzlement in his voice.

'You must try,' said Devi. 'It is because you do not try that you do not get better.'

'But I am better. Never felt better,' said Mr Koshy, his puzzlement deepening.

'You are not what you were,' said Devi.

'No man is what he was,' replied Mr Koshy, summoning Zen to his defence. 'We are the same. And yet we are not the same.'

'Mamma needs your help. I need your help. Lalu needs your help.'

'I need my help,' said Mr Koshy.

'Most of all,' said Devi, hoping she was getting somewhere.

'But where am I?' asked Mr Koshy, looking around the room in bewilderment. 'I am not in that flower vase. I'm not in that . . . .'

'Stop,' said Devi, suddenly stern. 'No more of this. You see our pain and yet do nothing.'

'Is wisdom nothing?'

'Wisdom from a sick bed! I want wisdom from a healthy father.'

Argument was useless. Her father always scuttled into his Zen bolt hole.

It was Devi's first quarrel with her father.

Devi discussed her father with Dr Vareed later that day.

'His nerves couldn't take it,' said Dr Vareed. 'The flood, the quarrel with Thampy, the thugs, the new land . . . .'

'He was the kindest of men.'

'The usual victims,' said Dr Vareed. 'But was it kindness or just good manners?'

'Neither,' said Devi.

'Neither?'

'It was love,' said Devi.

Dr Vareed thought he had done wrong to discuss the patient with his daughter. 'I have no doubt that you are right,' he said.

'Until now I have never looked at him critically as a human being. I am sorry to do it now,' said Devi. 'To me father was just father.'

'A great compliment,' said Dr Vareed. 'To father.'

'There must be a cure,' said Devi.

'Do you know that in a case like this, it is rare to trust Western medicine alone?'

'You're not suggesting witchcraft?'

'I was thinking of a *vaidyan* (naturopath),' said Dr Vareed. Devi looked troubled.

'No,' said Dr Vareed, 'I wasn't suggesting devil dancers. A good *vaidyan* knows all about massages. He has a trunk-load of medicine, *arishatams* mostly. Usually harmless and often quite useless. It is the massages that really help.'

'I don't think we can afford a *vaidyan*. Mamma spends hours at night over the accounts. We are clearly living beyond our means.'

'There's always Thankam.'

'Mamma dislikes charity, especially when it begins at home,' said Devi.

Dr Vareed was a doctor of a kind that the Koshys had not

known in Malaysia. There, doctors were brisk figures behind desks, paid by the government to minister to the sick strictly by the rules. Patients, especially Malay and Indian patients, tried to entice the doctors into 'involvement', begging for extra time or playing for sympathy. Doctors for their part, lived in terror of hypochondriacs and sympathy seekers. The Malaysian health service was made in the image of the British National Health Service and suffered from similar problems of uneasy doctor-patient rapport. Mercenaries, Mr Koshy used to say, may make good soldiers but they rarely make good doctors.

Dr Vareed never gave the appearance of having sprung out of a cash register. He always had time for you, never having to 'find time' for you in the manner of more busy doctors. He had inherited money and was therefore freed from the need to earn it. Dr Vareed had not married—for reasons of lethargy, he said. His mother, a fierce woman, continued to try to get him married. He was thirty now, but his mother hadn't lost hope, wouldn't lose hope.

'Thampy wants us out of this house,' said Devi. 'Maybe, he wants to make an ashram of the house for American bhaktas.'

'He smells easy money,' said Dr Vareed.

'Mamma is stubborn. She will not leave the house. My uncles support her.'

'Of course you mustn't leave the house,' said Dr Vareed.

'But what is the point?'

'Never ask,' said Dr Vareed. 'I suppose there is such a thing as not yielding to a bully.'

'With the house a battle ground.'

'Not the house merely,' said Dr Vareed, 'but all of us too.'

'There are ruffians on both sides. There can be little to choose between Kunnukuzhi Mohan and Madhavan Thampy.'

'I don't care a lot for Kunnukuzhi Mohan,' said Dr Vareed. 'But if he is on our side . . . .'

'The usual argument,' said Devi.
'Yes, the usual argument.'
'A pity,' said Devi.


A team of labourers hired by Avrachen began work on the kitchen. Avrachen himself came to consult the *mesthri*. The labourers squatted in the compound, chewing paan, as the *mesthri* worked out how much material, wood, cement, and plaster he would need. He drew figures with his forefinger on the loose sand. He was an old style *mesthri* who thought that paper and pencil only added to what one might call the 'overheads', though he didn't worry about wasting his labourers' time. Wiping out one set of calculations with a sweep of his hand over the sand, he set to work on another set. Sometimes he muttered over the results of his calculations; sometimes he brooded over them in silence. Anyone not familiar with the ways of the *mesthri* would have thought that the *mesthri* was an astrologer casting a tricky horoscope. The *mesthri's* mysterious sums pointed to a stock of knowledge, of literacy that set him apart from his crew. His face grew tight with concentration as he worked out the sums.

'Too much!' said Avrachen. 'Five bags of cement! I could build a *kottaram* (palace) with that and still have something left over.'

The *mesthri* returned to his squiggles in the sand and announced that perhaps four bags would do after all.

'Three,' said Avrachen. He held the *mesthri's* hand before it could go back to the sums. 'You do your sums in such a way that you get an answer of three bags. Understand?'

*Mesthri* understood. Then there was similar haggling over wood and *chunam* (lime) paste. Avrachen waited patiently for the *mesthri* to complete his sums and then went on to cut each answer to a third or a half. The *mesthri* gave in each time after weak resistance.

'There!' said Avrachen impolitely. 'I work out these things

in my head and I get them right. No school arithmetic for me.'

The *mesthri* did not like to be ridiculed before his men. He saw in Avrachen's banter a challenge to his authority and a possible loss of face.

'Master,' said the *mesthri*, 'I did the sums. You only divided by two or three. Master divides better than he adds.'

'Divide when you pay. Multiply when you ask,' said Avrachen.

'So master knows,' said the *mesthri*.


'We are building a new kitchen,' wrote Lalu.

> It is going to be grand. There is going to be a huge work place, and an area outside the work place for the servants to eat in. And within the servants' part of the kitchen there is going to be a place for the high caste servants and a place for the low caste. Pappa says caste is all a matter of silly nose-in-the-air pride. But Mamma says that if you want to keep your servants you must give them their different kitchens. It is a bore because we have to build two, almost three, kitchens, instead of one. We have masses of servants. In Malaysia we had a maid-of-all-work. But here we have servants behind every chair. You feel spied upon. I can't write this without a servant wanting to bring me ink and paper. I bet we have more servants than the Sultan of Johore or even Tunku Hasina, and Lord she does have servants, doesn't she? Mamma said that Tunku Hasina needs servants to keep her pretty for the Sultan. But if you ask me, not all the servants in the world can do that for her. Her seventy-year-old face is going to pieces. Do you remember how she came for Prize Giving and kept powdering herself unendingly on stage?

Lalu ended with a cryptic private joke. 'But there are some things that cannot be made to look better no matter how much powder and paint you put on them. But one tries. One always tries . . . .'


Avrachen and Thankam came often to inspect the work on the kitchen. Thankam usually brought food, mounds of rice, idlies, sambar and vegetable *thoran*. There was always a dessert, a sickly sweet *payasam* in a flood of jaggery treacle. Mrs Koshy and Devi always pronounced the food excellent. They were beginning to learn how to handle Thankam. Thankam liked thank yous, the louder the better. Mrs Koshy and Devi sometimes even rehearsed their compliments, laughing at their exaggerations. Some of the shame that Mrs Koshy felt in having to play up to her own sister, leaked away in laughter.

'How strange our life has become,' said Devi.

'I have to play-act with my own sister. And Pappa play-acts with all of us.'

Later Mrs Koshy told Dr Vareed that she was disappointed that Pappa was not 'improving'. Sometimes the adult in him went into hiding and he kept talking about half-forgotten happenings as if they were the stuff of the grandest sort of autobiography: Lalu's sprained ankle at the foot of the St. Francis Xavier statue in Malacca: the beehive in the rambuttan tree that burst open without warning: the fire in the Run Run Shaw Cathay Theatre during the second part of Mel Ferrer's *War and Peace*. 'And remember,' he said, 'the awful row there was when I wrote to the *Straits Times* saying that such a picture needed such a singeing. 'Whore and Piss' I called Mel Ferrer's nonsense . . . . ' Mr Koshy had giggled contentedly at the memory all morning. Tolstoy was his favourite novelist. And *War and Peace* his favourite Tolstoy novel. He considered Tolstoy a brother spirit. Tolstoy had been horribly misunderstood all his life.

'Did Mr Koshy ever have these problems in Malaysia?' asked Dr Vareed.

'Never,' said Mrs Koshy.

'You do miss your life in Malaysia don't you?' asked Dr Vareed.

'Perhaps Mr Koshy misses it most of all.'

'Yes, but I doubt whether I would like to go back.'

'Why not?'

'We were a shallow people there.'

'Then there is something to be said for the shallow life,' said Dr Vareed. 'Something to be said for Cathay Theatre and Run Run Shaw.'

'One can tire of life lived entirely on the surface,' said Mrs Koshy.

'I was talking to Devi about seeing a *vaidyan* for Mr Koshy,' said Dr Vareed. 'A *vaidyan* has massages that we allopaths know nothing about. A body that is massaged gets all the right signals.'

'I will have to ask Thankam,' said Mrs Koshy.

'That is not a way of saying no, is it?'

'Can I afford to say no?'

'I am afraid not.'

'I hope the *vaidyan* won't upset Pappa.'

'A *vaidyan* talks with his hands. An oil bath. A good massage, and we may be able to rout the Zen master.'

Dr Vareed laughed.

But Mrs Koshy had no answering laughter.


The *vaidyan's* 'pharmacy', so a signboard outside described it, was in Kodapanakunnu, about ten miles outside Tiruvananthapuram. The pharmacy was set in the middle of a coconut *thop* (grove) cut across by a brook. The coconut palms grew so close to one another that the leaves meshed, forming several arcades of shade. The *vaidyan's* thatched cottage stood at the far end of the *thop*. You reached the cottage by following a beaten path down the middle arcade until you were pulled up short by a brook. A coconut tree trunk served as a bridge of sorts over the brook. Dr Vareed, Mrs Koshy and Devi took the precaution of using the coconut trunk one at a time.

The *vaidyan* was good advertisement for his trade. He was powerfully built but without the showy muscles of the body builder. His skin was smooth and unwrinkled. It had a lustre that no doubt came of constant application of oil. His skin resembled nothing so much as polished mahogany.

The *vaidyan's* cottage had no more than two rooms, a living-room which was also used as a bedroom and a room at the back which served as kitchen and storeroom. The living-room was bare except for mats spread on the floor from end to end, skipping a rectangular area round the door. The walls of the living-room were, however, very far from bare. Kathakali masks of various sizes, stared down from every wall. The masks had hypnotic eyes and realistic mops of coconut fibre hair. But the coarsely thickened lips and the exaggeration of the cheeks, reminded you of the pantomime character of Kathakali.

'They are my friends,' said the *vaidyan*, pointing to the masks.

'I wouldn't like to meet them in the dark,' Dr Vareed.

The *vaidyan* laughed. He clapped his hands and his daughter appeared. The *vaidyan* ordered his daughter to bring them four tender coconuts.

'There is no better drink,' said the *vaidyan*. 'Now, which of you is sick?'

'I've come about my husband. He is not quite himself.'

'It is usually the family that is sick, not one among them merely.'

'I assure you . . . ' protested Dr Vareed.

'There are exceptions of course,' said the *vaidyan* hastily. 'One sick person can drag a family after him.'

'Exactly my worry,' said Mrs Koshy.

'Sometimes one sick man can drag a whole country after

him,' said the *vaidyan*. 'Think of Hitler.' The *vaidyan* pronounced the name as Hittiler.

'There are days when my husband thinks he is a Zen master.'

'Zen?' asked the *vaidyan*.

'It's a form of Buddhism.'

'Ah, then you have less to fear than you think. It is a benign confusion. Think what trouble he would have been if he thought himself Hittiler.'

'Sometimes he is a grumbling old man, far older than his years.'

'Is he not being treated?' asked the *vaidyan*.

'I'm his doctor,' said Dr Vareed.

'You admit failure,' said the *vaidyan*, with a laugh. 'You 'Inglish' doctors, you treat the body, but never the whole man. Of course 'Inglish' medicine is wonderful. You don't spend five years studying nothing. But forgive me for saying that we are better doctors because we make health our work. You make disease your work, and when you fail you come to us.'

'We seek our cures everywhere,' said Dr Vareed, irritably, 'even in a witch-doctor's hut.'

'My knowledge,' said the *vaidyan*, 'compared with your knowledge, would appear too much like ignorance. I will not even try to argue. But allow me one question, how old am I?'

'Forty-five maybe,' said Dr Vareed.

'I was sixty-three last week. And you, Doctor, you are about thirty, are you not? Yet you look older. It's the tiredness about your eyes that makes you look older.'

'I'm sure,' said Dr Vareed drily.

'And, Doctor,' continued the *vaidyan*, 'you must do something about that tiredness round the eyes.'

Dr Vareed's eyebrows rose.

'Tired eyes may mean a tired body. And never in your life have you needed to look younger, feel younger.'

'But we haven't come to you to have our horoscopes cast,' said Dr Vareed, disliking the *vaidyan's* cocksureness.

The *vaidyan's* daughter came in with an armful of tender coconuts.

'Please drink,' said the *vaidyan*, 'you have come a long way. I mustn't tire you with my old man arguments.'

'Can you help my husband?' asked Mr Koshy.

'A good *vaidyan* like a good wife never says no,' said the *vaidyan*. 'I have business in Tiruvananthapuram. I can visit you from time to time, maybe stay overnight when you can have me. I don't need a room. Just a veranda and a mat. I know a few massages. But the best massage I know is kind and loving conversation. People think I have spells and mantras. I don't. I just try to persuade people to be kinder to one another.'

'Does it work?' asked Devi.

'There are people who think that they must be as nasty as they can to one another, the way to get on they think. This describes all of us at least some of the time. Those Kathakali masks are really about us.'

The *vaidyan* went to his gallery of masks. '*Pacha* (green) for Indra, Nala, Krishna and Kubera. Red beards for nastiness, for Dussasana and Bakasura. I jumble them together. Red beards and greens, we have to live together.'

The *vaidyan* said he would start his visits as soon as he could.

'I would have liked to stay with my patient,' said the *vaidyan*. 'But this village has claims on me. I am their medicine man. I arrange their marriages. I work out their horoscopes. They need me. Perhaps I need them too, more than I let them know.'

'It is nice to be wanted,' said Mrs Koshy, politely.

'Did you know that an 'Inglish medicine' doctor set up practice in this village? He lasted two weeks.'

'He couldn't have known much about horoscopes,' said Dr Vareed.

'Worse. We discovered that he knew nothing about human beings. A pity. He had such beautifully coloured liquids in bottles. Such reds! Such greens! Even my Kathakali masks looked dull beside such peacock colours. But he was gone in two weeks. He hasn't taken his name board away yet—MBBS it reads.'

The *vaidyan* stuck out the tip of his tongue at Dr Vareed mischievously.

On the way back, Dr Vareed said, 'The *vaidyan's* manners are odd. But his heart is in the right place. More or less.'

# Chapter Eight

THE KITCHEN WAS coming up nicely. But the *mesthri's* idea of a kitchen was not Mrs Koshy's.

'Women should kneel when they cook food,' said the *mesthri* dogmatically. The *mesthri* had designed a traditional work place.

Mrs Koshy said that she knelt only to pray.

The *mesthri* said that he could put in a kitchen seat. It was a concession. His manner was grudging. A seat was decadence. Women were born to kneel.

The *mesthri* made a toadstool-like seat with *chunam* and plaster. The top sloped off like an umbrella. The stem of the seat looked unsteady. It might have been thought up by a *farceur*.

There were other skirmishes. The *mesthri* wanted to have an open firewood chula. Thankam tried to explain that an open chula wasn't necessary. Mrs Koshy used kerosene.

'Kerosene, muckasene,' retorted the *mesthri*. 'Food cooked on a kerosene fire tastes of kerosene.'

The *mesthri* went on to build a full-blown open chula. Mrs Koshy sighed. Well, it wasn't 'her' kitchen. She wondered when she would have her own kitchen. 'When' seemed to be yielding to 'if'. The question marks over their lives seemed to be deepening. Devi joked that even the question marks had been chased away by exclamation marks.

The chula was a warren of round and square wells for pots and pans, and firewood entry points. There was a fan shaped receptacle area for ash and slag. A row of chimneys rose out of each fire-well. These were the lungs of the chula. A chula is only as good as its chimneys. A wrong rise here, a false dip there and the chula can wheeze and splutter. Worse, those who work beside an asthmatic chula soon begin to wheeze and splutter with it.

The *mesthri* tried to explain that the chula only looked complicated. In truth, he was proud of its complexities. He thought his chula a thing of cunning beauty.

The *mesthri* wanted to make a ceremony of the lighting of the fire. He gathered his workers. He lined them up beside the chula. He invited Avrachen, Thankam and Mrs Koshy. He brushed up his 'rocking-horse' mantras. He filled his lungs. He threw back his head. He started chanting—and as he did so he began to fill the first fire-well with coconut fibre and coconut shell. Then he lit a fire and raised it to a high flame with a pipe bellows.

The fire crackled in the first fire-well and then abruptly went out. The *mesthri* looked puzzled. He lit another fire which went out exactly like the first. The fire seemed to get lost in stagnant pools despite the *mesthri's* huffing and puffing. The chula was built on the prairie fire principle. The fire had to spread rapidly. The flames had to be sucked along quickly from fire-well to fire-well.

'Poor show,' said Avrachen brutally.

The *mesthri* did not care to have his work disparaged. He began a long explanation. A house without a morning-sun-facing-door, he said, gets the kitchen fire it deserves. Fire comes of the sun. You can't thumb a nose at the sun and hope to be forgiven.

'Excuses!' retorted Thankam. She stared scornfully at the *mesthri*. She was glad that it wasn't her nice kitchen that the *mesthri* was playing games with.

'We have, it seems, made enemies not only of the wind and water gods,' said Avrachen, 'but also of the sun and fire gods. Add Madhavan Thampy to the list of our enemies and what a list of angry gods we have!' He was laughing at the *mesthri*.

The workers sniggered behind upraised palms.

'Forgive me, master,' said the *mesthri* almost tartly, 'if I say that I do not entirely see the joke.'

'That is not surprising,' said Avrachen. 'After all, your fires have gone out.' There was insult in the double meaning.

'No, master. Not all my fires,' said the *mesthri*. He spoke through gritted teeth.

The shamed *mesthri* worked all that night on the chula. He made new mouldings. He carved and he broke. It was a bloody business.

'Murder! It is like killing a child,' said the *mesthri*. 'It had looked so pretty.'

Even as the *mesthri* worked, he complained to Mrs Koshy about the lack of a morning-sun-facing-door.

'Never have I heard so much about the morning sun,' said Mrs Koshy to Thankam. She said it was almost a case of sun stroke.

'This is how our people think,' said Thankam.

'The Chinese were so down to earth,' said Mrs Koshy. 'They never let heaven bother them. The troubles of this world were enough for them.'

'But Koshy's Zen is Chinese,' retorted Thankam. Thankam didn't like what she called her sister's Malaysian pedestal. Nor did she much like the godless Chinese. She had heard it said of them that the only good and bad they recognized was good and bad food.

'Pappa's Zen is just Pappa,' said Mrs Koshy.

'I think it is a Chinese infection he has picked up,' said Thankam stubbornly. She was suggesting that you couldn't live so long with the godless and not pick up a godless flea or two. Zen to her was a form of Chinese godlessness. The *mesthri's* mumbo-jumbo was at least god-worship of a kind.

'Well, didn't our grandmother say,' said Mrs Koshy, 'that you have to put up with at least twenty-four kinds of silliness if you want to get through a twenty-four-hour day. Not counting our own silliness.'

'I have far less patience for silliness than you have,' said Thankam. 'Not least for my own.'

Mrs Koshy greeted the remark with a tight smile. Thankam liked to think that she was the tougher sister.


It took a whole week for the *mesthri* to knock the chula into shape. The *mesthri* said that it was the longest week in his life. He had to endure a lot of snide talk from Avrachen and some sneering from Chechamma who was disappointed in the *mesthri*. Avrachen said that a good *mesthri* got it right the first time. 'Better to destroy bad workmanship than try to correct it,' he said. In certain moods Avrachen could sting harder than an angry bee.

The *mesthri* said that he had been up against no mere chula. It was against a hostile universe that he had struggled and won. The sun kept thwarting him all the time—until he discovered the mantra that finally tempered its anger. Sometimes Mrs Koshy found herself plugging her ears against his babble.

The *mesthri* enjoined a ceremony. The kitchen fire had to be lit with proper *pietas*. Mrs Koshy yielded only because she felt it would be cruel to snub such enthusiasm. The *mesthri* wanted to show off his new chula.

The *mesthri* ordered sandalwood, *kunthrikam* (bazaar frankincense) and two headloads of *kothumbu* (coconut fibre). He also ordered an audience. Lalu, Devi and Mrs Koshy came. Thankam grumbled but came. Avrachen grumbled and did not come. The *vaidyan* who was visiting, came. He was given a place of honour. He was an esoteric man. It was an esoteric ceremony.

The *mesthri* laid a coconut fibre trail through the tunnels that joined chula with chula. Secretly, very secretly, he had taken the precaution of dipping the coconut fibre in kerosene. A proper chula should do without such adventitious help. But the *mesthri* didn't want to risk any more stumbles.

The *mesthri* murmured soothingly at the chula. He might have been handling a very difficult child.

111

Chechamma brought in a pan of milk still warm from the udders of the cow tethered in the courtyard. The pan was placed over the first fire-well. Thankam's servants brought in a big mud pot of rice *payasam*. Many strong arms hoisted the pot to the chula.

Mrs Koshy was invited to light the fire. This she did to the drone of a mantra. The *mesthri's* eyes were closed in prayer. The worker's heads were bowed.

Mrs Koshy stoked the fire with a heavy iron prod. The prod had belonged to her grandmother. It was a thing of some beauty and character. It was elaborate wooden handle at one end and vicious-looking brass claw at the other. It had followed her through many kitchens. It was a survivor, a sturdy companion in a tottery world.

Mrs Koshy stirred the fire again. With a dry whistle, it leapt into flame, and it ate up the coconut fibre greedily. You could hear it chomp and chew.

The fire spread from fire-well to fire-well. The *mesthri* wrapped his arms round himself, as if congratulating himself. It was a beautifully behaved fire.

But then quite abruptly the fire stopped behaving itself. With a growl, it sprang tigerishly from one fire-well to another, tearing out of the tunnels that should have contained it. It set up strange fire bridges in the air between fire-well and fire-well.

The workers were goggle-eyed. It was pretty, but was it part of the *mesthri's* show?

The *mesthri* stared at the fire as if 'reading' it for meanings and portents. His lips twitched.

Mrs Koshy sniffed the air. There was a thin reek of kerosene. Mrs Koshy bent over the chula. She looked like a sniffer dog closing in on a quarry.

The *mesthri* looked at her through a corner of his eyes.

The flames danced higher and higher, growing unlovely cobra hoods. The cobra hoods spat sparks and cinder-flecks.

The *mesthri* looked anxious. Absent-mindedly he threw more frankincense into the fire as if trying to appease an anger.

The fire leaped about, full of a huge animal life.

'Don't feed the rogue any more!' cried Chechamma.

'Save the *payasam*!' ordered Thankam.

'Save the milk!' It would be inauspicious for the milk to boil over.

Soon the cry changed to 'Save the chula'.

'Let the fire burn itself out,' said the *mesthri* stolidly. 'That's the only way.'

'And do you want the kichen to burn out with it?' asked Mrs Koshy sharply.

Thankam ordered the workers to bring buckets of water. She was edgy. Mrs Koshy feared hysteria. Thankam crumbled easily in a crisis.

'There is a simpler way,' said Mrs Koshy.'

She picked up the iron prod and taking aim she fiercely smashed the mud pot. *Payasam* cascaded from the broken pot into the chula. A thick lava of *payasam* sluiced into fire-well after fire-well, smothering the fire as it went along. The fire was dead in about two minutes.

The *mesthri* opened his mouth and then shut it. Perhaps, thought Devi, there was no appropriate mantra for spilt *payasam*. None too for a spilt reputation.

'So much good *payasam* gone to waste!' grumbled Thankam. 'And I stirred in the jaggery myself.'

'Shame,' said Chechamma.

'Now we will have to buy our *payasam* from a shop,' said Thankam, 'though it won't be the same thing at all.'

'The sun god is not mocked,' said the *mesthri* irrelevantly.

'Neither are the rest of us,' said Mrs Koshy, speaking with a rasp.

The workers nodded. Mrs Koshy spoke for them all.

It was only an extreme sort of compassion that made Mrs Koshy say no more about the *mesthri's* sneaky kerosene-oblation to the sun god.

A few days after work on the kitchen was over, Avrachen said that now they had rebuilt the kitchen they might go on and rebuild the rest of the house. 'I've got the builder's itch,' he laughed. 'One brick invites other bricks.'

But Avrachen wasn't speaking entirely in jest. He argued that the house was really built all wrong. A house that is situated deep in a bowl of hills, should be built on stilts. It should stand like an egret in a paddy field, high and dry above the mud and water below.

'And not least,' said Avrachen sardonically, 'rebuilding the house would give Thampy something to think about. That man is best behaved when he is hung up to dry from a tall hook.'

Mrs Koshy said that she did not care for house-grabbing talk. Didn't their grandmother say better the sky above for a roof than a stolen roof? Thankam nodded. To the two sisters their grandmother was uncanonized goodness and hugely quotable.

'Your grandmother could never think outside pretty little proverbs,' said Avrachen. Avrachen disliked having wet wisdom thrown in his teeth especially when he was discussing 'commerce'.

Avrachen had attacks of what Thankam called 'money-lust'—if it wasn't money-lust it was another more deplorable kind of lust. And when in a 'money' rut, Avrachen was full of eloquent strategems. Avrachen always said that it is an instinct with businessmen to ride an advantage as hard as they can whenever they can. 'Hard riding' rather described his love life too.

Avrachen listed the advantages of the house to Mrs Koshy. It was in a good part of town, less than a mile from Kawdiar Palace where the Travancore Royal Family still lived. On a clear day you could see the pale green roofs of the Palace and if you squinted, maybe even the royal washing put out to dry. No house in Tiruvananthapuram could ask for more.

Avrachen said that the property market had never been so topsy-turvy. Newly rich Malayalis from Dubai and Muscat were buying up every bit of decent property. The Koshys were unlikely to be able to afford a house of their own for a long while to come, and certainly not in competition with the Gulf 'sheikhs' and 'emirs'. Why shouldn't the Koshys keep what they had? They had the law on their side. They had Kunnukuzhi Mohan on their side. Both the law and the 'outlaw', joked Avrachen.

Mrs Koshy said convenience was not the law.

'That's only your grandmother's conscience talking again,' said Avrachen. 'We have to live in the times we are born into.'

'Do you think that Thampy would ever leave us alone if we grabbed his house?' asked Mrs Koshy.

'Let me make that my problem,' said Avrachen.

'No,' said Mrs Koshy. Sometimes Avrachen had a horribly direct way with problems. It was rather like inviting a hangman to catch a thief.

'I wish we had a larger outhouse to spare for Sosamma,' said Thankam. 'But our *pathayam* takes up most of our outhouse. And where there is paddy there are rats. The outhouse has come to belong to the rats. It is all teeming rat colonies.'

'I don't think we will fit into any outhouse,' said Mrs Koshy. Thankam was being tactless. Outhouses are for servants and rats.

'Of course you deserve a house of your own,' said Thankam. 'But houses don't fall from cracks in the sky.'

'They don't,' said Avrachen stoutly.

'Perhaps we could buy the house from Thampy for a fair price,' said Thankam. 'I know he can out-talk a Chettiar . . . .'

'Well,' smirked Avrachen, 'I have nothing against a very fair price.'

After some argument it was agreed that they would try to

strike a deal with Thampy. 'And the fairer the price the better' was how Avrachen summed up their strategy, revelling in his cleverness.

Avrachen sent his accounts clerk to Thampy the next day. Thampy played haughty. He made the clerk come several times. At first he refused to negotiate saying that there was nothing to negotiate about. Then he began to negotiate unreasonably.

'One lakh or nothing,' Thampy said. It was pure stand up and deliver.

'That's Gulf money,' protested Avrachen. 'My sister-in-law doesn't have that kind of money.'

'Then she mustn't try to live in that kind of house,' retorted Thampy.

And there matters stood growlingly for a week.

Then Thampy sent word that he might consider just a little less than a lakh. But the precise figure would have to be arrived at astrologically. His astrologer was waiting for a good time for negotiations. All that week *Shani* (Saturn) was in the fourth house of Jupiter. It was a bad time for business deals. The heavens were overcast. The stars were brooding.

Avrachen knew that Thampy wasn't an astrology man at all. He used to joke that a doctor with his stethoscope could tell you more about your future than an astrologer with his horoscope. But for all that Thampy never went into any negotiation without an astrologer by his side. An astrologer was a useful psychic second string. When sense failed in negotiations, he was happy to see nonsense take over. Irrational argument sometimes did better than rational argument. Numerology did better than mere numbers.

Avrachen consulted the *vaidyan* who said that he knew something about astrology. He also knew something about tenancy law, and also something about how to brew the two together.

'Can the stars be persuaded to suggest twenty-five thousand?' Avrachen asked the *vaidyan*.

116

'The stars have no mouths, no ears,' said the *vaidyan* in his self-consciously delphic style. 'They have only auras. And auras are best read with the eyes half shut.'

The *vaidyan* winked. Avrachen winked.

Mrs Koshy redoubled her prayers to the Gethsemane Christ. She didn't think it right that so much should be left to a disturbing form of heathenism.

Mrs Koshy sat down that night to attack her account books or rather to let her account books attack her. Devi sat beside her. Three hours into the night and they had still no answer to three nasty debits. And how, asked Mrs Koshy, would they find the twenty-five thousand which Avrachen said was a fair price for the house?

Her account-book worries led Mrs Koshy like a hapless bird in a storm to her camphor wood chest. The chest was almost her last purchase in Singapore's Change Alley. It had a large and complicated brass lock. She had insisted on the lock which the shopkeeper had called the 'Tower of London' lock. Mr Koshy had tried to point out the superfluity of the purchase. 'You are going home, remember,' he had said. That was his innocence then. The Chinese shopkeeper had answered for her, 'This camphor wood box is for home, lah.'

Mrs Koshy kept her jewellery in the top drawer of the chest. Fifty-five years of her life were contained in a few ebony boxes—her baby *arignanam* (waist chain), her wedding chain, her twenty-one carat birthday gift chains, her mother's bangles. They were a sort of autobiography. Each piece had a freight of memory, a story to tell. Her mother's three bangles had been a death bed gift. Thankam had got her mother's earrings.

'No one sells off this kind of jewellery,' said Devi.

'No, but you will find some trinkets among them,' said Mrs Koshy. And she added after a pause, 'Particularly if you look hard enough.'

117

'But they have been your friends. You have talked so much about them. Talked to them even.'

'I'm too old for these games,' said Mrs Koshy. 'A sovereign fetches almost two thousand. It will buy us a breathing spell at least.'

'Pappa won't like it at all.'

'He mustn't know.'

Mrs Koshy picked up a mango pendant. 'That was Thankam's gift to me. Never have liked it very much. Some kinds of gold can be too loud.'

Then she picked a butterfly brooch. 'I don't like winged things on me.' The butterfly brooch was a farewell present from the Malayali Association in Johore Bahru.

The last victim was an over-heavy necklace. 'It's like wearing a gold halter.' It was a hand-me-down piece, a less well-loved part of her wedding trousseau.

'Not that,' said Devi.

'It is best to say as little as possible,' said Mrs Koshy. She wrapped the three pieces in a handkerchief. She shut the camphor wood box. There was nothing more to be said.

The goldsmith was called in the next day. He weighed the three pieces in his small brass scales. He was a fussy man. He played with what seemed like tiny toy weights. He did his sums on his palms. 'Six sovereigns,' he announced. 'Twelve thousand rupees. No promissory-dormissory notes. I deal in ready money.'

Mrs Koshy counted the money. Twelve thousand rupees was a strange sensation. Mrs Koshy had forgotten what it was to handle so much money.

'If ever you have more jewellery to sell, Ammachy,' said the goldsmith as he left, 'come to me first before you go to anyone else. I have the most honest weights in the business. And I have weights on my tongue. I buy. I sell. I forget. I forget from whom I have bought and to whom I have sold.'

'We don't usually sell our jewellery,' said Mrs Koshy. 'And we don't want to make a habit of it.'

'Gold,' said the goldsmith, 'is our best friend in hard times. Sometimes the only friend. There is no shame in turning to it in trouble.'

Mrs Koshy put the money away in the camphor wood box. But it went into the bottom drawer. She had broken the first of the proverbial rules of her grandmother. No sensible housewife ever sold her jewellery, she used to say. There could be no excuses. No extenuating circumstances.

'This money is not just for the house,' Mrs Koshy told Devi, as if apologizing for what she had done. 'A wedding costs money. Two days and two nights of money-splurging. And we have been eating into the money that we had put away for your dowry. It started as a nibble. Then we could hardly help ourselves.'

Devi blushed as she always did when her marriage was discussed.

Mrs Koshy stroked the back of Devi's head. 'Though why I am selling off jewellery that I should, rightly speaking, save up for you I do not know. Maybe I am as confused as Pappa is sometimes.'

'No, Mamma,' said Devi. 'You don't have that excuse. I'm afraid you know exactly what you are doing.'

Generously, Mrs Koshy allowed her daughter the last word.


Avrachen invited Thampy for what he called a face-to-face talk. He would have said man-to-man, but a person with only one what's-what wasn't really a man at all.

Thampy brought his astrologer, and Avrachen the *vaidyan*. It was going to be an elaborately old-fashioned occasion. They would do their haggling through their mediators.

Thampy's astrologer was an old Brahmin. He came with his charts and his *jathakams* (horoscopes). He carried a bundle of palm leaf manuscripts in what looked like a very battered violin case. He spread out the palm leaves on the ground.

Thankam served coffee. The Brahmin asked whether he
could have coconut water. It need not be poured into a glass,
he said. He was only being tactful. He really meant 'must not'.
As a Brahmin he wouldn't eat or drink from a non-Brahmin's
hands.

The Brahmin began by saying that selling a house was
rather like cutting off an arm. Thampy nodded vigorously.

The *vaidyan* was ready with his counter thrust. 'But must a
man have ten arms? Even Vishnu has only four arms.' The
*vaidyan* was referring to the well-known though still unproven
story that Thampy owned ten houses in Tiruvananthapuram
alone.

'There are those who say that Madhavan Thampy sar owns
Kawdiar Palace itself,' said the Brahmin, 'and that our maha-
rajah stays there only because Thampy sar allows him to. You
may believe the rumour or you may not. For my part I do
not.'

'What if I do own Kawdiar Palace and Bockinharm Palace
as well?' asked Thampy belligerently. 'The pain of losing a
small finger is not less because a man has a thumb.'

'At least you have both your thumbs,' said Avrachen. He
was in the most literal sense hitting below the belt.

The *vaidyan* said that sour words were inauspicious. He
took his betel box from a fold in his *mundu*. 'For those who
want to sweeten their spittle I have some sweet paan. For
those who do not, I would counsel silence.'

The Brahmin said that it was best that their clients did not
speak directly to one another. 'They should speak either
through us or not at all.'

The *vaidyan* began to crack a betel nut with a silver nut
cracker and to lay out fresh betel leaves. He worked with a
tranquil industry that he hoped would quieten the nerves of
the company.

The Brahmin shuffled his palm-leaf manuscripts. He held
whispered consultations with Thampy and then announced
in a sweet voice that Rs 99,669.92 was, numerologically

speaking, the right price. 'And if you think that price too high, I give you an alternative . . . Rs 99,662.21.'

'But 99,661.21 would be numerologically wrong, I suppose,' Avrachen snorted.

'Is that your counter offer?' asked the Brahmin, looking at the *vaidyan.*

Avrachen thought that this was cheek. 'No,' he said. He wrote furiously on a piece of paper. 'My counter offer!' he said. 'And what numbers could be rounder and prettier?'

The paper read 00,000.00.

Thampy looked at the paper, his head held at a quizzical slant.

'That's a lot of marbles,' he said. 'But marbles don't buy anything but marbles.'

The Brahmin said that between the two prices there was room enough for all heaven and earth to slip in. 'This is the way to argue, not negotiate.'

The *vaidyan* spread *chunam* paste on a betel leaf, threw in a few betel shavings, stuck in a clove and offered it to Thampy. 'Let us be sensible,' he said. 'You know that we know, and we know that you know that neither 99,999 nor 00,000 is right. There is a figure in between that is right and we must find that figure.'

'Must,' echoed the Brahmin. 'But not we alone. We need help from the stars.' He pointed to the pile of palm-leaf manuscripts.

'Then you must ask your stars to show more common sense,' said Avrachen. His irritation with the sly Brahmin was increasing.

The *vaidyan* and the Brahmin looked at each other. They were losing control over their turbulent clients. It was rather like trying to put lids on two snorting heads of steam.

'Whatever the stars might say,' continued Avrachen, 'we do not have a paise more than 30,000 to spare.'

'That doesn't sound like the price of my house at all,' said Thampy.

'And it is a most inauspicious number,' said the Brahmin. 'Too many zeros, too many hangman's nooses.'

'I will go down to 99,000 but no further,' said Thampy. 'You know that if our Gulf 'emirs' knew that this house is for sale, they would be queueing up outside my door.'

'But it will take quite a few of the strongest Arab camels to drag us out of this house,' said Avrachen.

'So we come back to threats, do we?' asked Thampy.

'Street language!' said the Brahmin, wrinkling his nose.

'You forget we have the law on our side,' said Avrachen.

'Only the law as Kunnukuzhi Mohan understands it,' said Thampy.

'Kunnukuzhi Mohan,' said Avrachen, 'has a truer understanding of the law than most.'

Thampy made a lewd gesture waistwards. 'That's what I think of Kunnukuzhi Mohan when I do think of him at all.'

The *vaidyan* put up his hands. 'Street language!' he said, throwing the Brahmin's phrase at him.

The Brahmin sighed. 'I do not think even the stars can make 99,000 of 30,000. There is too much of a too much between the two.' He paused. 'I have handled many difficult negotiations but none so difficult as this.'

Thampy, nose in air, said that he had nothing to say to 30,000. '99,000 doesn't speak to 30,000.' He left abruptly.

Thampy, Avrachen jeered, looked like a hundred thousand thunders.

'I wouldn't laugh all that loudly if I were you,' said the Brahmin. 'You have made a dangerous enemy.'

'I have?' mocked Avrachen.

'The stars foretell trouble,' said the Brahmin, putting his palm-leaf manuscripts away in his violin case.

'Do your stars also foretell that if Thampy tried anything, the rest of his life will be all *Shani*, all sun and moon eclipse?'

'Do not jeer at the stars,' said the Brahmin. 'These palm-leaf inscriptions are not written on water.'

But Avrachen's laughter was very rude.

# Chapter Nine

IT WAS THE cashew season. The cashew trees were heavy with fruit. Poaching crows looped in and out of the trees. There was at least one greedy crow for every ripe cashew fruit. The cashew trees seemed a flutter of black crow-feather. Crows damaged as much as they ate. The compound was littered with pecked-at fruit. What the crows dropped the annan squirrels scavenged.

Mrs Koshy asked Lalu to pick some ripe cashew fruit. It seemed such a shame to lose so much good fruit to the crow, the least lovable of Indian birds.

'Cashew juice makes a refreshing beer,' said Mrs Koshy. 'It may be good for Pappa. We must try everything, I promise myself.'

When Lalu had left the room, Mrs Koshy told Dr Vareed with a smile, 'We couldn't discuss the boy in his hearing, could we?' Mrs Koshy leaned back in her chair. 'Lalu's so worried about Pappa. He talks in his sleep. And what a lot of small-boy-talking there is. He has, I am afraid, far less to say during the day. He keeps scribbling rather in the way that Pappa had. He writes such fanciful letters.'

'He is a worried little boy,' said Devi.

'Children cope with fear so badly,' said Dr Vareed. 'We shouldn't admit him into our worries.'

'Mathaichen doesn't approve at all of Lalu's scribbling,' said Mrs Koshy. 'He fears that the boy will take after Pappa. Mathaichen says that the boy has too many books. Pappa of course says that nobody can have too many books. Lalu is such a greedy reader, and if we don't give him the right books he will read all the wrong books. But I can't buy Lalu as many books as he was used to in Malaysia. Well, I try not to stint on books . . . and fruits and milk. But it is hard. Pappa has only a pension, a bread-but-no-butter pension.'

In the end all discussions of money returned to Mr Koshy's pension. Mrs Koshy said that the pension like all fixed incomes seemed to dwindle from month to month. The Malaysian Government ungenerously refused to proof its overseas pensions against inflation, arguing that its burden of pension payments was already too heavy. Mr Koshy had once remarked that the Malaysian Government should come clean and declare itself in favour of a programme of euthanasia for its overseas pensioners. Mrs Koshy was shocked when she discovered what euthanasia meant. She thought it in poor taste that Mr Koshy should suggest it even in bitter joke.

'It is so dispiriting to have to think of economies all the time,' said Mrs Koshy. 'A little less soap, a little less butter. A rupee here, a rupee there. I can't soap-pare, butter-pare, money-pare. Some women can. Some women can't.'

'What do you say to a boarding-school for Lalu,' said Dr Vareed. 'Children are happier with other children.' He meant that Lalu needed a break from his father. 'If you can't afford a public school we can find something in between. A Catholic school of quality, but inexpensive. I know a school in Tangaserri.'

'Isn't Tangaserri where the Anglo-Indians live?' asked Mrs Koshy. Tangaserri had a reputation. It was known for its exotic women—too light-skinned to be Malayali and too dark to be European and therefore the stuff of fantasies.

'I must ask what Mathaichen thinks of Tangaserri,' said Mrs Koshy. But she knew what strong views Mathaichen had about boarding-schools. He thought a boarding-school no better than a football mob. And a mob that comes from everywhere, from every class and caste. He said that parents must bring up their children on their own, not pay others to do it for them.

It didn't seem right to Dr Vareed that the Koshys should

surrender all judgement to Mrs Koshy's Kuttanad brothers.
'What is right for the Kuttanad man,' said Dr Vareed, 'may
not be so very right for others.' His tone suggested that there
was something faintly neolithic about the Kuttanad man.

'You know we consult my brothers on everything,' said
Mrs Koshy. 'Especially with Pappa so.'

'You do not have to wait for a *muhurtham* to ask them?'
said Dr Vareed.

Mrs Koshy didn't care for the joke. There were times when
she found Dr Vareed's jocularity a little trying.

When Lalu came in with the cashews, Mrs Koshy cut the
head of a cashew fruit with some show of irritation. She
squirted the juice into a glass. She swirled the cloudy white
juice about. 'Clears the mind. Bridles the tongue, they say.
Would you like some, Doctor?' Dr Vareed fell silent.

Mrs Koshy knew something about bridling tongues.

Dr Vareed and Devi exchanged glances. Mrs Koshy noticed
the sympathetic telegraphing.

The doctor, thought Mrs Koshy, was galloping into their
lives. Devi had to be protected more closely than she thought
necessary. Dr Vareed was a friend of the family, but he must
know that every family had its reticences. Not everything
could be told. Even friends of the family could not resist
passing on a neat gossipy anecdote and more reputations have
been ruined by neat anecdotes than anything else.

How could she explain that she had begun to depend on
her brothers in many ways, big and small? Such arrangements
are never very tidy, and do not bear talking about. Mr Koshy
was still head of the family, but he was consulted less and less,
and more often than not, only for the sake of form. Sometimes
Mr Koshy did mutter under his breath that Kunjunj and
Mathaichen were stealing his family from him. Mrs Koshy
did not contradict him. That was an argument that she didn't
want to have.

And, not to put too fine a point on it, when there was a
financial panic it was her brothers who were her lever to

Avrachen's money. She was too shy, too proud, to do the asking herself. Usually, Avrachen, the keeper of the family purse, was asked, ordered even, by Mathaichen and Kunjunj and Thankam, the keepers of the family conscience, to find the money. And Avrachen, thanks to Thankam's bullying, always did so. Avrachen was a generous man but his generosity needed priming. The tap never seemed to flow on its own. Sadly, Avrachen's generosity tended to be eccentric. He got his kicks from wasting money, on pointless tips, on undeserving servants, on greedy hangers-on and on seedy friends. But he became strangely tight-fisted when a constructive purpose was mentioned. He left that kind of charity to Thankam who, Avrachen joked to his friends, pillow-talked with angels.

A family, Mrs Koshy often said, repeating a Malayali proverb, is at once the strangest and the most wonderful of God's creations. The domestic nest must find uncomplaining space for its cuckoos. And God give her strength to handle the cuckoos.


Pragasam's description of delicious Chinese-Malay school-tuck, *meehoon*, *satay*, *nasih goreng* was long and salivating. Pragasam was crowing. He was saying that Lalu shouldn't have left Malaysia.

Lalu told Mrs Koshy that he felt homesick for Malaysia.

'But do try to remember that we have come home,' said Mrs Koshy.

'Perhaps there is only one cure for homesickness,' Lalu announced solemnly. 'I must write it out of me.'

'Well, if you must, then you must . . . .'

'I haven't seen any tigers yet,' Lalu wrote to Pragasam.

> Of course tigers in the zoo don't count. But there is a tiger in the zoo, a large fierce beast whose roars fill the town. He is calling out to his fellows in the

wild. He is homesick they say. Not long ago he broke out of his cage. The town was terrified. Everybody hid behind bolted doors. But the tiger was captured in the end . . . but only after he had killed a visitor to the zoo who had spat at him. How he tracked down the visitor no one can say. The tiger was not put down. In fact there are some visitors to the zoo who actually worship the tiger. White tigers they say are special. So many things are special and holy in India, white tigers, cows, monkeys, snakes, even rats. India worships what the Chinese put into their cooking-pots. I would be careful what I eat from Chinese cooking-pots. Monkey in, monkey out, as they say.

That was one in the eye for Pragasam.
  Lalu added:

Pappa has bought a horse and goes riding every day. He manages a horse very well. He looks so very well on a horse. The open air suits him. I haven't started riding yet. I told Pappa I'd prefer an elephant. Riding an elephant seems so much easier. The Maharaja has an elephant. The elephant makes the motor car seem so boring. I hope to get an elephant for my birthday.

'I go to the Model School here,' concluded Lalu, drifting into a rougher kind of fantasy.

I have not made any friends yet. But I have made many enemies. The medals of war—one and a half broken teeth, one twisted thumb. I am a tough boy now. India has made me tough. It takes a tough country to make you tough. I tell you it takes more than *satey* and *nasih goreng* to make you tough.

127

But the humorous phrases hid real pain. His friendlessness seemed even to dry up the ink in the pen. Lalu put away his letter.

The truth was that at Model School Lalu didn't have a friend even among the teachers, which was where Lalu usually found his friends. It seemed to Lalu that a Model School teacher's best friend was his cane. No teacher was ever without his cane. They taught with their canes. One teacher with some pedantry joked about the school's Damocles' cane. Lalu was thrashed more soundly than the rest because he was different. His Malayalam accent was not Malayali enough. And his English accent was too 'Inglish'. Lalu felt that he could not open his mouth without provoking either anger or laughter. Lalu's beatings were a sad and humiliating secret kept from his mother.

In Malaysia, Lalu had been the teacher's favourite in every class he had been. Not once in Malaysia had he been beaten. He was the first with classwork, and always the least trouble in a racially mixed and turbulent class. But in Model School it was the toughest boy who received the teacher's affection. This tough boy kept the class in order when the teacher was away, and teachers in Model School seemed to be away more often than not. This tough boy had the right to beat the class and his beatings were often brutal. It was this system of gangster prefects that made Lalu loathe school. He wondered if Tangaserri had gangster prefects. He would ask Dr Vareed.

Troubled though he was, Lalu hated the thought of leaving home. It seemed so wrong to abandon his mother and sister. Going away seemed so much like running away. If only Pappa could ride a horse. If only Pappa loved the open air instead of his dull books. Conversation was impossible with Pappa. Zen, he spoke chiefly of Zen. Lalu wondered why. Perhaps everybody needs a white tiger. Zen was Pappa's white tiger. Lalu disapproved of Zen. Zen, Zen, Zen, Zen, Lalu muttered to himself. The word was meaningless. He could not abandon his mother and sister to this white tiger.

Lalu wondered whether it would not have been better for them to have chosen to settle in Kuttanad, where Mamma's brothers were. Lalu was willing to forgive Kuttanad its rough manners. His uncles, Mathaichen and Kunjunj, were terrible belchers. He knew that their belching horrified Pappa and Devi. But Lalu thought their belching manly. He thought everything about Mathaichen and Kunjunj manly. Mathaichen was very much a boy's man. He was always in command, always the captain. Kunjunj Ammachen spoke little, and in grunts mostly. But Lalu preferred his grunts to Pappa's careful speech.

Mathaichen Ammachen had 'knowingness', not bookish opinion. Lalu thought of Mathaichen Ammachen's hairy forearms, his operatic belches. Only a real man had such thick hair. Only a real man could produce belches like that. Pappa had no hair, no hair on his arms, hardly any on his chest. And he did not belch. His gastric juices were decorous.

Only if Mathaichen Ammachen approved of Tangaserri, would he go. But he would have a man-to-man talk about his mother and sister with his uncle. Man-to-man, Mathaichen Ammachen would tell him what to do. He would place himself entirely in Mathaichen Ammachen's hands. Those hairy forearms were strength itself. And after the milk and water of Zen, he needed strength.

Mathaichen Ammachen had a winner's way with money; he never allowed himself to be intimidated by it—so very unlike Pappa, Lalu thought. When Mathaichen Ammachen came to Tiruvananthapuram, he scorned to travel by the town's bone-shaker buses. He hired taxis and never haggled over their charges. He had tips for the servants; he had presents for the family, not stinting token presents such as relatives frequently give, but presents of things that you really wanted. His 'knowingness' seemed to be something that grew into him from the red earth of Kuttanad.

True, Mathaichen Ammachen had a violent temper. But his rages, though terrible, were rare. For the most part he was

good-humoured and placid. Small things did not fray his good
humour; he could ignore a raised voice, an occasional familiarity of speech from the young, a failure of household management. You thought he expected things to go wrong and
was thankful when they didn't. He wasn't a bundle of Zen
irritabilities.

Mathaichen Ammachen made admiration, even love possible. A boy could love such an uncle without trying. Loving
a father was a duty.


Mathaichen arrived from Kuttanad a little before supper. He
had travelled, as Lalu knew he would, in a taxi. Mrs Koshy
paid off the taxi because Mathaichen seemed too preoccupied
with Devi and Lalu to heed the ticking meter. But Mathaichen
remembered to throw in a tip. Unnecessarily, Mrs Koshy
thought. But tips were in Mathaichen's style. The driver
flagged down the meter. Ting-a-ling it went, and ting-a-ling
again, the extra note no doubt contributed by sneak wiring.
Taxi drivers in Tiruvananthapuram called the extra wiring,
the *Ganesharahasyam*, or the secret of Ganesh. If it had been
Mr Koshy there would have been a scene. He would have
threatened to call the police, and even made good his threat.
But Mathaichen had, blessed word, 'knowingness'. There
would be other times and places to settle scores.

'Aa,' said Mathaichen. It was his usual greeting.

'Ahi,' said Mrs Koshy.

It was brother-sister argot which had the advantage of
making private conversation possible in company.

'Ahaa,' said Mathaichen, in clarification.

'Ammm,' responded Mrs Koshy.

'So they are thinking of sending you to Tangaserri?'
Mathaichen asked Lalu.

'We do nothing without your saying so,' said Mrs Koshy.

'Whose idea was it?' asked Mathaichen.

'Dr Vareed's,' said Mrs Koshy.

'I haven't met Dr Vareed,' said Mathaichen, almost in rebuke. 'Pazhaymootil Thomachen's son he is, isn't he?'

Mrs Koshy said he was.

'Then he is a rich man,' said Mathaichen. 'Is he married?'

'No,' said Mrs Koshy in quiet voice.

'Hmmmmmm,' said Mathaichen.

Mrs Koshy fidgeted with the hem of her sari.

'I will not have Lalu go to a boarding-school,' said Mathaichen. 'Not even if it is run by nuns under the direct eye of the Virgin herself. There is more to education than living in a slum dormitory with boys of every caste, kink and stink. I have made my position clear?'

'You have,' said Mrs Koshy.

'And how is Koshy?' asked Mathaichen with the air of one moving briskly down a list of sticky subjects.

Mathaichen had never understood Mr Koshy. He thought it was well that Mr Koshy had taken himself away to Malaysia. Mr Koshy had been a clerk there, doing just the thing that clerks are good at, scribbling. India was a trickier climate. Here the poor man had become sick. Mathaichen pitied his sister. It was a good thing that she did not pity herself. For his sister's sake he hoped Koshy would pull himself together. It was a shame about Zen whatever. Religion, he felt, is best left to priests and women: it is unnatural for a man, a real man, to muddle himself with religion.

'We've got Pappa a *vaidyan*,' said Mrs Koshy.

'There are many fakes among *vaidyans*,' said Mathaichen. 'Some are mad. Most are only pedlars of love potions and charms.'

'Dr Vareed recommended this *vaidyan* . . . .' Mrs Koshy's voice trailed away.

Mathaichen looked questioningly at her. 'Dr Vareed again?'

'Dr Vareed is helpful.'

'You mean only that he has a ready tongue. Any son of Pazhaymootil Thomachen would,' said Mathaichen.

'Thomachen could talk a man's shirt off his back. The Pazhaymootils are all rich now. But not all their wealth will bury their moneylending past.'

'Dr Vareed cannot be blamed for what he cannot help.'

'The usual argument,' said Mathaichen with an impatient flip of his hand. 'Don't allow him to get too close to Devi or we may soon have reason to blame him for what he can help. His father, Thomachen, had a wandering eye. He may have passed on to his son something more than his wealth.'

'Even a Pazhaymootil has a right to his reputation,' said Mrs Koshy. 'Wealth cannot buy a man a reputation. But wealth should not lose a man his reputation either.'

'Maybe. But we who have only our reputation for honour left to us have to be more careful than most about the company we keep. We had our elephants once. Now the only elephant we have is our family honour.'

'The world did look different from the top of an elephant,' said Mrs Koshy.

'Very different,' said Mathaichen. 'You know I have come to borrow again from Avrachen. I haven't paid my labourers for two weeks.'

Mrs Koshy shook her head. She had suspected that her brothers' circumstances were bad but this was worse than anything she had feared.

'Once we fed our elephants better than we fed our labourers. There was sugar cane for the elephants and sugary elephant piss for the labourers. Now our labourers are Communist. They demand to be fed.'

'Communists?' asked Mrs Koshy. 'There were Communists in the jungles of Malaysia. The British killed them all.'

'Our Communists do not hide. They are respectable.' Mathaichen was contemptuous. 'It is we who have lost our respectability.'

'Is there nothing we can do?' asked Mrs Koshy.

'Nothing. Except pray.'

'The Lord have mercy upon us.'

'The Lord hasn't abandoned us all. Avrachen has his cardamom estates. He has no trouble.' Mathaichen always spoke grudgingly of Avrachen's luck.

'Has he killed his Communists?' asked Mrs Koshy.

'Avrachen employs Tamils. It is the Malayalis who are Communists. Malayalis read and write, read and write all the wrong things.' Mathaichen suspected reading. 'Consider what has happened to Koshy. We must know what to read. Not Communism. Not Zen.'

'I will send word to Thankam that you have come,' said Mrs Koshy.

'Thank the Lord that girl understands me,' said Mathaichen. 'But I do not like living off a sister.' But his words were only a half-hearted formula. Mathaichen thought that a sister as rich as Thankam had a duty to help a brother down on his luck. It was not his fault that paddy had the Communist disease and cardamom didn't.

When Thankam came, Mathaichen, with his usual exaggerated delicacy, did not mention money. He talked only of family honour and how it was threatened by his increasingly conspicuous poverty. Yet, last year he had spent six thousand rupees on the *chundan vallam* (snake boat) race at Aranmula. The family had always taken part in the race. He could not break with tradition. But there was a price for everything. He could not sell the family copper and silver, could he?

Thankam, like Mathaichen, felt strongly about family honour. But with her, there was another festering—her personal honour. Avrachen had tired of her body. She had tried prayer, nagging and pleading, but nothing could cure Avrachen of his shameless liaisons with his estate women. True, she hadn't kept her figure, but surely a marriage isn't about curves.

Love, assuming there had been love, had dried up. There was still some meagre companionship, but that was all. How could she forget that Avrachen might have lain beside some fallen women, but the previous night, that he might yet be hot with illicit passion? Only Thankam's love for her brothers made her life seem worth living. Mathaichen had not fathered his nine children by panting after other women. Kunjunj's private life was more of a mystery. Thankam preferred to believe that Kunjunj didn't have a private life. In her eyes he lived wholly in public, a pillar of the Syrian Church, the chairman of the local panchayat, a paid-up member of the Indian National Congress.

'Thankam,' said Mathaichen. 'You are sure it is not going to be difficult for you?' Thankam had offered five thousand rupees as a loan, and Mathaichen as usual made a show of diffidence.

'Avrachen owes it to you to find the money,' said Thankam. It was a point she always made. Avrachen made the money. She found honourable ways of spending it.

'And there is another matter,' said Mathaichen. 'Sosamma might need a little help too. Koshy's pension does not always see them through to the end of every month. A thousand will be a nice thought.'

Thankam pouted like a little girl. She was ready enough to help her brothers, but far less ready, for many complicated reasons, to help her sister. Thankam reserved her unquestioning love and generosity for her brothers alone.

'You shouldn't have asked,' said Mrs Koshy to Mathaichen. 'Thankam will no doubt say that money doesn't grow on coconut trees. We must learn to manage on our own.' She had never cared for Thankam's grudging manner towards her.

'No, wait,' said Mathaichen. Thankam had to be steered into generosity, not quarrelled into it.

'I try my best to help,' said Thankam, pouting a little. 'But do I ever receive any thanks?'

'You know we are thankful,' said Mrs Koshy.

'I had to fish for that,' said Thankam. She blew her nose delicately. Being a providing sister was a tricky business. And then, quite suddenly there were tears.

'Devi, Lalu, leave the room,' said Mrs Koshy.

There was going to be a scene. With tears would come confessions and recrimination. Thankam had always needed handkerchiefs even as a child.

'Thankam, you know we love you,' said Mrs Koshy.

'But no one wants to know how impossible my life is. No one wants to know.'

Usually Thankam's tears were just aggravated nerves. But these tears seemed to have deeper springs.

'Avrachen, you know it is Avrachen!' said Thankam. 'I try not to notice, but his estate women, they chase me everywhere.'

Chase only after a manner of speaking perhaps, thought Mrs Koshy.

'But Avrachen has put all that behind him,' said Mathaichen. It was only a formula of consolation.

'No,' cried Thankam, 'he hasn't. You know he hasn't. He has only become more sly. More deceitful. Harder. Why does he do this to me?'

'What do you know?' asked Mathaichen.

'Everything,' said Thankam. And there were fresh tears. 'The driver tells me everything.'

Desperation has its own excuses, but Mathaichen thought it most undignified to use a driver as a spy. Rephrasing his thoughts, Mathaichen asked, 'And if Avrachen should find out?'

'Find out?' asked Thankam in surprise.

'About the driver,' said Mathaichen.

'Servants always exaggerate,' said Mrs Koshy.

'I don't believe everything,' said Thankam.

'I suppose you pay the driver extra for his information,' said Mathaichen.

'A little something.'

'You have been most unwise,' said Mathaichen. 'It is Chacko, isn't it?'

'Yes.'

'He has a drink habit, and now he has found a way of affording it.'

'But everybody is talking about Avrachen,' said Thankam.

'Not everybody,' said Mathaichen. 'Only one person. Chacko the driver. And only one person is listening, my dear silly sister, Thankam.'

'You think so?' asked Thankam.

'I'll have a word with Chacko,' said Mathaichen. 'I'll sew up his mouth if need be. And I will have a talk with Avrachen. And I will tell him everything that can decently be said.'

Thankam smiled wanly. Mathaichen had steadied her nerves. 'I'll help Sosamma as much as I can,' she said.

'Thank you,' said Mrs Koshy. Once it would have cost her an effort to say it, but now it seemed easier. She had thought that Thankam had everything, cars, servants, a rich husband. But Thankam didn't have everything. No one has everything. Somewhere something has a way of giving. Avrachen's fornication on the estates, despite Mathaichen's brave effort to comfort Thankam, was still fornication. Perhaps Thankam needed her money in a sense that she, Sosamma, didn't.

Mathaichen sat at the kitchen table, sipping his afternoon tea. Mrs Koshy was tidying up the kitchen almirah. Chechamma had gone away to take part, or so she said, in a festival at a *bhutasthanam* (spirit temple) in her village. There always seemed to be a festival in her village, usually of devil dancing, when her nerves got overwrought. But since she came back a quieter person, Mrs Koshy didn't ask too many questions. Today the kitchen was Mrs Koshy's own, and she was determined to make the most of it.

Mrs Koshy gathered her pyrex plates and put them away on the top shelf. She did little cooking in the oven now. Cooking in the oven had been one of Mrs Koshy's delights. Mr Koshy had wanted to sell the oven since she used it so little. They needed the money, but selling the oven was rather like burying a style she had been used to. So, she had said 'no'. She couldn't explain herself to Mr Koshy. He had become very impatient. Mrs Koshy gave her pyrex plates an extra dab of the duster. The plates would go into the oven, and stay there, monument to the life she had lost.

'You were lucky to have saved your oven from the flood,' said Mathaichen.

'With seconds to spare,' said Mrs Koshy.

'You have been through a lot.'

'Sometimes it all seems so unfair.'

'And we had such a happy childhood,' said Mathaichen. 'I never wanted for money then. Never.'

'Our father was generous,' said Mrs Koshy.

'Perhaps if he had been less generous, his sons would have been left with more money. He didn't leave any debts but he didn't leave much money either.'

'Sometimes I think my life in Malaysia a continuation of my childhood, you know. Malaysia was childhood. This is growing up.'

'And growing up is painful at your age,' said Mathaichen.

'And Pappa! Look at Pappa! He is going to pieces before our eyes.' Mrs Koshy fought back her tears.

Mrs Koshy ran a cloth quickly over the almirah. The more she dusted, the more remorselessly the dust seemed to invade her kitchen. Sometimes she wondered where the stuff came from. She kept the windows shut most of the time and the doors too, but still there was dust, blankets of dust. And they had said Tiruvananthapuram had the least dust among towns in Kerala. Dust was a dreadful business. She was so much less kitchen proud than she had been. Dust seemed a part of her growing up.

'Keeping the windows shut makes the room hot,' said Mathaichen.

'It keeps out the dust.'

'You know you talk as if you were still a stranger in this land. No one worries about dust. I say accept it.'

'I don't think I can!'

'You remember how I hated mud. Other children made mud pies but I couldn't. Then one day I threw myself into a paddy field. Now I can stand as much mud as a water buffalo.'

'But you were a child then.'

'You can break yourself in at any age. Invented worlds are a mistake. Invented worlds like Koshy's Zen. Plunge into the mud. There is no other way.'

'You are a regular water buffalo now,' said Mrs Koshy.

'Do you think that Kuttanad would settle for less?'

Kuttanad, the rice bowl of Kerala, is a land of mud-flats and sandy outcrops, and water everywhere. Kuttanad is land wrested from the water. But it is also an invented world. The pioneers built their houses on the mud-flats and planted coconut trees on the sandy outcrops. Mathaichen's father was one of the pioneers. But water isn't easily defeated. There are floods in the lagoons, insane in their fury. Mud is the stuff of Kuttanad. Mathaichen was right to baptize himself in mud.

Mrs Koshy passed a moist chamois over the top of the oven. The chamois was a treasure from Malaysia. She couldn't afford another in Tiruvananthapuram. It was curious how much little things, especially the adjuncts of hygiene and health, cost in India.

Mathaichen wiped his hands on his shirt sleeves. 'Hot, it is hot. Do you have any of the Tiger beer from Malaysia left?'

Mrs Koshy rummaged in a Lifebuoy cardboard box and produced a can.

'It is a pity about your refrigerator. I like my beer chilled,' said Mathaichen.

'We liked our water and almost everything else chilled,' said Mrs Koshy. 'But we have got used to drinking tepid water from the tap.'

'Keep the water to cool in a *kooja* (mud-pot) first,' said Mathaichen. 'It may be the only Westinghouse we will be able to afford for a long time.'

Mathaichen drank the beer gurglingly. He belched re-soundingly. 'Sosamma, keep an eye on Dr Vareed,' he said, wiping his mouth of beer-surf. 'His father came from Kuttanad too. If the thought that he might make a good son-in-law has crossed your mind, put it out at once. His blood is all wrong. Inferior blood does not become good blood merely because it becomes rich blood.'

'I don't think anyone has mentioned marriage.'

'A man of experience rarely wants to settle down,' said Mathaichen.

'Then you know something?'

'I'll be fair. I know nothing. But a rich man of thirty doesn't spend his time playing draughts.'

Mathaichen was terrible about inferior ancestries, thought Mrs Koshy. For the most part, Mathaichen was a lovable water-buffalo of a man, happy enough to wallow in his Kuttanad mud. But there were times when the water buffalo became a snappy crocodile. The crocodile's teeth were bared the most when family ancestries were discussed and Mathaichen was ready to make a meal of anyone foolish enough to want to argue with him. The crocodile had no mercy for inferior ancestries.

Mrs Koshy half wished that Mathaichen didn't know as much as he did about the Pazhaymootils. She didn't want a 'cheap money' marriage for Devi of course. But there is more to match-making than matching old stock with old stock. Families deteriorate. Noble rot was still rot. She thought of Pappa's gibbering sister. She had had to be strait-jacketed in her thirty-third year. And could Devi find a husband with her father so? Arranging marriages is a fussy business and Mathaichen was already supplying the fuss. She would need strength. Was it a bad sign that in her prayers she worshipped God as strength? Strength first. Compassion next.

A telegram from Kunjunj asked Mathaichen to return to

Kuttanad at once. Labour trouble had broken out again in Kuttanad. The Marxists were threatening to burn down the granaries of every landlord.

Mathaichen cursed. He said philosophies, Marxism, Zen, whatever, only addled a man's mind. A man had no right to throw his life away on a brain fever. He knew what his workers had been like before Marxism. He knew what they were like after Marxism. Marxism had made killing-machines of his workers. His father's servants had been faith and loyalty in the feudal flesh. They would never speak to any one of the *janmi* (landlord) family without hunching their backs or cupping their mouths with their hands. Some would make their bodies tremble in a panto-mime of fear. That pantomime of fear had yielded to a pantomime of hate. Today, in the Marxist class war, even ordinary civilities were forgotten. And they called it pro-gress.

The Marxists had made battle fields of the rice fields of Kuttanad. Absurdly, they were quoting Russian wage rates at Kuttanad landlords. Mathaichen said that Kuttanad's Marxists should be packed away to their Soviet fairy land. Hobgoblins belonged to fairy land not to the real world. He made an eloquent anti-Soviet speech. The Russian Revolu-tion, he said, was threatening to happen again, this time in Kuttanad. It is India's lot to pick up cast-off clothing, usually the fancy dress clothing, of the white man.

As for Zen, that other brain fever, privately Mathaichen thought that his sister was not entirely without blame for her husband's Zen-strangeness. She had not tried hard enough to pluck her husband away from his funny books. Not to put too fine a point on it, if a man didn't live through his body then he would want to live through his mind. A man whose body sang with health didn't need to live his life through books. A swelling groin, a healthy thirst and what need for books? Books are usually about other people's worries. As if our own worries aren't enough, we are punished by the books we read, by the philosophies and religions we muddle our heads with.

Mrs Koshy said that high blood pressure ran in the family and that Mathaichen should try to keep cool. But Mathaichen would not calm down. He left for Kuttanad as if he were going out to a war.


Dr Vareed had stopped calling during the week of Mathaichen's visit. He had feared a shouting match. The spoken and unspoken slurs would rankle ever afterwards. Mathaichen who complained about his workers' lack of civility, could himself be horribly blunt. Kuttanad was the home of colourful speech, and Mathaichen had no equal in colourful argument. Dr Vareed had heard it said of Mathaichen that he had everybody's paternity down to the fifth generation at the tip of his tongue, and was ready to spit it out at any who crossed his path. Paternities lend themselves to the most colourful abuse. Even a civilized drawing-room can become a gutter during a shouting match about family and ancestry.

But Dr Vareed saw clearly enough that Mathaichen and Kunjunj were Devi's *dwarapalika* (gatekeeper) uncles. And no one who wanted to get into the house quarrelled with the gatekeepers. So, it was not until Dr Vareed heard that Mathaichen had been called away to Kuttanad that he called again.

'The doctor has come back,' muttered Mr Koshy. 'Now he will want the disease to come back too.'

In his most polite voice, so as to rule out irony altogether, Dr Vareed asked Mrs Koshy about Mathaichen's health, alert to hints about what Mathaichen might have said about him. He knew he was a condemned man in Mathaichen's eyes, but had Mrs Koshy allowed him to be led up to his execution? But Mrs Koshy would give nothing away. She was rather good at sudden iron curtain silences.

And what, persevered Dr Vareed, had Mathaichen said about Tangaserri school? Mrs Koshy repeated Mathaichen's thundering judgement about boarding-schools. Dr Vareed said that Mathaichen had got his arguments very wrong. Mrs Koshy said that there really was no appeal. Dr Vareed shrugged his shoulders. Even the unsilliest families can be silly about some things.

'Pappa says books are the best teachers,' said Mrs Koshy. 'I suppose he is right. Schools everywhere are in such a poor way nowadays that we will have to go back to books.'

'If nothing else,' said Dr Vareed, 'we must get Lalu away from his concentration camp school. I travel a lot. Lalu can come with me. He must see something of our land.' Dr Vareed said Lalu was still stranded somewhere between Kerala and Malaysia. Between destinations is an uncomfortable place to be at. Dr Vareed cleared his throat. 'Devi can come too. She doesn't travel much, does she?'

Mrs Koshy flushed. 'I am afraid Devi cannot come. It is quite out of the question.'

Dr Vareed groaned. Kuttanad was laying down the law with the roughest of peasant sticks.

'My grandfather used to say,' said Mrs Koshy in a voice that seemed to say that it was herself she was quoting not her grandfather, 'that with most families there are fences that outsiders mustn't climb or want to climb. A healthy distance is no bad thing . . . I am putting it very badly.'

Dr Vareed was being accused of familiarity.

# Chapter Ten

' . . . I HAVE WRITTEN to you,' wrote Lalu,

> about white tigers, sacred cows, elephants grey and
> white, but little about the naughtiest animal in the
> zoo, our landlord. This animal can kneel in elabo-
> rate prayer, curl up in long pujas, but he can also
> butt harder than a goat. Pappa with his funny kind
> of goodness is no match for him.

> The landlord came to speak to us yesterday. He
> spoke and we didn't much listen . . . and we spoke
> and he didn't much listen. But I heard all that I
> wanted to hear. My ears turned red at the land-
> lord's language. God help us, it was very animal.
> Pappa muttered something about the law. The
> landlord said there is no such thing. But, oh God,
> I always thought there was . . . .

Madhavan Thampy was on his knees before a stone idol of
Saraswati. Saraswati was his *ishta devata* (special diety).
'Woo a goddess as you would woo a woman.' So his mother
used to say. *Nirmalayum vilakkum* (flowers and lamps) and
long obeisances, were the way to favour with the goddess.

Thampy had bought the largest marigold garland in the
bazaar. The marigold garland hung on the idol like soft and
wavy yellow fire. The goddess had been in the family for
generations. His mother used to have the idol coated with
sandal paste in imitation of the *muzhukappu* (bathing the

diety) ceremony in some temples. It was after a *muzhukappu* of the goddess that he, Thampy, was conceived.

Thampy had his own special way with the goddess. He treated her as his mother said he should, but he went further than his mother would have thought right. Indeed, his poor mother would have fainted away if she knew how special his special way was. He flirted with the goddess. He was not afraid to touch her.

Thampy spread himself on the floor before the goddess, flat as a prayer mat. He made his voice crack prayerfully. Why had he been let down so often? he moaned. He made a recitation of his losses. A house lost to a family of sheep. Five thousand rupees lost to a whore. Some of his pride lost to Kunnukuzhi Mohan. He did not add, though his heart hurt with the unfairness of it, that somewhat earlier in his life he had lost some part of his male clockwork to the freedom movement—as if the Mahatma had any use for that particular sort of thing. That was the sick joke. He had given more than most men would give to any cause, and what had he got in return except the laughter of the town? Only yesterday an urchin had told him in the horrible jeering way of these urchins that he had mislaid his handball and would he, Thampy, help him find it? The rascal had, as they say, spun a pun into every word.

Thampy knocked his head thrice against the feet of the goddess. In life there is a so much and no more rule. Every vessel has a brim.

He lit three *sambrani* (incense) sticks and offered a silk shawl to the goddess. He waited for a sign from Saraswati. The incense smoke curled into many pig-tails. One pig-tail rode on the goddess's upper lip. It thickened into a moustache. Was it a bad omen? Or was it just his overheated brain?

Thampy's cook bustled in with a breakfast of idli, sambar, *pootu*, coffee and plantain. There was a rattling of stainless steel plates.

Thampy ordered the cook to look at the goddess and tell him what he saw.

'What do I see?' said the cook. Playing for time, he poured the coffee into a tumbler.

'The incense smoke . . .' prompted Thampy.

'Oh Master!' cried the cook almost in alarm.

Thampy stubbed out the incense sticks. Two brains cannot overheat in the same way. The smoke-graffiti melted away.

'It was only my impious eyes,' said the cook.

'Our impious eyes,' said Thampy drily. He caught himself staring at the goddess' very thin blouse. The goddess had breasts like swollen and ripe mangoes. They seemed to ache to be plucked.

The cook peeled a plantain slowly and slid the *pootu* from its cylindrical moulds with his thumb. The *pootu* was perfectly formed. He clucked proudly, like a hen over a well-formed egg. 'Hunger will only feed your anger,' said the cook. 'We mustn't add heat to heat.' The cook peeled the plantain to the last seductive inch. Thampy laid the plantain at the feet of Saraswati. The cook pulled the peeled skin back over the plantain. There must be no suggestion of nakedness before the goddess. Thampy smiled at his cook's delicacy.

'Call in the priests and do a regular puja,' said the cook. The cook did not care for Thampy's religious improvisations.

'But maybe I'm an irregular man,' said Thampy.

The cook shook his head.

'Tomorrow I am getting my house back,' said Thampy.

'In an irregular way, master?'

'That's the only way I know or care to know.'

'Wait for an answer from the goddess,' said the cook.

'What if I already have my answer?' Thampy spoke quietly. The mango breasts were swelling at him.

'I did not hear her speak,' said the cook.

'It wasn't her lips, you . . . ' said Thampy.

The cook twitched with disapproval. This was no way to speak in the hearing of the goddess. Sadly he was beginning to think that the master was right about himself. He was a most irregular man.


Thampy hired nine *chattambis* (thugs). The young toughs looked all hip and shoulder and very little head. It was curious how pyramidal the fellows looked. The more pyramidal a man, the more criminal, Thampy always said. He himself was more playing card than pyramid. In folk psychology, a playing card figure was respectability.

Thampy explained his plan to the *chattambi* chief and his men. They were to use fright not fight to throw out the Koshys. No knives. No *kodalis* (axes). No bicycle chains. But these would be on heavy show. 'They have eggshell bones. You don't.' Thampy spoke in the manner of a Master, smooth and sharp but hard as nails.

A lorry would be waiting in the frontyard. The driver had been told to take the Koshys wherever they wanted to go. No doubt, the Koshys would take refuge in simper and Gandhian non-cooperation. They wouldn't be respectable middle class if they didn't. They would shed tears. The women might even offer to shed their clothes. 'These in-between classes will shed anything, down to the last *cheela* (loincloth) and more. But no shedding of blood please, we are too respectable. That's how respectable these respectables are!'

Thampy said the lorry driver was to drive straight to a warehouse in Chalai and dump the Koshys' belongings there.

'No mistakes. I am not paying good money for mistakes.' Nine men at fifty rupees a head for a day's work, not to speak of a thanksgiving round of toddies, at the end of it all, added up to four hundred and fifty rupees. Thampy thought he was pissing money almost. But he was pitted against Kunnukuzhi Mohan, who was a bigger pisser, of money, of blood, of *chattambis*. Mohan's private army was fifty strong. Mohan boasted that his army was ever ready. It was therefore important that Mohan's 'ever readies' did not know of the operation until it was all over. The *chattambis* had to strike in the same way a skilled butcher cut a goat's throat—entirely without warning.

The *chattambi* chief wore a long mala round his neck. Little skull-like pendants hung from the mala. He worked the mala through his fingers as if it were a rosary. He said that it was always easier if they began with a little roughness. His men were warm-blooded animals, not sanyasis. They needed a little roughness to get their fighting juices flowing. But Thampy said no. His gruffness astonished the chief. The chief saw that Thampy was afraid.

'Remember,' said Thampy, 'not even so thick a neck as yours can snap out of a hangman's noose.'

Thampy was truly afraid, thought the chief. A man smells different when he is afraid, almost like a cornered skunk.

The chief cracked his knuckles against his knees, explosively. 'I don't want to put my hand into a cobra's nest either,' he said.

'These people are not cobras,' said Thampy. 'Chickens, they are no more than chickens. Perhaps chickens with sharp beaks,'

'Chickens they may be, perhaps even newly hatched chickens with the eggshell still on them, but what if they have a cobra watching over them?'

'So your blood is running thin already . . . .'

'I must know the name of the cobra.'

'Kunnukuzhi Mohan,' said Thampy, letting the name drop casually.

'Ishwara! That is the name of a python, not a cobra. The biggest python in Tiruvananthapuram. This python has too many stomachs.'

'You have a big mouth,' said Thampy. 'But how much bigness do you have lower down?'

'I don't know whether Master will call it a python or a cobra.'

Not to be outdone, for skill in ribald exchanges is one test

147

of toughness, Thampy said, 'It depends on whether it crushes or whether it pecks.'

'It is trained to do both,' said the chief.

'You look more like a pecker than a crusher.'

'And Master must forgive me for saying that Master looks more like a rusher than a crusher.'

Thampy had no come-back. 'You have the dirtier tongue,' he said.

'Only the dirtier mind, Master,' said the chief.

The *chattambi* chief held up the skulls on his mala. 'Each time I score, I give myself a skull. First, I will complete one row and then a second. But Kunnukuzhi Mohan is a bigger skull than all the skulls on my mala put together.'

'You are risking nothing, and you know it,' said Thampy. 'If Kunnukuzhi Mohan catches up with you, you will cringe like a dog. If he beats you, you will roll over like a good dog, for another beating. When Mohan thinks that you have rolled in the dust long enough, he will let you go. If he spits into your mouth you will swallow it saying it is amrit and open your mouth for more. So what risk are you running?'

'Master is making me out to be more of a dog than I am.'

'It is I who will be running all the risks,' said Thampy. 'Because I will refuse to cringe before Mohan. All my life I have kicked out at pi-dogs that have come in my way. I cannot change the habits of a lifetime and go down on my knees before pi-dogs now, even if they are rich and powerful pi-dogs.' Thampy exploded into a many-coloured oath in which he questioned, as is usual in such Malayali oaths, Kunnukuzhi Mohan's paternity and sanity and masculinity for ten generations.

The chief ran his fingers over the skull-pendants. Suitably shrunk, Thampy would have made a fine upper-caste skull. But perhaps more than his skull, it was his smoking tongue that was worth preserving.

The *chattambi* chief said that the house was easiest to take from the rear. The front had a veranda: it would make sense to rush the veranda and use it as a first base. The veranda snaked round the front of the house and one could jump off its considerable length into almost any part of the house. But the veranda was shut off with mosquito meshing and bamboo trellising. The *chattambi* chief wanted to knock down part of the meshing nearest to the outer door but Thampy said no. The house was his. The *chattambi* chief wasn't to forget that, said Thampy. A bird does not foul its own nest.

Thampy said that at a signal from him, the *chattambi* chief and his men would stream into the back garden of the house through the wicket gate. It was now close to two o'clock. The members of the household would be settling down for their afternoon nap. A back door or window would be open: you could always count on such carelessness. One man would slip into the house and let in the others. Then they would start piling the family's belongings into the lorry.

Thampy held up a clutch of jute strings. The jute strings were cut into lengths of about twelve feet each. 'Truss them up like fowls if they resist,' said Thampy. 'But before they make too much of a squawk, you must be away. No broken bones. Understood?'

The *chattambi* chief lined up his men in the narrow lane outside the wicket gate. He looked them up and down in the manner of a colonel inspecting his men. Each man touched the chief's feet as he passed, and then straightened up. The chief punched one distracted man in the shoulder. The man bowed low from the waist. The discipline was feudal.

The men then took their shirts off and smeared their arms and chests with oil. They had heavy, muscular bodies, but thanks to some trick of criminal evolution their heads were the smallest *vellakais* (unripe coconuts).

'Not an oil bath?' asked Thampy.

149

'The oil,' said the chief, 'is only to make them more slippery in a fight. It isn't easy to get a hold on my men.'

The *chattambis* formed a two column file behind their chief. The chief jogged his men through the wicket gate. The well-oiled bodies of the men shone in the sun. Dust rose like a thin mist around them. One man coughed. The dust was throat tickling. The *chattambi* chief made a rude sign with his thumb at the man. It was part of the chief's conceit of leadership to bring to every 'job', however small, a touch of storm trooper discipline. That was the way to lick a bazaar rabble into shape and keep their hand in for the big tasks. Throwing a family out of their home was child's play really, but the chief liked to make it seem like hard work.

Thampy pointed to the back garden. The chief and his men moved into the back garden, following Thampy's pointing finger. The *chattambi* chief had gone into battle with beautiful spit and polish. Thampy tremblingly lit a cigarette.

There were two open windows in the house. Two *chattambis* climbed in through the windows and threw open the kitchen door.

It was Chechamma who raised the alarm. '*Chattambis*, Ammachy,' she cried, '*chattambis*.'

'Grab that whore,' ordered Thampy rushing into the kitchen. 'But be careful with the others. There is a man, more vegetable than man, really. He thinks that he is breakable and I don't want him to break in our hands.'

Chechamma was jostled roughly. One *chattambi* tried to lay a familiar hand on Chechamma's blouse. Chechamma slapped away the *chattambi's* hands. Thampy planted himself between Chechamma and the *chattambi*. Chechamma brushed her blouse clean as if of invisible smuts. 'This man has enough oil on him to fry fish for a wedding party!'

'And you have enough flesh on you to provide for all of them together,' said the *chattambi*.

'Yes, it would take all of you and more . . .' retorted Chechamma.

The *chattambi* gang began to carry away the furniture, boxes, pictures, saucepans, pots and pans into the lorry.

'It is the curse of the *thattinpuram*,' said Chechamma lugubriously. 'The unexorcized evil of the *thattinpuram* won't leave us alone.' The Koshys had thrown away a chance to exorcize the evil by putting in an east-facing door. An east-facing door would have opened the house to the sun, and the sun would have chased away the shadows in the house. But no, the Koshys worshipped their own gods, gods no doubt as thick-headed as they were. Didn't it say a lot that the *chattambis* had come into the house from two south-facing windows, the inauspicious direction?

Two *chattambis* carried the fridge, wondering why it had no lead wire. 'It is a fridge and yet it is not a fridge,' said one *chattambi*. 'It's a cheat. Just to impress the neighbours. But I wouldn't mind one myself.'

'Keep it if you want it,' said the other *chattambi*. 'Everything need not go into the lorry.'

Trunks and boxes that could not be picked up were trundled across the floor. And those that were too heavy to be moved were burst open. Their contents were flung out until the boxes were light enough to be carried into the lorry. There were jetsams of paper, clothing and broken glass everywhere in the house.

The six sturdy metal trunks that held Mr Koshy's books made the *chattambis* curse. 'Gold bars,' said one *chattambi*, 'you would have thought the trunks had gold bars.'

'That sort of luck is not for us,' said another. 'We have to be happy with books.' He spat in a stringy jet.

'Drop these trunks on a man and you will have him flatter than an anna coin.'

The *chattambis* burst open the trunks, levering the locks out of their places with an iron bar. 'By Shatan's mother's coconuts!' they said, seeing the neatly packed books inside. Dr Suzuki, Tolstoy and Christmas Humphreys were pulled out of their coffin-trunks and tossed into the air. They landed horribly on their spines. 'Such heaviness!' said the *chattambis*. Such heaviness, they seemed to say, should not go unpunished.

'The *vaidyan* has gone to Kunnukuzhi Mohan to get help,' said Mrs Koshy to Devi. 'He took Lalu along. I am glad for that. I don't want Lalu to see all this. There are nicer ways of growing up.'

'Didn't the *vaidyan* go to the police?' asked Devi.

'No,' said Mrs Koshy. She looked away from Devi in embarrassment.

'Oh?'

'The police may want to take their own time to come,' said Mrs Koshy.

'Thieves, have we become a nation of thieves and *pindaris* (bandits)?' cried Mr Koshy.

'We'll pull through,' said Mrs Koshy quietly.

All kinds of sounds were coming from the house—the animal rowdiness of the *chattambis*, the clatter of crates, and most of all it seemed the cries for help of a half-strangled house. But with something like a smile Mrs Koshy noticed certain seemingly uninterruptible domesticities. A neighbour's cat walked in and out of the house. Sometimes the cat stopped to lick its paws and scratch for lice, or stroke itself against a door jamb. And, through the din rather than above it, Mrs Koshy could hear the funny extra-loud tick-tock of the burnt brass kitchen wall clock in the kitchen. Life in a basic sense does have a stubborn way of going on despite our many madnesses. She saw the cliché happening.

'Everything we have is gone or is going,' said Devi.

'It is so unfair,' said Mr Koshy. 'These animals are tearing away our very skins.' His voice was close to breaking.

'The jungle has come home,' said Mrs Koshy. 'Perhaps to stay. Once I said our life is a circus. Then I called it a zoo. Now I see it for what it is. It is a jungle.'

'A jungle is full of unanswered prayers,' said Mr Koshy.

'But we must not let the jungle win,' said Mrs Koshy. 'Must not let it win.' Mrs Koshy might have been talking to herself. Her voice was just a little trembly. No, it wasn't fear, thought Devi. It was more like anger, anger that has passed the relief of mere hysteria.

The lorry was half-loaded now. The driver kept cursing the *chattambis*. The *chattambis* seemed to want to take all afternoon to decide on what they wanted to keep for themselves and what they would leave. 'Hurry up,' he cried. 'You are not women choosing things at a *chantay* (market)!'

Two *chattambis* were pushing a timber cot into the lorry. It collided with the drawing-room divan. The *chattambis* pushed the cot, urging it sideways. The mattress fell out of the cot. The divan ripped open the mattress. The mattress leaked white feather stuffing all over the lorry. The *chattambis* cursed. They pulled the ripped mattress out of the lorry and dragged it back into the house. There was a blizzard of feathers in the veranda. A brisk wind swept the feathers through the house. Mr Koshy chased the feathers from room to room. 'They are almost like snow-flakes,' he said. Mrs Koshy remarked in a dry voice that these snow-flakes looked alarmingly like the feathers from their softest mattress. Mr Koshy let go of a fistful of feathers. They danced round him. Some sat down in his hair, some on his hands. Poor little snowman, thought Mrs Koshy. How white and lost he looked.

'The *vaidyan* has gone to get help,' said Mrs Koshy.

'What good would that do?' asked Mr Koshy. 'After all this is the end of the world.'

No good at all, muttered Mrs Koshy. Mr Koshy was hopeless in a crisis. He had a way of making soothing fairy tales of their worst troubles.

'I had a very loud argument with Thampy,' said Mrs Koshy. 'Didn't you hear?'

Mrs Koshy had threatened Thampy with the law. He had smiled. She had threatened him with the anger of her Kuttanad brothers. He had smiled. 'Aren't you going to threaten me with the anger of your husband?' Thampy had asked in his politest voice. Mrs Koshy had gulped down her anger. Mrs Koshy hadn't mentioned Kunnukuzhi Mohan. She feared that this would only make a mad bull of Thampy.

'Pappa,' said Mrs Koshy, 'we will soon be on the streets. Wherever the lorry dumps us.'

'Streets!' said Mr Koshy, twisting uncomfortably. The streets, he had always thought, were for other people.

'This may be much less than the end of the world.'

Mr Koshy slapped away the feathers on his shirt sleeves and blew away a feather that seemed to want to dance on the tip of his nose.

'Kunnukuzhi Mohan is our only hope,' said Mrs Koshy.

'It's come to that?' asked Devi.

'Yes,' said Mrs Koshy. 'Avrachen is away at his estates. The *vaidyan* is arranging to send a message to Kunjunj *chetan* (elder brother) and Mathaichen.'

'But Mohan is not our kind at all,' declared Mr Koshy.

'Maybe that is why he is the only one who can save us,' said Mrs Koshy.

Mr Koshy buried his head on his wife's shoulders. 'I have failed you,' he whimpered. 'You, Devi, myself.'

Mrs Koshy picked a feather from his hair.

'I have failed my books too,' Mr Koshy added. 'These gangsters have been flinging them about. They are no better than waste paper now.'

'And you were trying hard not to notice?' asked Mrs Koshy.

Mr Koshy burrowed like a child into his wife's shoulders.

Mrs Koshy stroked the back of his neck. She should have allowed him to play with his snow-flakes. Her poor little snowman!

Kunnukuzhi Mohan's men came in a mini-bus. Their 'Captain' was a tough-talking lieutenant of Mohan's. His skin seemed a rough sort of bark. There were knots and knobs all over his forehead and body. Kunnukuzhi Mohan joked that if you looked hard enough you could see the dead wood in his heart. The Captain was a useful lieutenant.

'The Master wants to teach Thampy a lesson,' said the Captain to his men, 'maybe the last lesson Thampy will ever need to be taught. But remember, we use only our lathis on him.'

'Do you want to make policemen of us?' Someone laughed derisively.

'Does anyone want to argue this out to the end?' asked the Captain.

'We were only joking,' said one man.

'Make sure that next time I see the joke just as soon as you do,' said the Captain. 'The Master wants to finish this business with his own hands. The Master will come in an hour's time. Meanwhile we will have some fun with Thampy, but no more than that.'

The *chattambis*, with Thampy at their head, came rushing out of the house. Some of the *chattambis* picked up stones.

'You don't want it to be said that you threw stones at Kunnukuzhi Mohan's Captain,' said the Captain.

'By my mother and her mother,' said the *chattambi* chief. 'Not Kunnukuzhi Mohan.' He tugged at his ears in self-abasement. The *chattambis* flinched away as if from a whip. They dropped their stones.

The veins on Thampy's head stood up, tall enough to be counted. 'So you come from the pi-dog!' he said.

The Captain struck Thampy across the face. It was a limp slap, more humiliation than physical hurt.

'Get him!' shouted Thampy to the *chattambis*.

'Get him yourself!' replied the *chattambi* chief. When a cobra fights a mongoose, it is only commonsense to keep out of the flying spittle.

'Bhagwan,' said Thampy looking skywards. 'There was a time when hot lead would have been poured down your nostrils for daring to strike a man of my caste. And heaven would have sent lightning.' Thampy rolled his eyes like a Kathakali dancer.

'There are only two castes today, man and woman,' said the Captain, 'Perhaps not even these, seeing how some men behave. Shrill as women some men can be, but when it comes to a proper fight you wouldn't believe they had anything more than hot air between their legs.'

'Yes, only two castes!' said Thampy. 'Those who know the scriptures and those who don't. Tell your Master that even he, limb of Shatan though he may be, cannot take my caste and my home away from me. Caste is what Bhagwan has put into this world and only Bhagwan can take away what Bhagwan has given. As for my house, the cement in this house has set all the harder because it is mixed with my sweat. Add my blood to it and it will only set all the harder.' He spoke his hate with an upper-caste lilt as if trying to cast a blue blood spell on his audience.

Determined to mock his speech and his caste, the Captain's men surrounded Thampy. The men locked arms.

'When you catch a dog by its tail, it either bites or licks your hands,' said the Captain. 'But here comes the Master . . . .'

A space was cleared for Mohan's Mercedes. Everybody namasted the red car. Mohan climbed out, pot belly first.

'The scrapes you manage to get into,' said Mohan to Thampy.

'The scrapes you manage to get me into,' said Thampy.

Mohan had expected a less placid man. 'I very nearly did not recognize you,' said Mohan.

'I very nearly did not recognize you either,' said Thampy. 'You own a good car. You have grown a good paunch. It was not always so.' He would allow Mohan no conversational advantage.

'You have started keeping very low company,' said

Mohan, looking at the *chattambis*. 'It was not always so either. Once you had no friends outside the *kottaram*. Now you have no friends outside the gutter.'

'Maybe the gutter must be fought with the gutter,' said Thampy.

Mohan reared forward like an angry cobra. Each of his blows stung. Mohan aimed at Thampy's double belly. His knuckles hit a wadding of cloth. 'Has your belly grown a dewlap,' Mohan asked, waiting for laughter between questions, 'or is it with child? Or is it a chastity belt? Do you have trouble with your small one, your very small one at this age?' The laughter came obediently on cue. Then like a *mantravadi* (magician), Mohan pulled out a cloth pouch from under Thampy's belly. Thampy snatched at the pouch but Mohan had the firmer grip. 'Or is your pouch standing in for your missing one?' The laughter was jeering. Mohan fished out of the pouch two tightly rubber-banded wads of notes. 'All in hundreds,' said Mohan. 'That is how the best people keep their money.' Mohan tossed the money to the Captain. 'You might be able to afford some very high-caste whisky tonight.'

'Bastard!' said Thampy. His eyes popped horribly. They looked like hard boiled eggs.

'This is more like the man we all know. You can tell a man by his eyes.'

'Your mother,' said Thampy, 'used to sell herself for four annas a time.'

Mohan chopped Thampy on the neck.

'But I used to pay her eight annas. She always earned a tip.'

There was another chop.

'She knew how to do a good job, especially on young bodies.'

Mohan felled Thampy with a blow in the stomach.

'Stop!' said Mrs Koshy, hurrying out of the house. 'This is murder.'

'But still better than he deserves,' said Mohan.

'Jungle,' said Mrs Koshy, 'what a jungle!'

Mohan said that jungle law was the only law that Thampy cared for. 'You know that too. You wouldn't have come to me otherwise.'

Mrs Koshy made no answer. Mohan had jabbed home.

Thampy was down but he would argue still. He couldn't lose his argument with Mohan, couldn't lose caste. 'How many more bones must I break before you know you are defeated?' asked Mohan. He clenched his fists again. Thampy put out all his fingers. It was a defiant answer. The Captain had trouble keeping Mohan back.

'As long as there is one breath of life in the dog,' said the Captain, 'his caste pride will live on. You can kill him but not his caste pride.'

'Take the dog away,' said Mohan. 'I fear he may tempt me into killing him. He is only two heartbeats away from death.'

'You can kill him with the back of your hand, Master, but you won't,' said the Captain. He was applauding his master's mercy.

Three men bore Thampy away. Thampy's fingers were spread out like dark exclamation marks. And as he passed Mohan's red Mercedes, one crooked forefinger greeted the car rudely.

Kunjunj and Mathaichen hurried to Tiruvananthapuram from Kuttanad in a fast taxi as soon as they got the *vaidyan's* message. Ready for battle, they brought three family retainers with them. Mathaichen said in a pompous voice, that even he would not have recognized as his own, that it was upsetting that it was Kunnukuzhi Mohan who had saved their 'family honour'.

'Sometimes,' said Kunjunj in jokey condescension, 'it is not the lap-dog but the pi-dog that bites and barks best.' But, secretly, they were relieved that the battle was over. Family honour is a good cause but they were not as light on their feet as they once were. Their retainers were fierce but only in a decorative way.

Kunjunj did what he was good at. He called a crisis family council. Thankam and Avrachen were summoned. The family sat in the kitchen, surrounded by cardboard boxes brimming with rubbish, broken furniture, and the spilt stuffing of cushions and pillows. Thankam dabbed her eyes. 'If only,' she said, 'Avrachen had been here when it happened. But of course he had to go away to his estates. His estates are his home now. Not his second home as we used to hope they were. Perhaps I am merely his other wife or will be soon . . . .'

Avrachen, who sat opposite her, sucked at his teeth hecklingly.

'Thankam,' said Kunjunj sternly, 'this is not what the family council was called to discuss.'

'To think that a pariah has saved us from a wolf,' said Mathaichen, as if he had made up his mind never to get used to the indignity of it. He looked accusingly at Avrachen.

Mathaichen was taking up for Thankam. Kunjunj recognized the storm signals. 'I won't have anyone discuss anything except business,' he said.

'If by business you mean Thampy,' said Avrachen in a sulky voice, 'there is not much busy-ness left in that business. The man is recovering very slowly. Kunnukuzhi Mohan was settling a personal score. I would not have dared to do half as much as he did to Thampy. So Thankam has less reason to complain than she thinks.'

'I have more reason to complain than you think, and not on this matter alone,' said Thankam.

'A cobra perhaps is never more dangerous than when it is wounded,' said Kunjunj, trying to head the conversation away from husband-wife bickering.

'Those who say,' said Thankam, speaking in a muddle of double meanings, 'that some houses have dark lives of their own, just like some men have dark and secret lives of their own, may be right. Chechamma says that the stench of the evil in the *thattinpuram* is never far from her nostrils. I say we must break out of this house before it breaks us. A man

159

must in the end break clean with evil if he does not want the evil to swallow him.'

'But we have put money into this house,' said Avrachen, ignoring his wife's snide meanings. 'We have rebuilt the kitchen walls. We have put in a new roof. And the drains cost a pretty sum. We have all but rebuilt the house.'

'I'm sure you have the bills somewhere,' said Kunjunj drily.

'We may have rebuilt the house,' said Thankam, 'but we will never be able to do anything about the pall that hangs over this house.'

'You are being fanciful,' said Avrachen, still thinking of his investments.

'When a house gets rotten, the lives of those within it rot too,' said Thankam, refusing to back down from her argument. 'It takes a woman to see that.'

'But are you strong enough for another beginning?' Kunjunj asked Mrs Koshy. 'You know that Koshy is no strength to anyone of us, least of all to you.'

'Perhaps we will have to make ourselves strong enough for another beginning,' said Mrs Koshy. 'This land is merciless with those who cannot begin again and again. We must begin again. In hope.'

There was silence round the table. The optimism of that seemed a little thin. Kunjunj stroked his chin. 'Ahem,' he said. It sounded rather like an amen.

Devi marvelled at her mother. The debris of battle still surrounded them, ripped mattresses, torn books and clothing. Mr Koshy had kept saying that he didn't dare to look his vandalized books in the eye. Devi felt the same about some of her knick-knack possessions. Her Chinese musical box which played the "Negara-ku", the Malaysian national anthem; her Max Factor make-up set which was almost her last purchase in Singapore; her prize books, the leather bound copy of Shakespeare with a smart zip-up cover and the specially inscribed copy of the Bible: where were they? Perspiring quietly under a pile of rubbish, perhaps. She felt too tired to think of hunting for them. But already her mother was talking imperturbably of another house. Another beginning. She would 'carry on'.

Thankam said that she had seen a house in Kawdiar. It had a good kitchen. And drains. She hadn't noticed a pall.

'I have never cared for towns,' said Mathaichen. 'Are you sure you do not want to return to Kuttanad?'

'Yes,' said Mrs Koshy. She could never return to villlage life. 'I can't think of one nice thing to say about town life and yet I cannot go back to Kuttanad.'

Mathaichen shook his head impatiently. 'That isn't logic. But I won't argue.'

'Pappa has been in bed all yesterday,' said Mrs Koshy.

'I suppose his nervous system is out of joint again,' said Kunjunj.

'God seems to have given him a nervousness system, I sometimes think,' said Mathaichen.

'I would be very careful about my nerves if I were you,' said Thankam to Mrs Koshy. 'Nerves can snap without warning.'

'I thought I could hear my nerves this morning when I discovered that the door of my electric stove was missing!'

'And I was admiring it only last week!' said Thankam.

'Electric stove doors are sturdy things!' said Avrachen. 'They are built to stand a lot of heat and wear.'

'Not our kind of heat and wear,' said Mrs Koshy. 'It is easy to blame the *chattambis*. It is more than the *chattambis*. It is something in the air.'

Kunjunj drank his coffee from a saucer, noisily. He didn't usually allow this sort of 'intense' comment at family councils. He always said that discussions should grow out of the head, not the blood. But Mrs Koshy had been through a lot. She had earned the right to a bout of 'intensity'. Better a flame-of-the-forest than a weeping willow, as his father used to say.

'Mathaichen,' said Kunjunj, winding up the council, 'you must remember to thank Kunnukuzhi Mohan. Who would have thought that such an outcaste would do us a favour. But he has. We mustn't grudge him a thank you. After all we are a family of honour.' He might have been ironizing Mathaichen's phrase.

After the council, the family prayed together. Thankam looked anxiously at Mrs Koshy out of a corner of her eye, afraid that her sister would cry. But Mrs Koshy said her prayers with a strength of voice that astonished Thankam. In her place, Thankam thought, could she have brought herself to form her lips to such plaintiveness as 'Let us seek peace with a strong heart . . . ?' In her place Thankam would have speedily surrendered to the joys of hysteria.

Stray newspapers flapped around them. Mrs Koshy was briefly distracted. I must remember to clean all that up tomorrow, she thought. 'The Lord is my shepherd,' she began, 'I shall not want . . . .' The others took up the words after her.

# Chapter Eleven

MY DEAR PRAGASAM, thunder and lightning have happened to us. I will put some of the story down and you try to make sense of it if you can. A robber gang broke into our house. They started pulling the house apart. I was disappointed in Pappa. He just stood about, he has such a knack for doing this, saying that it was the end of the world. The Last Judgement, he said. The Last Fudgement, I almost said. I sneaked away with a friend of the family to fetch the leader of another gang. Not the police as you might have thought, but the leader of another gang. Only gangsters can fight gangsters. This other gang broke the first gang. I saw our landlord being half-murdered. But we are safe for now because the biggest gang in town is on our side. That's our comfort. Our very strange comfort. Now you know how we really live. There are no horses, no elephants, no tigers, only endlessly strange human beings.

But the good side of a bad story is that my uncle has found a new house for us. The house sits on top of a hill. It will take a very large flood to flood this house. Our new landlord is another endlessly strange human being. He likes cats and dogs better than he likes most human beings. Pappa says that is very good taste. A disfiguring motor car accident gave him the excuse to break with human beings. He built himself a hideaway in Kodaikanal, a hill station not far from Madras. The hideaway is a thing of tunnels and many curious basements. It might have been built for a light-hating mole. Half bricked up in his Kodaikanal house, the landlord will see nobody, except for his cats and his dogs and an ancient caretaker. He has lost interest in his house in Tiruvananthapuram. My uncle says that it is to his cats and dogs that he will leave his house. But my uncle, working through his estate friendships, has got us the house on rent. Our new house is full of cat and dog pictures.

Well, how much stranger can the world get! Nothing makes much sense to me anymore. Maybe Pappa is right after all. It's a nonsense world that we live in. Mamma wants everything to make sense. Pappa wants nothing to make sense. I feel so trapped between sense and nonsense. Between the lioness and the unicorn. Here I am slipping into writing nonsense even when I make up my mind to write sense. But in Pappa's phrase, when one writes one must write with the horn of the unicorn. He says that is the only way to write . . . .

Mrs Koshy declared that clearing up after the *chattambis* was like clearing up after a herd of elephants. Everything was so squashed, so flattened. And a stench of body vapour hung over everything. No broom can deal with such a steaminess. She had to wait for brisk winds.

The goose feather from the ripped mattress was everywhere. Mr Koshy had complained that he had found a feather in his morning tea.

'I want tea, not bird soup,' he had said.

'I will ask Chechamma to use a strainer,' Mrs Koshy had replied. 'If we can find the strainer.'

Later, at dinner, a feather had got as far as Mrs Koshy's throat before she had felt its tickle. She had decided to wash it down with soup rather than make a fuss at the table.

Mr Koshy was playing nurse to his books. He bandaged broken spines and pasted together torn pages. There is no vandalism worse than book vandalism, he muttered. Each time he discovered a new tear he exclaimed in horror. He saw in every tear a raw wound. Book-blood lay around him in little swamps. It was silliness to say that books don't bleed. 'They bleed through their pores,' Mr Koshy said in a whisper to Devi as if revealing a detail of intimate anatomy. Or did she hear 'prose'? 'Prose' too would have made equal Zen-sense. He cradled Christmas Humphreys and *Anna Karenina* in his arms. *Zen and the Art of Motorcycle Maintenance* lay in at least two pieces. 'Zen and the Art of Book Repair' might have been more to the point, thought Devi.

Mr Koshy squatted in the midst of gum bottles, brown paper, plaster, two pairs of scissors. A little atelier had grown up around him. He had a cobbler's needle in one hand and he unskilfully stitched together stray sheets of paper. Devi noticed that her father had cobbled together six pages of *Anna Karenina* with the *Ramayana*; but then he was a rather jerky jackdaw reader.

Across the room from Mr Koshy's atelier, Mrs Koshy, Devi and Lalu went through all their possessions, trunk by trunk, box by box, suitcase by suitcase. Anything that could be saved was put away into a large, wooden crate. Rubbish went into a jute sack. The crate filled faster than the jute sack.

Two very ragged copies of *Tit Bits* went into the jute bag. Mr Koshy used to buy *Tit Bits* for the weekly short story. He said that it gave him ideas for the book of short stories that he planned to write some day. But the pages outside the short story page made Mrs Koshy blush. Jayne Mansfield's clothes were a very short story indeed.

'Ammachy,' said Chechamma. 'Waste paper is two rupees a pound.'

But Mrs Koshy refused to rescue Jayne Mansfield. That woman had coarsened a whole generation in Malaysia. She deserved the jute bag.

The family worked through the crates all morning. They were sitting in judgement on the rag-bag accumulations of their life in Malaysia. Baby clothes, broken kitchen appliances, a Twyfords sink set, there was no saying what would come out of the packing. So little went into the jute bag. They seemed to want to save the smallest Malaysian bauble. Devi said countries don't let go of you all that easily. They have more 'cling' than a field of burrs. Even a cracked Chinese tea cup has 'cling', homesick memory.

Lalu discovered two Mary Mouse Enid Blytons and a Malay reader. These were the first books that he had ever had. They had slipped out of his life a long while and had now surfaced in tattery good condition. Tattery, but still chattery in the way of some well loved books. Lalu had written his name in a half-baby scrawl in at least ten places in the books. The books belonged to a beautiful innocence.

'And now I must have quiet,' said Mr Koshy, from his atelier.

'Why, Pappa?' asked Devi.

'*Anna Karenina* has just been run over by a train. I have bandaged her. She needs all the rest she can get.'

'Yes, Pappa,' said Devi. It was another of Pappa's Zen Commandments.


Avrachen sent a team of workers from his estate to move the Koshys, scattered wits, scattered belongings and all, into the house on the hill.

'The house on the hill' pleased Mr Koshy. It was open to the sky. There was not so much as a tree or roof to come in the way of a clear view of the sky. He said that now at least he had the sky to himself, he did not have to share it with grudging neighbours. A house that owned so many acres of good sky, must be a good house.

On Mr Koshy's first visit to the house, it was the ripe evening sky that claimed his attention. Pink-diamond stars. A water-melon moon. A rose sky. Mr Koshy declared that he hadn't seen anything so good.

Devi thought their new house an emancipation. She had a view of the sea from her bedroom, though the view was more telescopic than panoramic. 'It's only a very thin ribbon, but it is still the sea,' she told Dr Vareed.

'Can you smell it?' asked Dr Vareed. 'That's the usual test for the sea.'

'Not through so much cat and dog,' said Devi.

'But that's what the sea smells like sometimes.'

The house announced its cat-and-dog history in every room. There were photographs of cats and dogs everywhere. Every photograph had a caption in English. Avrachen said that the landlord had gone to a university in England and had come back something of an Englishman. 'The people of England,' explained Avrachen, 'like animal life more than anything else. They say that if an Englishman has to choose between saving his drowning wife and a drowning pet, he will choose the pet.'

'Especially if the pet is another woman,' said Mrs Koshy, gently mocking Avrachen's race psychologies. He hadn't, after all, travelled further than Madras.

Avrachen told the story of how the landlord had insisted that the two dogs that were with him when his car crashed, should precede him into the ambulance. And his face had been horribly cut too. 'He is a gentleman,' said Avrachen. 'An English saheb.'

Some of the captions to the photographs were quaint. It was family album crossed with *Punch*. 'Flouncie at play'. 'Minnie smiles'. 'Hun'. 'Tip-top'. 'Zip-up'. 'Funny Bunny'. 'The Queen Mother'. And, under a photograph of a poodle being trimmed, 'God shaving the Queen'.

The animals looked happy, though happy wasn't a word one used of animals. They seemed to know that they were wanted. They had an air of sturdy animal confidence. Mrs Koshy looked at Tip-top, a handsome brute of an alsatian. A real *chattambi*. Its mouth was top-dog haughty. There was a hint of fang. It had an expression that was almost intelligent. Dogs that have lived closely with human beings tend to acquire seeing, knowing eyes. This animal had that sort of eyes.

That evening after their sorting out work was over, Mrs Koshy and Devi lit a bonfire. All the rubbish in the 'throw away' jute sack went into the bonfire. There was a lot of cardboard, some rags of cloth and paper, and every feather that they could sweep up. Dr Vareed stirred the fire with a stick. The flames rose higher and higher.

'My mother used to have bonfires almost every evening,' said Mrs Koshy. 'A good way to keep mosquitoes away.' Mrs Koshy threw a little *kunthrikam* (bazaar incense) into the fire. The fire crackled and spat. A sickly-sweet incense smoke rose in thin spirals. 'Mosquitoes are terrified of incense smoke they say.'

'I don't think the mosquitoes of Tiruvananthapuram are terrified of anything,' said Dr Vareed.

'But everybody is frightened of something. Or should be,' said Mrs Koshy with a laugh.

'And what are you frightened of?' asked Dr Vareed.

'The jungle, I think,' said Mrs Koshy. 'In Malaysia the jungle was where the bandits hid. But I think the jungle is everywhere. As the Malays say, man is so recently come down from the trees. Some of us are such terrible orang-utans, people of the jungle.'

Mrs Koshy looked over the wall of the garden into the green valley below. Little oil-lamp and electric lights were coming out everywhere. Tiruvananthapuram lay spread out at their feet like an orderly toy town. From their hill-top the town seemed almost well-behaved. It was a town of trees, coconut, cashew and tamarind. The orang-utans had the decency to disappear into the trees.

Mrs Koshy thought of the gallery of cat-and-dog photo-graphs in the house and of Avrachen's story of the dog-loving landlord who had wanted his dogs to be carried into the ambulance before him. It was a touch of compassion, eccentric, 'English' compassion Avrachen had thought it was. But it beat the jungle. Perhaps there were people beating the jungle everywhere.

She took a deep breath. 'Top of the hill' it seemed a saner air.

Mathaichen said that the house-on-the-hill was a stroke of luck. He told Mrs Koshy he wished he had a house-on-a-hill too. But he was stuck in Kuttanad mud. 'Perhaps a water buffalo's place is the mud. He mustn't want to climb to the top of a hill.' But, he added, running his fingers nervously through his hair, he feared that he would soon drown in Kuttanad mud.

He said in a whisper that he had come to Tiruvananthapuram on a sad and secret mission. He had run out of money again. 'I can't go to Thankam,' he declared. 'I owe her more money than I can repay in a hundred years.'

Mathaichen's labourers were refusing to bring in the harvests unless they were paid their bonuses. The Communist party, though a party of unbelievers, believed in bonuses for Onam and Christmas. 'I have to play both Mahabali and Santa Claus to my workers,' moaned Mathaichen. Mahabali, the legendary king of Kerala, was banished to the nether world by Vishnu but Malayalis believe that he comes to visit his people once a year at Onam. It is a time of good cheer, well, for some.

Mathaichen drew in his breath sharply. 'I am thinking of going to Kunnukuzhi Mohan for a loan.'

'You must be desperate,' said Mrs Koshy.

'If I do not find the money the harvests will be spoilt and that will be the end of the end for me,' said Mathaichen.

'There is a red flag on every tree and the party says that they will not rest until there is a landlord corpse to keep the flag company. Their language is that of unspeakable threat.'

Mathaichen beat a sad tom-tom on the kitchen table.

'You must save your harvest,' said Mrs Koshy.

'My life depends on it,' said Mathaichen. 'Money has no caste. Besides, it is not charity that I am asking. I will repay every paisa when the harvest comes in. I have the honour of the family to think about.'

His resolutions were always sincere enough, thought Mrs Koshy, but the debtor who incurs debt to repay debt never repays a new debt in any hurry.

Clutching his long-handled umbrella, Mathaichen shambled out of the house. Mrs Koshy felt sorry for her brother. All that was left to him now was the honour of an ancient name. That was the last of his gods. Every other god had turned its back on him.


Kunnukuzhi Mohan received Mathaichen in his air-conditioned 'reception' room. He lolled against heavy cushions on the floor.

'I am honoured,' said Mohan.

'Kunjunj *chetan* wanted me to thank you for helping our sister.' Mathaichen chose his words carefully. He would not be fulsome. The family had its pride.

'I too had a score to settle with Madhavan Thampy,' said Mohan.

'Thampy is a very hateable man.'

'I hate him less when I remember that he is a piece of upper-caste turd. No one should waste time over shit. You may become what you hate.'

Mathaichen nodded although he thought the proposition altogether too radically put.

'But no more about that shitbag man,' asked Mohan. 'Now, sar, I must ask whether you will stay for a meal with me.'

A most unnatural mixing of conversational strands, thought Mathaichen. Mohan had little conversational finesse. And there was some comedy in an ex-shitpot man denouncing a shitbag man.

'No,' said Mathaichen, uncomfortably. 'I have to return to Kuttanad tonight.' He wasn't ready for the equality of a shared meal. That wouldn't come in this life time.

'Oh,' said Mohan. He was disappointed. Mathaichen's 'gratitude' hadn't done very much to chip away at the invisible wall of caste.

Mohan cuddled a giant cushion as he would cuddle a woman.

'It is best to travel by night,' said Mathaichen. 'It is cooler. I can't remember a summer so hot.' These were his excuses for not staying behind for a meal.

'Thank the Lord for the air-conditioning,' said Mohan. He spoke with a small suggestion of boasting.

'You have much to be thankful to the Lord for!' said Mathaichen. 'But cling to what you have. I too had my elephants.'

'Now no one can afford elephants. Not even the Travancore Maharaja. Now we have only money, then you had wealth.'

'I have seen what tricks fortune plays,' said Mathaichen. 'It rewards you for no cause. It punishes you for no cause. Once I rode on elephants. Now the Communists ride me.'

'Perhaps the Communists are elephants too,' said Mohan, playing with a bolster. 'Those who do not ride them or ride with them, may be trampled under them.'

'The Communists are not elephants,' said Mathaichen. 'Only a hammer-and-sickle. You can't ride a hammer-and-sickle. You either hammer them down or be ready to be hammered down. That is the sort of hell that Kuttanad is now. Perhaps Kuttanad should declare itself a hammer-and-sickle republic!' He growled.

'You are very angry,' said Mohan.

'Angry enough to twist the neck of any Communist republic!' said Mathaichen. 'The Communists will not reason. They will not argue. They will only state their propaganda against us over and over again. That's how they win. The red of their flag will be redder yet.'

'Redder?'

'With landlord blood.'

'Beer?' asked Mohan, trying to change the subject.

'Yes,' said Mathaichen. A beer was not a meal.

'We live in changing times,' said Mohan. 'Yet, for some the changes do not come fast enough. After all some of us have had to wait for twenty centuries. You made us wait for twenty centuries. Perhaps we are still waiting. Untouchables yesterday. Harijans today.'

Mathaichen thought it was tactless of Mohan to want to personalize an argument in this way. But Mohan was never unintentionally rude. He was trying to make a point in his own way.

'You know that this isn't about you and me,' said Mohan. 'But do you know what Madhavan Thampy calls me still? The hiding that he received at my hands has taught him nothing.'

'It is disgusting the way he talks.'

'But he is not alone. There are other Thampys. Their mouths must be washed out with soap.'

'Laws,' said Mathaichen. 'We need proper laws.'

'There are laws. Proper laws even. What we don't have is power. Another beer?'

Mathaichen feared he was being patronized. His stomach rumbled for the beer in a horrible low-caste way, as if determined to undermine his dignity.

'I don't understand political parties,' said Mathaichen. 'They are always screaming at one another.'

'I have been tempted . . .' Mohan paused, ' . . . by politics.'

'Well, why shouldn't you? You have money to throw away . . . .'

172

'I'm an investing sort of man. Money that doesn't grow, dies.'

'Is there such a thing as investing wisely in politics?'

'If you choose the future, yes!'

'But how can you know what the future is?'

'In Kuttanad, would you say that the landlords are the future?'

'Uncremated corpses cannot be the future,' said Mathaichen warmly. Mathaichen was as bitter about Kuttanad's landlords for their lack of spirit, as he was angry with Kuttanad's Communists for their excess of spirit, excess of revolutionary spirit.

'You will not blame me then if I refuse to throw in my lot with uncremated corpses. I had a difficult choice. I had after all to choose from what there was.'

'No!' said Mathaichen, springing from the cushions. 'It cannot be.'

'It was a difficult choice you must understand.'

'But this is a betrayal.'

'Of what?'

'Of friendship.'

'It would have been friendship, if you had allowed me to marry your niece.'

'I don't believe you have joined the Communists,' said Mathaichen in a ragged voice. 'Do you hate us so much?'

'The Communists have promised me a seat in Kuttanad.'

'Impossible!' said Mathaichen.

'We are on different sides of the fence. But we can still be friends.'

'The Communists are a blight on our land . . . the worst kind of paddy blight, I say. But even the worst blights must pass. Remember my words . . . you Communists are only a passing nuisance.'

'Like almost everything in this world.'

'I give you ten weeks in politics,' shouted Mathaichen. He put away his beer undrunk. He wasn't ready to toast Mohan's political career.

'But think, isn't the Communist you know better than the Communist you do not? I will not hurt you willingly. I do not drop my friends, whatever their politics. I can be of use to you in Kuttanad. I can calm the anger of the party against land-lords. If there is a strike by your workers, I can advise patience. Other politicians may want to stir up the workers all the more.'

'You forget that you will be the slave of the party,' said Mathaichen, scornfully.

'But even in the tightest parties, there is space for men to use their elbows in.'

'Not in the party you have joined.'

'You'll be surprised,' said Mohan.

'Every party makes its career out of dupes.'

'Like most people who do not understand politics, you are prejudiced against it,' said Mohan.

'Politics of your kind has made horrible rebels of my loyal workers.'

'Some may say, made men of slaves.'

'I'm disappointed in you. Horribly disappointed.'

'I'm sorry.'

'One day you will be disappointed in yourself.'

'Let us part as friends.'

'Never,' said Mathaichen, with a beery toss of his head.

'But if at any time you think I can be of service to you . . . .'

'Can a blight remove a blight?'

Mathaichen moved to the door. Mohan hurried ahead to open the door for him.

'No,' said Mathaichen. 'You stay in your air-conditioned room. It is warm outside.'

'You're hard on me,' said Mohan. He made a low namaskar, bending from the waist. Mathaichen swept out without returning the namaskar. He meant the breach to be complete.

'My driver will take you back,' said Mohan.

'I'll walk,' said Mathaichen.

'I'll not allow it,' said Mohan.

'I insist.'

'I touch your feet and beg you to travel in my car,' said Mohan. He moved to touch Mathaichen's feet. It was a Malayali gesture of submission, though not quite what a Communist should be doing.

'You are a strange animal,' said Mathaichen, with a sour smile. 'Your tail wags in friendship but your teeth are still sharp.'

'I dare not lose a friend. I make friends so slowly and as I grow older, less and less easily.'

Mathaichen allowed himself to be jostled into Mohan's car. Reclining in the back of the car, he made a fine figure. He hardly acknowledged Mohan's broken-backed namaskar.

'Stiff-neck,' said Mohan to himself when the car was out of the drive. If he hadn't been superstitious about losing friends, Mathaichen would have fared less well at his hands. Politics is not about losing friends. Even an uncremated corpse, so long as it has a vote, has its uses. Mohan returned to his air-conditioning. Was it terribly wrong for a Communist to want to keep cool?

As he kicked the giant cushions into place, Mohan wondered what it was that had brought Mathaichen to see him. He had mentioned no particular business. Was it money or women? These were the usual things that people came to see him about. Mohan stretched himself like a langurous cat on the giant cushions. It was six o'clock. Too late for a beer? Too early for a woman? He liked to think that he led an orderly life. He had until midnight to kill. He clapped his hands.

The head servant answered his summons.

'Yes, Master?'

'Bring her in.'

'Yes, Master.'

Lalitha was a film extra. She was out of work, and while she waited for something to turn up, she stayed with friends. She had lovely eyes and legs.

'Found any work today?' he asked.

'No.'

'You are not afraid of hard work, are you?'

She sniggered.

They made love to the panting rhythm of the air-conditioner. For no particular reason, that curiously ambiguous phrase 'workers of the world unite' kept ticking in Mohan's mind. Landlords had little to fear from his kind of Marxism. If only Mathaichen knew!

'Open your eyes, Lalitha,' he whispered. 'Keep them open.' He would say the same to Mathaichen. 'Keep them open,' he commanded, as they climbed the cushions together.

# Chapter Twelve

'YOU KNEW!' SAID Thankam. It was Thankam's style to use 'accusation marks'. Thankam pulled her top lip against her teeth irritably.

'Mathaichen said that he couldn't live off you for ever.' Mrs Koshy tried to speak calmly. Thankam was working herself into a state. Her cobra hood was opening out. There was hot venom in her eyes. This was the strange way that Thankam's affection for the family sometimes expressed itself.

Holding her face well away from Mrs Koshy, Thankam said, 'You allowed him to go with cupped palms to an outcaste. Where is our pride!' There were more accusation marks.

Mrs Koshy didn't want to quarrel. Thankam insisted on winning all her quarrels even or particularly those which she had no business or right to win. This made her a very awkward sort of sister to have. She knew nothing of the art of amiable squabbling. All her quarrels, all her affections, were very do or die.

Mrs Koshy said that Mathaichen had argued that money has no caste. She found herself speaking chiefly to the back of Thankam's head.

'Money,' said Thankam, her face goosefleshing irritably in the strange way it had, 'like everything else in life, has caste. There is low-born money. There is well-born money. No money is better than the man who has it. I'm only repeating Mathaichen's own arguments, arguments that we all know by heart. If Mathaichen has chosen to forget these arguments it is only because of the state he is in. A desperate man will think anything, do anything. And you know how Mathaichen is when he has his frets. I always see it as my duty to talk him out of his frets. No doubt you don't.'

Big sister him out of his frets, thought Mrs Koshy.

'To stay together,' said Thankam, 'with so close a family such as ours, you must know how to think together with the rest of us. Thinking together is an instinct. Sometimes I wonder if your Malaysian years have not deadened some part of your family instinct.'

To Thankam, Mathaichen was the eternal baby of the family. Their mother had died young. Thankam had brought up Mathaichen. Mathaichen to her was half-son, half-brother. Anyone who suggested that Mathaichen might have grown up over the years and needed less big sistering than he was used to, always angered Thankam to the point of black unreason.

I won't quarrel, Mrs Koshy told herself. Even as a girl Thankam had wanted to manage other people's lives for them. Avrachen had once said rather unkindly that she was better at running other people's lives than her own, better at running the universe than her backyard. When Avrachen's sallies were reported back to her, Thankam put it down as another example of Avrachen's painful lack of wife-loyalty. Avrachen and, more recently, Sosamma were constantly sinning against the tribe.

'There is,' said Thankam, with a tightening of voice, 'another business that brought me here. Are you not worried that Dr Vareed has eyes only for Devi? A man of the world, a young girl . . . you don't leave them together any more than you would a tiger and a sheep . . . .'

Now, Mrs Koshy thought she heard intimidation marks.

'Mathaichen and I,' continued Thankam, 'agree that the doctor must be told that he need not call any more. And you must do the telling.'

'You know how bad I am at making enemies,' said Mrs Koshy with a hot little laugh.

'Must we then wait for the worst to happen before we drop this friend?'

'I am saying we must be sensible.'

'All your life you have wanted to be sensible. But this isn't a sensible situation. This might not even be a sensible sort of country.'

'Then that's one more reason to be sensible.'

Thankam thought that this was the sort of thing that Mr Koshy might have said. Most marriages, if one did not take care, slipped into becoming 'like husband, like wife' duets.

'And when did the doctor last call?' asked Thankam, ignoring her sister's silly cleverness.

'He did come yesterday evening.'

'And again this morning?'

Mrs Koshy nodded.

'Exactly,' said Thankam. 'I have nothing more to say. The doctor says it all against himself.'

Mrs Koshy feared that Thankam would have a lot to tale-carry to Mathaichen.


Thankam had a way of kneading facts together in the oddest ways. She had a hundred eyes for scandal. Thankam especially suspected laughter. Thankam had been solemn even as a baby, Mrs Koshy remembered. Never a dimple.

Thankam had seen Dr Vareed and Devi once or twice in laughing conversation. She knew just what to think. Laughter was an undressing of the personality, and it was too easy for a man and a woman to slip from that kind of undressing to another kind of undressing.

Thankam always argued from her 'wronged wife' bitterness. Mrs Koshy was worried that Thankam's bitterness was getting into everything she said and did. She looked as if, as they say, even the spittle in her mouth were all vinegar.

But, thought Mrs Koshy, to be fair to Thankam, though so

few were ready to be fair to her, Thankam was also arguing from Kerala custom which decreed more or less that marriages must not just happen. They had to be 'arranged'. And so it was that strangers came to marry strangers. Only after marriage were bodies and minds explored. And some liked what they discovered less than others. Love where you must not marry, marry where you do not yet love. It was a hard formula. Arranged marriages hid many heartbreaks. Thankam, however, would see nothing of all that. Stoically she believed that marriages had to be made as they had always been made, by the *chetan* and other elders-over *paramparyyam* charts and envelopes of dowry money. Anything else or less was wrong. Marriage was a duty by the tribe and therefore best left to the tribe.

Mrs Koshy had hoped to keep the subject of Dr Vareed and Devi within a tactful conversational fence, but Thankam had kicked down the fence. And behind Thankam stood Mathaichen who was always ready to do battle for *paramparyyam*. Somewhat more than most, Mathaichen was a *paramparyyam* snob. *Paramparyyam* is family lineage, and introductions to *paramparyyam* come early in the life of Syrian Christians. You shall know your *paramparyyam*: they called it the First Commandment. Children were quickly screwed into the snobbery of *paramparyyam*. The family blood line, the family kennel charts were compulsory education.

That Mathaichen knew Dr Vareed's father, Pazhaymootil Thomachen, muddled matters still more. Pazhaymootil means 'ancient root' and Mathaichen sneered that the Pazhaymootil family was as ancient as this year's *kappa* (tapioca) harvest. Mathaichen said that the name came close to mocking joke.

As Mathaichen told the story, Pazhaymootil Thomachen had started life as a *kappiyar*, a church verger. Proverbially, only a church verger is poorer than a church mouse. But Thomachen had been a defiant sort of verger. He had said that poverty need be only the least of a verger's Christian virtues. Thomachen had taken to moneylending. He had used church collections to start himself off in business. He had used the church vestry for his business. But what he took from the collection plate he always replaced before accounts closed at the end of the month. He also paid interest on what he took from the Lord. Irregularity it was, but not quite dishonesty.

Moneylending takes a strong arm and Pazhaymootil Thomachen had what it took. Thomachen's big break came when a bishop had trouble finding money for building his *aramana* (palace). A moneylending verger had seemed an easy touch. The bishop had carelessly signed a sheaf of promissory notes. When the verger had asked for repayment of the debts, the bishop had said this was no way for a verger to talk to a prince of the church. Thomachen had apologized, but had said that if the bishop wouldn't pay up he would take him to court. He had been blunt. He had the arrogance of his new wealth. The bishop had threatened him with excommunication and, in due course, damnation. But Thomachen had retorted that he thought bankruptcy was but another way of going to the devil. In the end the bishop had repaid the money but not before he had thrown the verger out of his job and blackened him in an angry Sunday sermon. That Christ too had driven out the money changers, had made for a neat sermon.

Thomachen had gone on to become a full time money-lender. His business had grown into an office with a name board, 'Pazhaymootil Pawnbrokers'. A little airily, Thomachen had said 'Pazhaymootil Pawnbrokers' could buy anything. Even a *paramparyyam* could be bought. Worse, he seemed to say that even salvation could be bought. The disgraced verger had a fallen angel's pride.

But, Mathaichen said with relish, Pazhaymootil Thomachen had lived long enough to see that 'Pazhaymootil Pawnbro-kers' could not buy everything. Thomachen had grown richer and richer but his money offered no escape from the ranks of 'lesser breed' Syrian Christians. To old stock Syrian Christians a mongrel with gold in its teeth and brass in its arse was still a mongrel. When Thomachen, the newly rich mongrel, had offered to build an *aramana* for an impoverished bishop, the bishop had denounced his dirty money and flung it back at him. The bishop had said that you can't 'Judas kiss and make up with God'. Thus did the Church revenge itself on a scapegrace verger. Thomachen had wept in frustration.

We must be sensible, Mrs Koshy had told Thankam. Perhaps, thought Mrs Koshy, it was impossible to be sensible about blood and caste and race, impossible to be sensible about nonsense. These are the sad coffins we have made for ourselves. In a coffin all must rot.

Mrs Koshy wasn't altogether taken by surprise when Dr Vareed came to her with his proposal of marriage. She had seen it coming. Mrs Koshy said she had to consult her brothers.

'My brothers will worry about your age.' Mrs Koshy plunged bravely into the first objection.

'But will you argue for me?' asked Dr Vareed. Classically he had to win the bride's mother, before he could win the bride.

'There are ten years between my husband and me,' said Mrs Koshy, somewhat evasively. Her voice contained a small sigh. 'I was bewildered at first. He seemed to know everything. Not that he did of course. It was just that he had seen more of the world. But the gap between what he knew and what I knew began to close. Marriage is about closing gaps. But there are some gaps that cannot be closed. It would be foolish even to want to try.'

'Will you argue for me?' repeated Dr Vareed. He had to know.

'We must try to settle this without arguments,' said Mrs Koshy. 'Hurry and argument are wrong in these matters.'

'I will be patient, but do not ask me to be patient for too

long,' said Dr Vareed. It was a deliberately awkward sincerity. Mrs Koshy had to know that he was not going to allow the last word to Mrs Koshy's brothers. He liked to think that he was a modern sort of chap and he would go into this in a modern sort of way.

'Does your mother approve?' asked Mrs Koshy. She had heard Mrs Vareed being called a she-dragon.

'She must.'

'Must?'

'I leave her no choice,' said Dr Vareed. 'Perhaps that is the only way to win. I'm only joking of course.'

Mrs Koshy wished she could be sure that he was only joking. She found his approach rather too competitive.


Mathaichen was indignant. 'Already he shows his lack of breeding,' he declared. 'He came into this house as a doctor. Not as a hot-lipped lover! The doctor has behaved like a cad. He comes into the house with a stethoscope round his neck and steals out of it with the daughter of the house round his neck. Is lovemaking a branch of medicine I ask you! And has he sent you any bills for his doctoring?'

'No,' said Mrs Koshy.

'No,' growled Mathaichen. 'You see how much he tries to put you in his debt? The very tricks of his father. I once borrowed money from Thomachen, a moneylending animal if ever there was one. He had two hands when he lent you money, but when it came to getting back what he lent you, he had more hands than a spider! I hope you are not saying that a moneylender husband for Devi can be no bad thing . . . seeing how little money we have.'

'You are being unfair to me,' said Mrs Koshy. 'Uncharacteristically.'

'This is too serious a matter for foolish courtesy,' said Mathaichen. 'Remember what our father used to say, that you can sell family honour but not buy it.'

Mathaichen produced a roll of paper from his travelling-bag. He spread the paper on a table, smoothing out the edges reverentially. 'All our ancestors for eight generations starting with our Namboodiri Brahmin ancestor,' he said. 'Written out in the hand of our dear father. I am going to ask you to hang it up in the drawing-room. Let Father speak to you if I can't.'

'I'll have to make space for it on the drawing-room wall,' said Mrs Koshy lamely.

'Malaysia is a mongrel country, three races now but soon to be sure there will be only one mongrel race,' said Mathaichen. 'But now you are back where pedigrees matter. Put Father's family tree up beside those photographs of cats and dogs if you have nowhere else to put it. Let animal pedigree remind you of human pedigree. In the end you will have to choose between the Pazhaymootils and us. You can't have both.'

Oh Lord, thought Mrs Koshy, they were on the brink of a quarrel. 'Don't make it so difficult for me,' she cried.

The *vaidyan* came into the room. He held back the swing doors opening on Mr Koshy's room. Mr Koshy shuffled in. 'I was trying to sleep,' said Mr Koshy, twitching irritably. 'But my ears must sleep before the rest of my body does.'

'They must?' asked Mathaichen, more scornfully than solicitously.

'Maybe old stock hasn't done very much for my body,' said Mr Koshy.

'I am more than ready to believe that,' said Mathaichen. Mr Koshy always brought out the very rude man in Mathaichen.

'Old stock I may be,' said Mr Koshy, a slyness coming into his voice, 'but I'm trouble than anything else for my family. My sister died in a strait-jacket. I can hear her screams still, especially on new moon nights when the dogs bark. And look at Avrachen, running after gypsy skirts in the hills. How many more arguments against old stock do you want?'

'I have never said that old stock cannot go to seed,' snapped Mathaichen. 'It is corruptible like everything under heaven. But old stock is good stock in ways that non-old stock can never be. And let me say this, since the simplest things sometimes need saying to certain kinds of minds, old stock wasn't my only argument. Dr Vareed is thirty years old and not married. Has he been playing draughts these many years? Then he must have played many thousands of games with himself.' There was a lewd suggestion.

'Either people are in a rush to marry or they are not,' said Mr Koshy. 'I remember your marriage was very rushed, but just in time people said.'

The story of Mathaichen's marriage was thought too scandalous even for furtive joke within the family. Mathaichen had 'known' his wife, the daughter of an old stock landlord, before marriage. There had been a great fuss when the sinners were discovered. In these situations the wages of sin are a quick marriage. Their first child had been born in their eighth month of marriage. But tongues had wagged maliciously and there had been many jokes about dates.

Mrs Koshy thought it was scandalously poor judgement to bring up this blush-making history, but then her husband thought in irritabilities.

Mathaichen opened his mouth as if to shout. Then he seemed to think better of it. He said in an unnaturally low voice, 'I see that my advice is no longer wanted. Nor am I. I shall never come here any more.'

Mrs Koshy clutched Mathaichen by the shoulders. 'You know how Pappa talks. He is not himself.'

'Isn't he?' asked Mathaichen bitingly. 'Then he must teach himself to be himself.'

'Pappa,' said Mrs Koshy. 'Ask to be forgiven. You know you have spoken most wrongly.'

'I will not,' said Mr Koshy, sulkily.

'Calm yourself,' said Mathaichen. 'I'll take him at your word. I shall try to believe that he wasn't himself.'

185

Mathaichen walked out of the house with almost military energy.

'Say that you will come back,' Mrs Koshy called after him.

Mathaichen didn't look back.

Mrs Koshy turned on her husband.

'We've lost him for ever,' she moaned.

'I fear we haven't,' said Mr Koshy.

'Oh Lord! I'm married to a hard heart.'

'No, only to a mad man. If it is mad for a man to want to be free . . . to be free of his relatives at any rate.'

Mr Koshy returned to his room, quite forgetting to hobble.

It was a very grey evening. Night when it came seemed all mosquito ping. As Mrs Koshy snatched at sleep she felt she was more alone now than she could remember. She fell asleep to a low bugle of mosquitoes in her ear. She had been too tired to unfurl the mosquito nets.


Devi had never seen her mother so red-eyed and sad.

Mrs Koshy had complained that she could not sleep. She spent long hours before the Gethsemane Christ, but not in prayer for her lips hardly moved. Mrs Koshy always made conversations of her prayers. She had made a friend of the Gethsemane Christ. But now she sat before Him frozen. He didn't seem to have very much to say to her either.

Mrs Koshy feared a huge family row. Thankam would sulk furiously and Mathaichen would be as nasty as he dared about the Pazhaymootils. In the end their nerves would be left raw, but the argument would be still unwon by either side. One family row would soon lead soon to others. The sensible thing was not to allow the cannon ball to start rolling.

Mrs Koshy hoped that Kunjunj, the *chetan,* the head of the family, would be allowed the last word. She prayed that Kunjunj's would be a sensible last word. If not she would have to choose. Rebellion would see the loss of her Kuttanad family. She was not ready, would never be ready for such an amputation.

Kunjunj was on the whole a commonsense man. He belonged more to the commonsense wing of the family than to the blood and thunder nonsense wing. Though no one could out-nonsense Kunjunj on the subject of family honour, unlike Mathaichen he could stop the cock-a-doodle-do when he had to.

Mrs Koshy wrote a long letter to Kunjunj, pouring out her heart. This side of the Gethsemane Christ, Kunjunj was the last appeal.

She would not, wrote Mrs Koshy, live Devi's life for her. Maybe she and her family were different. Maybe their stay abroad had played tricks with them.

> I have brought up my children differently. I cannot ask them now to be different because Thankam wants them to be different. There are some things that are too late to help in life. Thankam has worked very hard on Avrachen, some may say too hard. But Avrachen remains Avrachen. Avrachen must have taught Thankam something. Or hasn't he?

Mrs Koshy quickly sealed the letter for fear that her pen might run away with her. Unlike her husband she distrusted an over-frisky pen.

Kunjunj disliked refereeing in family quarrels. You could please one side only by displeasing the other. Headship of the clan had its disagreeable moments.

Kunjunj thought that quarrels were always about the failure of common sense. Mathaichen's answer to most problems was loudness and frenzy. Mathaichen's vanities of blood and caste were the vanities of a man whose pride had been hurt. He saw surrender everywhere. Marrying a Pazhaymootil was surrender. Talking to the Communists of Kuttanad was surrender. In Kunjunj's experience in the end they surrender everything, who want to surrender nothing.

Kunjunj had made discreet enquiries about Dr Vareed. He had discovered nothing shameful. Perhaps Dr Vareed did indeed play draughts in his leisure. That might well be the answer to Mathaichen's jeering question. If Dr Vareed visited women of a certain kind, no one knew of it. Kunjunj himself knew what it was to have no one to turn to on a hot night.

Of course, the Pazhaymootils were *poothukash*, new money. New money usually takes three generations to become old money, but it was unfair to ask Devi to wait that very long. Clearly, thought Kunjunj, they had to find a way of forgiving the Pazhaymootils the newness of their money. Mathaichen in particular was too easily angered by new money.

Kunjunj tried to reason with Mathaichen. Kunjunj said that even the best Kuttanad fields have to be manured. Many 'old stock' families were doing a Pazhaymootil too.

But Mathaichen would, as Kunjunj feared he would, only splutter. Was Kunjunj not afraid of the anger of their ancestors? It was uncomfortable to be poor, but even in seeking wealth there were rules. By the end of their argument, there were flecks of foam on the lips of both brothers.

Thankam was less argumentative.

'This is Sosamma's doing,' Thankam cried. 'This is her revenge.'

'What do you mean?' asked Kunjunj, alarmed by Thankam's crude hostility towards her sister.

'You are too innocent, *chetan*,' said Thankam. 'Sosamma has never cared for the family. I need the family to breathe. But she has always felt suffocated by the family. And she knows that you have been more brother to me than you have been brother to her. Now she has found a way of coming between us.'

Poor girl Thankam, thought Kunjunj, she was seeing ghosts again. Can brother-love ever make up for lack of husband-love?

'We mustn't insist on misunderstanding one another,' said Kunjunj. 'Sosamma and her family have lived away from us for so long that their ways are no longer our ways. I was always against Sosamma's going away to Malaysia, but some things no one can help. Our *vidhi* (fate), makes our lives according to plans only time reveals in its fullness. Sometimes our *vidhi* is a *viddhi* (joker).'

'But what will Mathaichen say? He is less of a philosopher than any of us.' Thankam was disappointed at Kunjunj's over-cool head.

'His feelings do him credit,' said Kunjunj. 'But he has tried everything. He has begged. He has threatened. Perhaps now we must leave it all to God.'

Kunjunj knew from experience as a *chetan* that when all arguments failed, it was best to pass the buck to God.

'Mathaichen says all Kuttanad will jeer at us.'

'I will make that my worry.'

'Yes, *chetan*.'

'And remember there are no losers in a patched-up family quarrel.' Kunjunj made it sound almost like a command. She was not to mope.

No losers. That was the cliché. But Thankam couldn't help thinking that Sosamma had won more than the others. Thankam decided that she would practise a reserve, a quiet hauteur, with Sosamma. Sosamma's pride had to be rebuked. Most of all her terrible independence of judgement, so wrong in a woman.

# Chapter Thirteen

'KUNJUNJ *CHETAN* THINKS that I'm a foolish little man,' said Mathaichen to Thankam. 'A foolish little man.'

It was evening. They were in the frontyard of Thankam's house. There was a small wind up such as wells out of nowhere at sunset. But it wasn't the honest kind of wind on which birds can glide and kites can fly. It was a darting wind, and full of fancy. It was a leaf-snatching wind. Leaves swirled like little sequins around Mathaichen. A leaf fell with a dry crackle on Mathaichen. He did not brush it away.

'A foolish little man? Did he really call you that?' Thankam asked.

'He does not always say what he thinks,' said Mathaichen. 'But I know. We haven't been brothers for fifty years for nothing.'

'Then he did not say what you say he said,' said Thankam. It depressed her to see her brothers drifting away from each other.

Mathaichen's reply was a deep and morose silence. He sat in his chair as if waiting for the night to swallow him up.

'But you are not going to stay away from the wedding?' asked Thankam. So public a break between the brothers would set tongues wagging. Their private sadness would become a public shame.

'We must save appearances, mustn't we?' Mathaichen spoke bitterly.

'My heart isn't in it at all. Kunjunj *chetan* has commanded only my head.'

'The usual head-heart argument,' said Mathaichen wearily.

'Don't use it. It isn't honest.' Mathaichen spoke from a deep sadness.

Thankam blanched.

Mathaichen touched the little bags of fat under his eyes. 'It is amazing how these little buggers grow. Yesterday they weren't there. Today they are. Is that how one grows old? One day young. The next day old. These bags have made slits of my eyes.'

Thankam switched on a veranda light.

'Don't,' said Mathaichen. 'Let this foolish little man sit here alone into the night.' He was determined to be tragic. He was very hurt.

Thankam sent for a thin cotton sheet. She spread the sheet over Mathaichen's shoulders. She picked a leaf out of his hair.

'I don't feel cold at all. There are warm currents dancing all around me. And have you noticed how the earth remains warm, well beyond sunset?'

Mathaichen played with the sand under his feet, piling and grooving it into ridges with his heels and toes.

'I shall suffocate if I do not feel the earth under me. I don't care if the bags round my eyes take away my sight. But leave me a patch of earth to call my own, and I will be happy. I am an earth man. Mud really, pure mud.'

A servant brought a mug of coffee. Mathaichen began to drink noisily.

'I am pure mud from top to bottom. You can tell Sosamma that. Mud men don't have to be taken seriously. That should please Sosamma.'

'She is already very pleased with herself,' said Thankam.

Frogs started croaking in the wetlands beyond the garden. Their opera would last most of the night, growing and dying with the moon.

'What did you say?' asked Mathaichen. 'I couldn't hear you for the croaking frogs.'

'I said Sosamma is very pleased with herself.'

'You don't like Sosamma much, do you?'

'Only as much as duty demands.'

'Then it can't be very much at all.'

'I don't like her independence. Women have no business to be that way. But who's to tell her?'

'Maybe at some stage in our lives we must stop being responsible for each other's upbringing. It is least painful that way.'

'You have never really believed that, have you?' said Thankam.

The servants switched on all the lights in the veranda.

'You fools!' shouted Mathaichen. The servants were taken aback. Mathaichen was usually polite and patient with them. 'Leave me alone with the croaking frogs. This croaking frog croaks best without light.'

The lights in the veranda stayed on. The servants did not know what to make of Mathaichen's curiously worded instructions. Mathaichen Master was known for his playful humour.

'Switch off the lights,' said Thankam.

The lights went out, except for one weak bulb.

'No one listens to me,' said Mathaichen.

'They didn't understand you.'

'No one understands me then.'

'I have always understood you,' said Thankam.

'You have been good to me. But maybe not even you have understood me.'

'I have understood you better than any human being alive.'

'I've something to tell you about myself.'

Thankam smiled easily. Her brother was an open book to her.

Mathaichen tried to keep his voice even. 'I'm going to sell out and leave Kuttanad.'

Thankam thought that she would be sick straightaway. Mathaichen's words seemed to hit her first in the stomach.

'You know that's impossible. We must think of the family . . . .'

'There will be Kunjunj *chetan*. Kuttanad can't need more.'

'But the boat race is only three months away.'

'Let Kunjunj *chetan* play at the boat race. Everyone knows that I have lost my race.'

'Bhagwanay, do I hear what I hear?'

'I don't think it was the croaking of frogs.'

'But you have a family to bring up.'

'I'm going into cardamom and tea.'

'But it is so low, so disreputable . . . .'

'And so profitable. Ask Avrachen.'

The frogs seemed to croak hysterically in Thankam's ears.

'Wicked frogs, I've never heard them so loud,' she said. 'Bhagwanay, not cardamom and tea!'

'Maybe the frogs approve of cardamom and tea.'

'Indeed it would take a frog to!' said Thankam with some asperity.

Avrachen's tea pluckers were ready to pluck her man away from her again. Already, Thankam could see the pretty little things at work on Mathaichen. The picture in her head was lurid. Scandalously, Mathaichen found the pretty little things' pretty little things irresistible.

'Would you rather that I struggled on picturesquely with paddy, with our Communists?' asked Mathaichen. 'Are you waiting to see me go down fighting hopelessly?'

Thankam almost said yes. For her Kuttanad was a gracious sort of cinema in which her brothers were forever the heroes. And there can be no heroes without villains and debt. There was a modest heroine too. But now the tea-picking whores had come crashing in.

'Can I live off you endlessly? Even landlords must have more than sister-provided pocket money.'

'I knew there was going to be trouble from the moment I heard from Sosamma that you had gone to Kunnukuzhi Mohan for a loan.'

'When you are in the bottom of a pit, you will do anything.'

'Not that sort of anything.'

'Even that sort of anything. That is the danger of my kind of moneylessness. You hardly notice how it robs you of your dignity, bit by bit. And for what? That Kunjunj *chetan* might sneer at me for being a foolish little man?'

'He didn't say that. Those are lines you have made up for him.'

'He would have said that if he had been a less polite man. I saw that I have lost his respect. If I ever had it.'

'You can't allow Father's lands to go under the hammer!' It was a last despairing argument.

'The hammer . . . and perhaps the sickle! But don't worry, there will be some lands left with Kunjunj *chetan*. Those lands can be our mannequin in the window.'

Thankam felt that she would explode into croaking like a bull frog.

'Cardamom,' muttered Mathaichen almost to himself, 'is the king of spices.' That was the last of his arguments. He was already dreaming of prosperity, of Avrachen-like prosperity. He had done wrong to allow his sister to subsidize him. A more honest brush with bankruptcy would have set him thinking more energetically of choices.

'This is all because of Sosamma,' said Thankam. 'If only she hadn't been so stubborn about this ill-omened marriage!'

'Don't blame her! Don't blame anybody!' said Mathaichen. 'All this could have happened in a dozen different ways. Sometimes I feel we are only corks that bob on water. We hardly know where we are going. We go where the water takes us. It is the fate of corks to be tossed about.'

'I shall blame Sosamma. Sosamma is selfish. If Kunjunj *chetan* hadn't commanded me, I would have had no part in this marriage, not the smallest part.'

'You must think that I have become selfish too, if it is selfish to stop living other people's dreams for them.'

Thankam said nothing mostly because she was afraid that anything she said would be angry, excessively angry.

Thankam returned to the house, and as she went in she put

out the one light in the veranda that was still burning, leaving Mathaichen engulfed in the night.

He's doing a Pazhaymootil too, thought Thankam, the blood croaking wildly in her head. They had in every sense a Pazhaymootil marriage upon them.

Mathaichen sat in the night, listening to the leaves fall around him. It was curious what the frogs were saying. It sounded so very much like 'cardamom' repeated again and again, like a rosary. A conceit, but he liked it.

Thankam's face is as stiff as a Kathakali mask, thought Mrs Koshy.

Thankam had come to discuss the arrangements for the wedding. She was quick to make plain that she had come only because Kunjunj *chetan* had wanted her to come. Thankam always wore a small jasmine garland in her hair. She picked the jasmine fresh from the garden and her maid wove the garland as Thankam wanted her to. The more jasmine, the better her mood. Today Thankam had no jasmine in her hair. She looked so very severe, so very sad and severe. And her hair was undone in the way mourners undid their hair at a funeral.

Mrs Koshy was determined not to surrender to Thankam's gloom.

'Should we have *pani*?' Mrs Koshy asked. It was customary to serve *pani*, a sweet palm syrup, with the plantain and curds course towards the end of a feast.

'*Pani*,' exclaimed Thankam, 'costs the earth. And although this is a wedding, *pani* somehow doesn't seem right.'

'But I will have *pani*,' said Mrs Koshy.

Mrs Koshy pulled out a paper on which she had put down a housewifely list of things to do. She ticked *pani* with some energy. She was also ticking off her sister.

'And who will hold the wedding feast?' asked Mrs Koshy, her pencil going down the list.

'We cannot allow the Pazhaymootils to hold the feast. They will hire every car in Tiruvananthapuram that can be hired. There might be a band from Madras. And drink will flow, especially foreign drink, and where there is drink there is lewdness. We will not live down the shame of it in a dozen generations.'

'It might not be like that at all,' said Mrs Koshy.

'But it will,' said Thankam stubbornly. 'They can show off their wealth if they want to, but not riding our backs.'

Quarrellingly, they went through the list. Thankam would allow the Pazhaymootils no more than a hundred guests. The Lord is the only guest we need to have,' she said in a tone that suggested that she already knew that the Lord was going to absent Himself conspicuously from the wedding. Mrs Koshy groaned at Thankam's sister-tyranny.

Next, Thankam went round the house on a quick inspection. She wanted the cat-and-dog photographs taken down. 'This is almost like a cat-and-dog museum. People will think that we are not right in the head.'

'I'll send you some photographs of Father and Grandfather to put up,' said Thankam.

'Grandfather will make a very handsome alsatian,' said Mrs Koshy, with a laugh.

'Alsatian enough to want to tear any mongrel to bits, I think,' retorted Thankam, with a bark.

'You always see more into things than I do,' said Mrs Koshy. 'Perhaps sometimes more than there is to see.'

'And you, Sosamma, see so much less than there is to see,' said Thankam. 'A wise mother should have eyes in the back of her head. But some mothers nowadays seem to want to keep closed even the two eyes that they have.'

Thankam was in the drawing-room now. 'These windows,' she said, 'look so naked without curtains. It is a naked sort of house.'

'What we did not lose in the flood, we lost to the *chattambis*,' said Mrs Koshy. 'But perhaps there is something to be said for the uncluttered house.'

'But not so uncluttered as to be taken for a peasant's *kudil*,' said Thankam. 'A family takes its character from the house it lives in. Live in a peasant's *kudil* and you will start behaving like a peasant. The house must at least have curtains. I will send the tailor round.'

Thankam paused before the fridge. 'You must take it out into the backyard. The Pazhaymootils will die of laughter to see such a wreck.'

'I once kept a good table, a neat kitchen,' said Mrs Koshy thoughtfully. 'I used to have such a rush of blood when I saw a cockroach wing or leg or a greasy sink. But I'm so much less upsettable now. I have come to ask for so little to be happy. First I lose my house. Next I lose Pappa to Zen. Now I am losing Devi. In the end what do we have left but God, if we have invested in God?' Was it quite God that she had or only the brown-framed Gethsemane Christ?

But Thankam wasn't listening. 'Look at the peeling walls,' she was saying. 'The house needs to be whitewashed. But some things can never be whitewashed.'

The two sisters were only pretending to talk to each other. Their minds kept sheering away from each other. Chalk-minds have trouble talking with cheese-minds.

Thankam ruled against a taxi. She said Devi would travel to church in Avrachen's vintage Studebaker. It had belonged to Avrachen's father and since his death it had been kept carefully garaged, for Avrachen had more than an eye on the Madras vintage car market. Thankam had convinced herself that the Pazhaymootils would come in their shiniest cars. You can judge a family by the cars they keep. The vintage Studebaker would stare down any of the Pazhaymootil's louder cars.

The Studebaker was first washed with lotion to keep the flies away and then garlanded with jasmine and marigold. The flowers were checked for buzzing insects. The car was polished till it half shouted out its superior pedigree. Thankam saw to everything with unnecessary ferocity as if driven by a dozen angry sprites that could be appeased only by ceaseless motion. One sort of fuss seemed to suggest another kind of fuss. Thankam did not want time to think, to brood. And as she rushed about she talked loudly to herself.

But loud though she was, she couldn't silence a terrible ticking in her ear. Was it a clock or a bomb? Sometimes the ticking found a nasty voice and it asked every kind of indecent, jeering question. The questions came in little hoots.

What, asked the nasty voice, are you going to do now that Mathaichen has gone whoring after another woman?

It is the same whores to whom you lost Avrachen, isn't it? The tea-pickers have run away, haven't they, with a second scalp? Something more than a scalp. Everyone knows how good the tea pickers are at trapping people in the little tea baskets between their legs.

Could Thankam face life without her man Mathaichen? Was there life without Mathaichen? Hoot followed hoot.

Thankam tried to run away from the voice. She swept into the kitchen like a typhoon. One maid was slapped for stirring too much jaggery into the *payasam*. Another was pinched for spitting in the kitchen. Pinching was Thankam's favourite form of corporal punishment. All except the most stout hearted servants were reduced to weeping. 'The richer the lizard, the more poisonous the spittle,' said one maid. 'And this lizard is losing both its tail and its head,' said another maid. 'And without a tail and a head, what's left except a belly ache?'

Thankam hurried Devi into the garlanded Studebaker. She was racing against the impossibly ticking clock in her head.

Mr Koshy rode beside Devi in the Studebaker. 'You must come and visit us as often as you can. Twice a day at least,' said Mr Koshy, almost formally.

'But of course, Pappa,' said Devi. 'I'm not leaving Tiruvananthapuram.'

'I know, I know,' said Mr Koshy. 'But will you want to come back to a cat-and-dog house? Yesterday, I could hardly sleep for the barking of the dogs. It was really a sort of moaning, the way dogs moan when they see passing phantoms.'

'Oh, Pappa,' said Devi.

'But there was more moaning in here,' Mr Koshy said, tapping his heart. 'Old men have only their daughters.'

Devi held her father's hands. Her father's conversation was as usual a jumble of sense and nonsense. Mr Koshy took a small packet from his shirt pocket and gave it to Devi. 'Don't open it now,' he said. 'It contains nineteen silver and gold coins. They belonged to my grandmother. There is one coin for every year of your life, and one more for luck. I don't want anyone to say that I was too poor to give my daughter a dowry. The coins are completely unusable of course. They are from the time of Maharaja Chitra Tirunal. I call it Zen money.' Mr Koshy giggled. 'It is not bazaar money, Zen hates the bazaar.' He giggled helplessly.

Dr Vareed came to church in a yellow-and-black Tiruvananthapuram taxi. Some of the Pazhaymootils had protested that it wasn't grand enough for a Pazhaymootil bridegroom. But Dr Vareed had insisted on the taxi.

'I am afraid they are playing a mock poverty joke on us,' remarked Thankam, when Dr Vareed drove up in the taxi. 'Everyone knows they have a dozen of those aeroplane-like American cars.'

'A dozen?' asked Avrachen. 'Are you sure?'

'I am sure,' said Thankam, putting an unnatural emphasis into her words.

Thankam's fever, thought Avrachen, was blazing like a fire. The man in Thankam's life had walked out on her. Not all the water pitchers in town could damp down this fever.

The St. George's Orthodox Syrian Church in the heart of Tiruvananthapuram, is typical of the small but sensibly de- signed Syrian churches in Kerala. There are no Roman stee- ples, no lush birthday cake shrines, no parade of church wealth. Inside, the church is bare of all furniture, except for rows of mats.

Mrs Koshy stood behind a pillar not far from the *katas- troma*, the chancel. The bare church agreed with her mood. Thankam might think poorly of naked houses: but Mrs Koshy thought that a house crammed with bric-à-brac is too dis- agreeably full and gorged. The emptiness of the Lord's house was not unlike the emptiness of her own. Mrs Koshy prayed for Devi. Let not her Pazhaymootil money crowd out what is good and true. Let her not have more and more of less and less.

The verger now came into the chancel and placed two chains and a *mantrakodi* (cloth used to veil the bride) on the table in front of the *mattuva* (main sanctuary).

Thankam sniffed at the sight of the verger. Devi was marrying into a verger's family and it was right in a symbolic way that the ceremony should start with the appearance of a verger. Thankam stole a glance at Devi who now stood just outside the chancel. She thought that Devi glowed most disgracefully, glowed only as a person living in a state of sin would glow. Frequent indulgence makes the skin glow un- healthily. She was full of the doctor's unspeakable tonic. Devi was almost crying aloud her state of sin.

The voice in her head got louder and louder. And huge, over-lively fantasies filled Thankam's mind. She could, heaven help her, see the doctor bending hungrily over Devi. And Avrachen's tea-pickers wearing nothing more than the baskets on their backs, dancing round the shameless couple, as in a witches' ritual of sin and death.

The priest appeared in the chancel to begin the service. Thankam stifled a scream. The priest was wearing nothing below his black rope girdle. The tea-pickers skipped round him in lewd invitation. The couple was hot with an animal lust that you could feel almost like a heat shimmer. And all in God's house. The ugliness of it. But then it was that sort of marriage.

Mrs Koshy did not wipe away the tears in her eyes. She allowed them to roll down her cheeks. She was losing a daughter, losing a part of her life with no obvious recompense. She sought refuge in the catechism of prayers bellowed back and forth between the priest and the congregation. Everyone knew their exits and entrances. No one had prayer books. They seemed to carry the order of service in their heads. Here were a people stitched into a tradition. Syrian Christians trace their origins to the mission of St. Thomas to Kerala in the first century. Religion is the biggest thing in their lives. They pray, therefore they are. They can make an epic of even a wedding service. Mrs Koshy felt herself pulled along on a tide of fervour and piety.

So many voices. So much laughter. Thankam heard the naughtiest suggestions. She thought that the thunder in her head would blow her scalp off.

Mrs Koshy crossed herself. The priest was placing the *minnu* round the bride's neck. The bridegroom knotted the thread passed through its eye. The *minnu* is a small, boat-shaped sliver of gold with tiny beads arranged in the shape of a cross; Syrian Christian women never remove their *minnus*. The placing of the *minnu* was the high point of the ceremony. May their love endure, prayed Mrs Koshy. May they grow old together.

'Behold,' intoned the priest, 'from this time on, we entrust you each to the other. God be witness between me and you, and if you break any of the laws of God, I am guiltless.'

'Guiltless indeed!' scoffed Thankam. She steadied herself against a pillar. She tried hard not to look below the priest's girdle. But she saw what she saw.

Three of the sauciest tea-pickers skulked wickedly in the aisle. They were waiting for companions. The priest disrobed with a laugh and rushed like a maddened bull towards one of

the tea-pickers. She made a delicious handful. Avrachen held
another tea-picker by the waist and let his tickling hands tickle
all over. Huge with lust, Mathaichen waddled towards the
third tea-picker. Mathaichen watched with an easy smile as
she did things to him. Thankam couldn't bear to see more. A
light went out in her head.

'It was the heat,' said Avrachen carrying Thankam out.

'It was more than the heat,' said Mathaichen.


A large pandal was put up in the garden of the house-on-
the-hill for the wedding feast. The Pazhaymootils swept up
the hill in their cars. Most of the Koshy relatives had to trudge
up the hill. 'Is this a wedding or a Sabarimalai pilgrimage?'
they muttered. The pilgrimage to Sabarimalai lay through
steep, uphill tracks.

Dr Vareed was chaffed about the house-on-the-hill by his
cousins. Was he marrying into a family of sherpas? And the
father of the bride certainly had a Himalayan remoteness.

The Koshy relatives for their part said that they had seen
a lot of twenty-two carat Pazhaymootil gold that day but not
a single heirloom. And gold hot from the goldsmith has a
brassy shine that only time can dull. It was the usual kind of
duelling between *benthukar* (in-law) families. Every bubble
of vanity was pricked without mercy. Only the bride and the
bridegroom were spared the worst of the ragging.

Mathaichen and Kunjunj *chetan* had a taxi to themselves.
To their great shame their taxi stopped with a horrible belch
half-way up the hill. The taxi was prevented from rolling
downhill by two bricks that the driver quickly wedged in
behind the back tyres.

'What a disaster!' said Mathaichen.

'We will have to walk up the hill,' said Kunjunj.

'Do we?' asked Mathaichen.

'Unless you want us to spend the wedding night together
in the car,' said Kunjunj.

Two Pazhaymootil cars swept past without stopping. 'They did not even slow down. They are jeering at us,' said Mathaichen.

Mathaichen put his head out of the window and bellowed at the driver. 'You should exchange your car for a bullock cart,' he said.

'Master, there is no point losing your temper with me,' said the taxi driver. 'You can whip a bullock. You can't do anything with a car that won't move.'

'Except whip the driver,' said Mathaichen.

'I will carry you piggy-back for the rest of the way, if you want, Master.'

'You will need an extra pair of legs to do that,' said Mathaichen.

A red Mercedes Benz screeched to a halt ahead of their taxi. Kunnukuzhi Mohan climbed out of the car.

'I did not know that we had invited him,' muttered Mathaichen.

'I invited him,' said Kunjunj. 'We must move with the times.'

'And he is the times?' asked Mathaichen sarcastically.

'He is in politics now and may be useful. To me if not to us.'

'But I will not befriend a Communist. I will not forget that it is his party that has flung me out of Kuttanad.'

'Oh what a sadness!' said Kunnukuzhi Mohan coming up to them. 'On such a day too! Come with me!'

'No,' said Mathaichen.

'Mathaichen,' said Kunjunj in a big brotherly voice, 'will stay behind to look to the car. I will come with you.'

The Mercedes Benz moved smoothly up the hill.

Mathaichen kicked the broken down taxi. 'Broken down,' he shouted angrily. 'We are a sad, broken down lot.'

The driver grabbed a spanner in case he had to defend himself.

# Chapter Fourteen

. . . PAPPA CALLED IT a Zen day,' wrote Lalu. 'A blue moon day. The three hundred and sixty seventh day of the year.

It was really two days in one. There was both sun and rain. Sun in the rain. Rain in the sun. Our lips were still wet with the wedding *payasam* when we went from the sun into the rain. The same priest, the same church, the same hard sky, the same cars. The Studebaker and the yellow and black taxis returned. We shed two sorts of tears, bitter and sweet . . . .

After the wedding, Mathaichen said that he had a bus to catch, and at once. It was a self-mocking excuse. Everyone knew that the Mathaichen *vahanam* (vehicle) was the taxi.

'Ammachen, may the bus that you want to catch never come,' said Devi. 'Forget your anger for one hour. Be ours for just one hour. A bride is allowed one wish at least.'

Devi put pleading into her voice.

'Not even a bride can ask me to surrender my pride. The values of a lifetime . . . .'

'Only the anger of a lifetime,' Devi interrupted. She thought prejudices. She said anger.

Mathaichen allowed himself to be led to a chair. He sat on a chair with his legs crossed. Only for an hour, he vowed. It would be the longest hour in his life. He wore his face long.

Mrs Koshy had spread four large *mettha payas* (straw

mats) on the lawn after the wedding was over. She had set up a copper samovar built in the bulbously large Central Travancore style on a table under the tamarind tree, to boil tea. She had set out some chairs for those whose bones were too creaky to squat down on the *mettha payas*. Paunches and pendulously large bottoms were better off on the chairs.

Chechamma had said that she would make meat dumplings. And she would buy strong tea leaf from the tea stall man who hawked smuggled Ceylon tea under the sarong as it were.

Dr Vareed did just what Mathaichen feared he would do. He shifted across the mat to where Mathaichen sat. Mathaichen shifted uncomfortably. Mathaichen crossed his legs tightly. He made a virile little fort of his legs. He was the father of seven sons, was he not? Seven fine strapping sons. Tighter, the legs crossed themselves still more tightly as if seething with their superiority.

Mathaichen suspected a trick. Did Sosamma think that if she threw people together in an ambush, they would then go on to throw themselves into each other's arms? A curious notion. A cat and dog will not make love simply because they are pushed together under a single blanket.

Devi put a hand on his shoulder. Mathaichen let it lie. If he hadn't been so out of sorts he would have taken her hand in his. Devi was his favourite niece. She would have made a good Kuttanad wife. He would have been proud of her. But that dream lay broken. She was from today a Pazhaymootil. She had been bought by Pazhaymootil money. Everything is for sale . . . the best women, the best houses, the best education. Perhaps there is only one caste . . . money. By this reckoning, he was an outcaste.

'You are still angry,' said Devi.

Mathaichen thought that if this was the script that Sosamma had written, then he wouldn't speak his allotted lines. Sosamma could play her little charade in her own way with no help from him. Besides, he had always tried to keep the children out of their quarrels, though the quarrels of the parents were visited sooner or later upon their children.

'It is too late for anger,' said Mathaichen stiffly.

Mr Koshy came into the garden with the *vaidyan*. Every charade needs a buffoon, thought Mathaichen contemptuously, and here he comes.

The evening shadows were beginning to fall. Everything in the sky and more so on the earth below was acquiring mascara. But the evening was not yet heavy shadow. All the birds blundering about in the sky looked like crows in the play of shadow. They were all crows now. One dark-feathered caste.

The little group on the lawn sat under the dimming sky, as if pinned down by the night.

'But what is keeping Sosamma?' asked Mathaichen. He thought it unfair that Mrs Koshy should have left him in the lurch like this. He had nothing to say to Dr Vareed. He looked blankly at Dr Vareed as if insisting on silence by mutual consent. Mutually consenting non-conversationalists. Mathaichen composed his face into an ungracious mask.

'Maybe Mamma is giving us time,' said Devi, speaking with an honesty that irritated Mathaichen. Mathaichen made a bull-like champing noise. It wouldn't work. Sosamma should know that. Her smart chess games with people put him off.

'Bhagwanay,' was Mathaichen's only comment. He made it sound crushing.

A long silence intervened. No one spoke for fear that anything anyone said would sound wrong and artificial. Devi thought she saw the evening crashing round them.

'And how is Thankam?' asked Mathaichen, to no one in particular.

'Avrachen Ammachen said there was nothing to worry about,' said Devi. 'Thankam Ammachy has always been so robust.'

'I will believe that many, many times over,' said Dr Vareed. 'She has an energy that must come from Saraswati herself.'

He intended the cautious joke to carry away the strain of the lack of conversation. Dr Vareed felt his natural convivality breaking out. Let two or three gather together and conversation would start dancing in his mouth.

It was then that Chechamma erupted on them.

'They have taken our jewel away from us,' wailed Chechamma. 'Our jewel.'

'What in the name of Bhagwan are you saying?' said Mathaichen.

'Aiyo, Thankam Ammachy is dead . . . . And most of me has died with her . . . .'

'Shut up you silly slut,' said Mathaichen bounding out of his chair. 'How dare you?'

But when Mathaichen saw Mrs Koshy running towards him, her arms outstretched, he flopped back into his chair, defeated.

'How did it happen?' he asked quietly.

'She never came to,' said Mrs Koshy.

Mathaichen hid his head in his hands. So much like a beaten animal. 'But that is not how it happened,' said Mathaichen in an eerie kind of whimper. 'Not how it happened . . , ,' The rest of the sentence fell into a huge silence.

'Don't try to talk,' said Mrs Koshy, caressing Mathaichen's hair.

Mathaichen began to rant. 'I tried to break with her. I only broke her. A son can never break with his mother. But I was her cuckoo child. Her ungrateful cuckoo child. Her murderously ungrateful cuckoo child.'

'Water, bring a jug of water,' said the *vaidyan*. There was danger in an overheating brain.

'I did not have the luck to say a civilized goodbye to her. She should have died in my arms . . . . That would have been family honour. But I keep failing all the tests . . . tonight I am lower than the lowest outcaste. I am a cheap and murderous little windbag . . . .' He thrashed his hands about on his chest.

Mrs Koshy clapped her hands on Mathaichen's mouth.

'There is so much grief ahead of us that we must not add to it,' she said.

Dr Vareed pinned down Mathaichen's hands. Mathaichen allowed himself to be pinned down, as if yielding to the strength of a stronger animal. He fell silent and stopped throwing himself about. The *vaidyan* splashed water all over Mathaichen.

'Drown me, drown me,' cried Mathaichen. 'This rat deserves a drowning.' Together, Mrs Koshy, Devi and Dr Vareed supported Mathaichen across the lawn and into the inner courtyard.

'Some things have to happen,' said the *vaidyan*. There is no dodging karma. It was difficult to say where and how a blow would fall, but fall it would. The *vaidyan* thought that he had been present at an execution. How suddenly the blade had dropped. He winced theatrically at the thought of the overhanging blade.

'She had to die on a wedding day!' said Mr Koshy. 'Poor dear girl. She never had a sense of timing. Or a sense of fun. Fun, that was one word she never learnt to spell. I will have a cup of tea, *vaidyan*. But should I really? Maybe I shouldn't . . . .'

The samovar hissed with the boiling water within. It sounded like a woman's suppressed shriek. The *vaidyan* took the samovar off the fire.

'. . . they buried her the day after the wedding,' wrote Lalu.

They covered her with a white cloth, the *kavani*, of the kind she always wore. It was odd, but when Mamma took Thankam Ammachy's best *kavani* from her mahogany chest, that dark box that none of us had ever seen opened, she found baby curls in it. They said that it was Mathaichen uncle's baby curls. Thankam Ammachy had kept them these fifty years and more. The *kavani* seemed to us a magical piece of cloth. Mathaichen uncle cried hugely. Avrachen Ammachen seemed much less disturbed. Thankam Ammachy kept us together, but she also kept us apart. She had a sense of duty, perhaps an overlarge sense of duty. Caste, duty, family honour, she gave a wild, frightening meaning to all these words. Mamma's answer was to try to be sensible at all times. But is keeping a cool head always the answer? But you wouldn't understand my sad gabble, would you? You happy little twerp . . . .

Printed at Rekha Printers Pvt. Ltd., New Delhi-110 020.